Florida
State Facts

Nickname:	Sunshine State
Date Entered Union:	March 3, 1845 (the 27th state)
Motto:	In God We Trust
Florida Men:	Pat Boone, *singer* Dwight Gooden, *baseball player* Jim Morrison, *singer* Sidney Poitier, *actor*
Flower:	Orange blossom
Song:	"Old Folks at Home" (Swanee River) (music and words by Stephen C. Foster)
Fun Fact:	Gatorade™ was named for the University of Florida Gators ...where it was first developed.

"Ladies and gentlemen, we're assembled here today to witness the marriage of Joe Brenner and Pamela Hayes. Now, you all know Joe. He's one heck of a fine fellow. Generous as the day is long—and right about now, the days are pretty long. Joe always fills the glass up to the rim. He always listens to a tale of woe, and he always laughs at a joke, no matter how poorly you tell it. I don't have to tell you what kind of a guy he is.

"Pamela, on the other hand, is new to the island. I've never met her, and I reckon most of you haven't, either. But she seems a charming young lady, and I'll tell you this—if Joe loves her, she's aces in my book, and I think we can all count her as a friend.

"Pamela, do you take Jonas Brenner to be your lawfully wedded husband through the good times and the bad, the ups and the downs, the high tides and low, the calm days and the hurricanes, to make this marriage a thing of joy and beauty?

"Joe, do you promise to take Pamela as your lawfully wedded wife, to honor and respect, to talk to and to listen to, to share the burdens and the blessings of each day with, to partner through the dance of life?"

American
HEROES
AGAINST ALL ODDS

Cry Uncle

JUDITH
ARNOLD

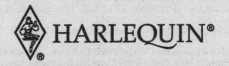

HARLEQUIN®

TORONTO • NEW YORK • LONDON
AMSTERDAM • PARIS • SYDNEY • HAMBURG
STOCKHOLM • ATHENS • TOKYO • MILAN • MADRID
PRAGUE • WARSAW • BUDAPEST • AUCKLAND

My thanks to Jo Anne Young of Moonstruck Travel
for her generosity and friendship.

This book is dedicated to my nieces,
Hannah and Rachel,
and my nephews,
Jacob, Sanders and Nahum.
Not a Lizard among them.

HARLEQUIN BOOKS
225 Duncan Mill Road, Don Mills,
Ontario, Canada M3B 3K9

ISBN 0-373-82207-3

CRY UNCLE

Visit us at www.eHarlequin.com

Printed in U.S.A.

About the Author

Since her first romance novel's publication in 1983, award-winning author Barbara Keiler has published nearly seventy novels, with more than seven million copies in print worldwide. She currently writes for Harlequin Books under the pen name **Judith Arnold.** Her novel *Barefoot in the Grass* has appeared on the recommended reading lists distributed by cancer support services at several hospitals. Barbara currently lives in Massachusetts with her husband and two teenage sons.

Dear Reader,

Joe Brenner.

Five years after the original publication of *Cry Uncle,* readers still tell me they're in love with Joe. I'm not sure what it is about him. He isn't rich. He isn't a genius. He isn't particularly dashing or talented or witty. His idea of dressing up is jeans that aren't torn, and his idea of a good night is one in which no fistfights erupt in the Shipwreck, the bar he owns and runs in Key West, Florida.

But oh, what a guy! I didn't create Joe; he came to me full-blown, and it was love at first sight. I learned from him that a man doesn't have to be dapper or polished, ambitious or affluent to be a hero. What he has to be is honest, courageous, willing to fight for the people he loves and…oh, yes. Sexy. Very sexy.

Meet Joe Brenner for yourself. I bet you'll fall in love with him, too.

Judith Arnold

Please address questions and book requests to:
Harlequin Reader Service
U.S.: 3010 Walden Ave., P.O. Box 1325, Buffalo, NY 14269
Canadian: P.O. Box 609, Fort Erie, Ont. L2A 5X3

PROLOGUE

JUST LEAVE, Pamela ordered herself. *Get out. Save your life.*

Two suitcases—a Pullman and a folding bag—stood by the door, her trench coat draped over them. The lights and the air conditioner had been turned off, the drapes drawn against the early morning fog. The traveler's checks she'd purchased yesterday were stashed carefully in an inner pocket of the Pullman. In her purse she had her passport, her driver's license and her credit cards, each of them required for travel, for escape.

She allowed herself a farewell look at the living room. Her gaze took in the dramatic abstract sculpture adorning the far corner, the wall of glass that faced Puget Sound, the gleaming hardwood floors. The sleek white L-shaped sofa. The glass-topped coffee table. The dhurrie rugs. The Waterford crystal coasters, stacked neatly beside the matching cut-crystal ice bucket on the wet bar. The embroidered silk throw pillows. The plants, a ficus and a couple of philodendrons, standing lush and green in ceramic pots.

Oh, Lord, the plants. She should have given them to someone to water in her absence.

But she'd been preoccupied by so much else: arranging to have all her mail forwarded to her attorney's office, discontinuing her newspaper delivery, emptying the refrigerator. Packing. Figuring out where on earth a woman could hide so a hit man wouldn't find her. Dreaming about when she could come back and resume her normal life.

If the plants die, they die, she thought. *Better them than me.*

She loathed running away like this, losing control over her existence, depending on the whims of fate to determine her course. But as long as Mick Morrow was out on bail, free to roam Seattle looking for her, she had no choice.

She checked her watch: six-thirty. She ought to be sipping a cup of fresh-brewed coffee right now and scanning the front page of the newspaper, after which she would don an elegant business suit and drive down to Murtaugh Associates, where she would take her place at her drafting table or behind her desk and contemplate her next assignment—an assignment she'd had to relinquish to Richard Duffy because Mick Morrow was on the loose. She'd done the preliminary designs for the strip-mall face-lift. She'd made the presentations and won the client, but now Richard was going to get to oversee the project. Pamela no longer had a say in it.

She no longer had a say in anything. Ever since she'd realized that the same car was following her for the third time in one week, driven by the same man she'd testified against in court, she'd lost her sense of safety.

The police thought she was paranoid, and maybe she was. They'd sworn they had an officer on Mick Morrow's tail twenty-four hours a day, and he hadn't been anywhere near her. She wished she could believe them, but she didn't.

Without her testimony, the district attorney would have a difficult time winning a murder conviction. Pamela had already seen Morrow commit murder once.

Was it really so paranoid to believe he'd commit murder a second time, if murdering her guaranteed his freedom?

She wasn't going to stick around to find out. She was going to disappear.

CHAPTER ONE

NONE OF THE WOMEN in the Shipwreck looked like wife material to Joe.

The usual crowd filled the tavern: sunburned beach bums, a few arty types, some navy guys, and the standard allotment of amateur fishermen, professional fishermen and big talkers eager to regale any sucker who wandered by with stories about the one that got away. The Shipwreck's female clientele fell into similar categories—boaters, navy personnel, beach bunnies, artistes. Joe knew at least half of them. The other half he figured he probably didn't want to know.

"She'll be here," Kitty promised, sidling up to the bar and slapping down her tray. "I need two rumrunners and a Cutty on ice."

Joe wrenched his attention from the noisy crowd and gazed around the dimly lit room. He took in the knotted plank flooring, the walls draped with weathered nets, and the ceiling, where broad-blade fans churned the sticky air without doing much to cool it. In front of him the bar stretched left and right, his personal, chest-high fortress. In front of the bar stood Kitty, his head waitress. Despite the heat, her skin was dry, her platinum blond hair only the slightest bit droopy.

"Two rumrunners and a Cutty on ice," he repeated, reaching for glasses. "What time did you tell her to come?"

"I didn't. She'll get here when she gets here, okay?"

"This is important, you know."

Kitty snorted. "If it's all that important, why don't you marry *me?*"

Grinning, Joe cascaded a generous portion of Scotch over the ice cubes in a highball glass. "That would make me what? Your fourth husband?"

"Fifth, but who's counting?"

"You know I love you, Kitty. But you're exactly what I don't need right now."

"Yeah, tell me about it." She returned his grin, then waltzed off, her tray balanced above her shoulder on the splayed fingers of one hand. Joe observed the sway of her hips with detached admiration. She had big curves top and bottom, and she dressed in clothing that flaunted them—tonight, a snug T-shirt and fire-engine-red shorts. Her legs were a tad thick, but her other dimensions were superlative enough to overcome that flaw. She probably would have been even more attractive if she didn't bleach her hair. Toward the end of every month, the dark roots made her look a little seedy.

Joe and Kitty had slept together once, years ago— between her second and third husbands if he wasn't mistaken. But they hadn't set the world on fire, and they'd decided that from that point on they would just be friends. In any case, a four-times-married bleached blonde whose brassiere cups runneth over wasn't the kind of woman Joe needed right now.

He needed someone proper and demure, someone stable and respectable and…boring. The woman Joe was looking for had to be bland and inoffensive. No dark roots, no wise-ass sense of humor, no D-cup bra and sassy hip-wiggling. The woman he was going to marry had to be exactly the sort of woman he'd never bother with if he had any choice in the matter.

But he didn't have a choice.

When she'd arrived at the Shipwreck for her shift that evening, Kitty had told him she'd found exactly the woman for him. "She moved into my building just a few days ago. Unattached, quiet, keeps to herself. I ran into her in the laundry room, introduced myself and said, 'I know a guy who's looking for a lady just like you.'"

"What did she say?"

"Nothing. She just kinda flinched."

"Great," Joe had retorted. At five o'clock, the bar had begun to perk up. The early-bird drinkers had staggered home to sleep off whatever they'd spent the daylight hours imbibing, and the evening drinkers were starting to trickle in. Joe had been filling bowls with peanuts when Kitty had sashayed in through the back door and filed her report on this new neighbor of hers.

"No, listen," Kitty had continued. "I said to her, 'The guy in question is my boss, and he's desperate to get married.'"

"Terrific," Joe had muttered. "You paint me as desperate, and she flinches at the mere thought of meeting me. You have such a way with people, Kitty."

Kitty had brushed off his sarcasm. "Damned right I do. Who gets the best tips around here?"

"They're tipping your anatomy, not your personality."

"Whatever works. So anyway, I said, 'Why don't you mosey on over to the Shipwreck tonight and check him out? He doesn't bite.'"

"That must have really reassured her."

"All right, look, you don't want my help? Just say the word, Joe. Stay single and see where that gets you."

Where that would get him was alone and bereft. His lawyer had told him that if he wanted to hold on to Lizard he would have to clean up his act and settle down, attach himself to a good woman and create a stable family situation. Joe knew all the good women in Key West, and most of them were married. The others, like Kitty, presented the sort of image that would have the majority of family court judges delivering Lizard to the Prescotts in no time flat. If this new neighbor of Kitty's worked out, Joe would be eternally grateful.

He wished he'd had more than a few hours' warning that he was going to be meeting a prospective bride that night. He'd shown up at the bar wearing his everyday garb—a loose cotton shirt, old jeans and sneakers without socks. If he'd known Kitty had invited a woman to stop by and meet him, he would have dressed in something a little nicer—and he would have shaved. As a rule he shaved only every third day. Tonight was day two.

He surveyed the room again. Two women huddled in front of the jukebox, their backs to him. Even in the dull amber light he recognized one of them from the pink-rose patch on the hip pocket of her shorts. Sabrina would have made a good wife, he supposed—at least she would have been a pleasure to find in his bed after a long day. She and Joe had been an item several years ago. But one long weekend, when he'd tagged along with a couple of buddies doing a round-trip sailing jaunt to Miami, Sabrina had taken up with a biker. Scuzzy guy, all tattoos and pecs. Sabrina had given him the boot after a few weeks, but her attempt to reconcile with Joe had gotten kind of complicated, and then Lizard had arrived, and Joe had found himself with more important things to worry about.

Sabrina had been damned good in bed, though—even if she had lousy taste in music, a fact he was reminded of when she shoved her quarters into the jukebox and the room filled with the nasal whine of Madonna begging her papa not to preach. One of these days, when Joe had a free minute, he was going to yank all the Madonna discs out of the jukebox so he'd never have to listen to them again.

Scanning the crowd once more, he noticed a woman entering the bar. She was on the heavy side, maybe a few years his senior, her hair a dark halo of frizz in the humid heat. Okay, he thought magnanimously. Assuming she wasn't too much older than him, she'd do. If Joe were to marry someone past, say, forty, a judge might not view it as a stable family situation. But mid-thirties probably wasn't too old. So what if his wife wasn't exactly heart-stoppingly gorgeous? This was strictly business. Joe didn't have to love the woman. He just had to marry her.

He watched her weave among the tables, heading toward him. Turning away, he checked his reflection in the mirror behind the bar. What with the atmospheric lighting and rows of liquor bottles lining the shelves in front of the mirror, he couldn't see much, and what he did see registered pretty low on the first-impression scale. He ran his fingers through his long, shaggy hair, scowled at the bristle of beard shading his jaw and straightened his shirt. Spinning back, he presented the woman with what he hoped was a congenial smile.

Except that she wasn't there to receive it. She had joined a group of guys at a table near the back. In fact, she was perched on one man's lap.

Suffering a twinge of regret tempered with relief, he nodded to Lois, his other primo waitress, as she hollered at him for a couple of Buds. He snapped off the tops of two bottles, set them on her tray and sent her off to serve her customers.

No sooner had she departed than Kitty was back, requesting two piña coladas. Joe busied himself with the blender. He didn't say a word, but Kitty apparently read volumes in his silence, because she said, "Stop worrying. She'll be here."

"What does she look like?" he asked, recalling with some shame his immediate response to the frizzy-haired woman who'd just come in.

"What do you mean, what does she look like?" Kitty arranged the frosty drinks on her tray and grinned slyly. "She's nowhere near as pretty as me, of course. But you could do worse. As a matter of fact—" she lifted the tray onto its one-handed perch "—you have done worse."

"Thanks." He watched Kitty saunter back into the crowd, then rinsed out the blender. His gaze strayed to the clock on the back wall. It resembled a ship's wheel, with thick wooden bars radiating out from a hub. It was actually quite tacky, which was why he'd bought it for the Shipwreck. Tacky was the ambience he was aiming for.

Right now the clock wasn't just tacky; it was annoying. It read 9:53. If this lady friend of Kitty's couldn't get her butt down to the bar at a reasonable hour when the subject was as momentous as her potential marriage to Joe, she wasn't going to work out. Joe was used to night owls, but he doubted a night-owl woman would make a wife decent and proper enough to persuade a judge to let Joe keep Lizard.

Brick arrived through the back door. Joe called a greeting to his second-in-command, and Brick grunted in response. Grunting was about the limit of Brick's communication skills, but he made the best tequila sunrises on the island, and at the Shipwreck such a talent was considered far more important than eloquence.

A trio of women entered the bar. Joe knew them all. He'd dated them all. One of them waved to him as the threesome worked their way through the room, looking for a table.

"Two shots of Cutty, neat!"

"I need a stinger, a boxcar and a gimlet!"

"Three rum-and-Cokes, hold the Coke!"

"A glass of chardonnay."

The noise level had increased as the ship's-wheel clock rounded 10:00 p.m., and Joe's skull was starting to echo. All the stools along the bar were occupied, and dozens of customers loomed behind them, waiting for someone to stand and free up a seat. On the jukebox Madonna was replaced by real music—Van Morrison—and the temperature in the crowded room ratcheted up a few degrees.

Kitty stood at the pickup station, smiling mysteriously. "I said, a glass of chardonnay."

"Who in this joint would order white wine?" Joe grumbled, rummaging through one of the refrigerators below the bar.

"Your fiancée," Kitty answered.

Joe stood bolt upright, the chilled bottle clutched in his hand. His heart did a tap dance against his ribs and his throat momentarily squeezed shut. He hated to admit how anxious he was. If this neighbor of Kitty's didn't work out, he was going to have to go shopping for a wife on the mainland. Things were getting tight.

Not desperate, though. He wasn't going to let on—to Kitty or anyone else—that he was close to desperation.

"A white-wine sipper, huh?" he murmured, sliding a goblet from the overhead rack and standing it on Kitty's tray. "Where is she?"

"Over near the front door. In case she wants to make a quick escape, I guess."

He peered through the mob of bodies in the dimly lit room, but he couldn't tell which one she might be. "I'll take her drink to her. What's she wearing?"

"A white dress."

"What's her name again?"

"Pamela."

"Pamela what?"

"How the hell should I know? I asked her if she'd consider marrying you, not what her last name was."

"Okay. Brick? Give me ten," he called to his assistant once he'd poured a hefty dose of wine into the goblet.

Brick grunted.

Joe managed a smile of thanks for Kitty, although he was feeling uncommonly nervous. It wasn't like him to get twisted in knots over a woman—or over anything, for that matter. Crises came and went, and when they were truly awful, he indulged in some intense moping. But then he got over it. Rolling with the punches was his preferred modus operandi.

But this was different. This was wife-hunting. Joe had never proposed to a woman before, and here he was, about to propose to a total stranger.

Not really propose, he reassured himself, strolling around the end of the bar and working his way through the throng, barely pausing to acknowledge the greetings the regulars hurled at him. What he was offering the woman was less a proposal than a proposition.

Scratch that. If she was a white-wine sipper in a white

dress—already dressed for her wedding, apparently—she wasn't the sort to be propositioned. He had to approach her in a classy way.

And he didn't even know her last name, damn it.

"Hey, Joey!" a man called out behind him. He smiled and waved vaguely, but his gaze was riveted on the screened front door that opened onto Southard Street. Standing next to it, looking incredibly out of place, was a woman in a white dress.

Not bad, he thought, one set of apprehensions fading and another set kicking in. The white dress she had on resembled a tank shirt that fell to midcalf, the hem notched a few inches on the side seams. The way the cotton cloth draped her body indicated that she was somewhat lacking in the curves department. Her arms were slim, her shoulders bony. Her feet were strapped into flat leather sandals. Her long, graceful neck was framed by ash-blond hair that fell to her shoulders with barely a ripple. Gold button earrings glinted through the silky locks. A matching gold bangle circled one slender wrist.

Her face was as angular as the rest of her, her nose and chin narrow, her cheeks hollow. Her eyes were a pale silver gray. In fact, everything about her had a pale, silver-gray quality. Obviously she was a recent arrival on the island. No one who'd been on Key West for any length of time could stay that pale.

A little washed-out, but definitely an interesting face. Not quite pretty, but intriguing. It was the sort of face a man could look at for a long time without growing tired of it.

Her expression was cautious. Maybe a touch skeptical. Haunted. Those eyes, so large and pale, seemed troubled.

The notion of marriage troubled *him* more than a little, too. But the alternative—losing Lizard—was far worse.

He took a step closer to her, and another step. In her search of the room, she stared at him, past him, and then at him again. Noticing the wineglass in his hand, she straightened up and eyed him warily. She bit her lip. Her teeth were as white as her dress.

"Hi," he said, sounding a hell of a lot more confident than he felt. "You must be Pamela. I'm the guy who wants to marry you."

OH, GOD. He looked like a bum.

The door frame dug into her spine as she backed away from him. Okay, she consoled herself, things could be worse. She hadn't agreed to anything yet. She'd made no commitments, no promises. And honestly, any danger this man posed couldn't be as bad as what she'd left behind when she'd escaped to Key West.

As bums went, she had to admit, the fellow extending the glass of wine toward her was actually rather handsome. Unfortunately, he was also scruffy and grungy, with a stubble of beard and hair that clearly hadn't had a close encounter with a pair of scissors in some time, a shapeless shirt and jeans faded to a powdery blue, the fabric split like a fraying grin across one knee. And that earring…oh, God. An earring.

She ordered herself to remain calm. Experience had taught her that just because a man was impeccably dressed didn't mean he was safe. And vice versa. Beneath the baggy shirt and the decrepit jeans she discerned a lithe, lean body. Behind the stubble of whiskers and the shaggy auburn hair this man…Joe…had a lively face, his smile producing a dimple on one side, his nose long and straight and his eyes as blue as a summer sky, two lovely spots of light in the gloom of his low-rent bar.

The Shipwreck, she recalled, glancing away from Joe long enough to remind herself of where she was. It was an apt name for the place. The rowdy, motley customers might well have washed ashore from some disaster.

As she had.

Joe continued to hold out the wineglass. If she took it, she might be tempted to consume its contents in one gulp—assuming the glass didn't slip from her hand and shatter on the floor. That was a strong possibility, given how slick with sweat her palms were.

His smile widened. It really was a charming smile, despite his rumpled appearance. Either that or she was rationalizing, trying to find a way to like this man.

She didn't have much choice. He was offering her exactly what she needed: some wine and a new identity. She might as well make the best of it.

"Hello," she said, discreetly wiping her hands on her dress.

He shot a quick look over his shoulder, then shrugged. "It's kind of crowded in here. If you'd like, we could go into my office to talk, or I could drag a couple of chairs outside. There's a little yard behind the building."

"It might be more pleasant outside." In truth, she wasn't sure she was ready to shut herself up inside an office with him.

He reached out and took her hand. Forget about being shut up with him in an office—she wasn't ready to be touched by him, yet she couldn't very well make a fuss simply because he wanted to hold hands with his future wife.

Besides, there was nothing threatening in his touch. His hand was as dry as hers was clammy, and his grip was warm and strong. If only he were barbered and well tailored and didn't have a silver hoop linked through his earlobe—and if only her life weren't completely out of kilter—she might have responded positively to the smooth, leathery surface of his palm, the thick bones of his fingers. She might have liked the deft way he navigated through the crowd, smiling innocuously at people who greeted him, ignoring one creep who gave him a salacious wink.

Pamela wished she could ignore the creep, too, but she couldn't. She was too tense, too conscious of how ludicrous this whole idea seemed.

Joe ushered her to the rear of the barroom and down a hall, past a pay phone and the men's and ladies' rooms to a door crowned by a glowing red Exit sign. He released her hand so he could grab two chairs from a nearby stack. Then he jammed his hip against the door and it swung open.

The outdoor air was nearly as dense and hot as the indoor air, but at least it wasn't stagnant. Instead of the acrid aromas of cigarettes and beer, it smelled of the ocean, rich and briny. Gravel and crushed sea shells crunched beneath her sandals as she followed Joe into a small lot bounded by a ramshackle fence that backed onto the buildings in the next block. A spotlight fastened to the rear wall of the bar glared down upon the yard, brighter than the moon.

She filled her lungs with the salty air, then attempted a smile for Joe, who was positioning the chairs so they faced each other a safe distance apart. He gestured toward one of the chairs and she lowered herself to sit. Settling into the other, he handed her the wine.

For a man dressed so disreputably, he had good manners, at least. And that smile, and those amazing blue eyes...

And that earring. She took a long sip of chardonnay and lowered the glass. And zeroed in once more on the silver earring. She wondered how he'd felt marching into a jewelry store and standing in line for ear-piercing with a bunch of prepubescent girls. Maybe he hadn't gone to a jeweler. Maybe he'd done it himself—plunged a needle into the heart of a flame and then into his own flesh.

Maybe a former lover had done it. Maybe a *present* lover had. But this evening's discussion was about marriage, not about lovers past and present, or monogamy, or fidelity, or anything like that.

All right, so Joe had an earring and—for all Pamela knew—hundreds of girlfriends. So he dressed like a bum. So he wasn't her style. Nothing about this encounter was her style. For that matter, nothing about the recent progression of her life was her style.

Things had gotten out of control. She didn't have many options left. The essential thing was to stay alive. If marrying a man with devastating blue eyes and an earring would provide the protection she needed, she'd be a fool not to give his offer a fair hearing.

"So," he said, his smile flagging slightly as he studied her in the pool of white light.

It occurred to Pamela that he could be judging her as harshly as she'd judged him. Perhaps he found her wanting. Kitty had said he was desperate for a wife, but she hadn't said he was desperate enough to settle for a skinny, panic-stricken architect from Seattle.

He spread his legs, rested his elbows on his knees and tapped his fingertips together. "I guess you're wondering why I called you here tonight," he quipped, then flashed her a smile that, for all its edginess, she found comforting. If nothing else, they had their anxiety in common.

The least she could do was help him out by contributing to the conversation. "Kitty told me you need to get married," she said.

He shrugged. "That about sums it up."

"Forgive me…Joe?" she half asked.

He smacked himself in the forehead, evidently disgusted by his lack of manners. "Jonas Brenner," he said, gently prying her fingers from their death grip on the stem of the wineglass and giving her a friendly handshake as she transferred the glass to her other hand. "Everyone calls me Joe. And you're Pamela. Kitty didn't mention your last name."

"Hayes," she said. "Pamela Hayes."

"Pleased to meet you."

She smiled diffidently. She couldn't quite say she was pleased to meet him, not yet. She wished he were a little less disheveled. She wished circumstances hadn't driven her to the opposite end of the continent, as far from her home as it was possible to be without leaving the country. But wishes weren't going to get her anywhere, so she accepted his firm grip as he shook her hand, and consoled herself with the thought that at least his fingernails were clean. As soon as he released her, she took another long sip of wine.

He leaned back in his chair, scrutinizing her. She wished he'd brought a beverage outside for himself, so she wouldn't be the only one drinking. She felt exposed, like a job applicant unprepared for an interview and doing everything wrong.

"Well," he said, then fell silent as a squadron of thundering motorcycles cruised down the street nearby, riders hooting and mufflers roaring. When the night air grew relatively tranquil once more, he began again. "The deal is, I have this niece."

She nodded.

"I've had custody of her for three years," he explained. "When I first got her, I thought it was just going to be for a few months, but when Lawton and Joyce—that's my brother-in-law's brother-in-law and sister—"

Pamela stopped nodding and held up her hand. "Your brother-in-law's brother-in-law?"

Joe smiled apologetically. "Okay," he drawled, as if speaking more slowly would clarify everything. "See, Lizard—that's my niece—"

"*Lizard?*"

"Elizabeth. But she likes to be called Lizard."

"Lizard," Pamela echoed quietly. If marrying Joe had seemed like an absurd idea before, it seemed even more absurd now. How on earth could she take seriously a man who had a niece named Lizard?

"Yeah. Now, Lizard's parents—that would be my sister and brother-in-law—died."

"Oh—I'm sorry."

He tried to disguise his sorrow behind a shrug that didn't hide much. His unbelievable blue eyes grew momentarily dark, the summer-sky irises obscured by storm clouds. Then the moment passed. "Well, anyway. That was three years ago. Lawton and Joyce said they'd take Lizard, which made sense. They were married, they were rich, they could afford nannies and all that stuff. Only problem was, they were involved in setting up some sort of development deal in Indonesia. So they asked me if I could keep Lizard for just a couple of months until they wrapped things up overseas. And I said sure. But then a couple of months turned into a couple of years.

Three years, to be exact. I suppose those Indonesian development deals can get complicated.''

So could stories about orphaned children named Lizard, Pamela thought, although she refrained from saying so. She only nodded again.

"Anyway, about a month ago, I got this letter from Joyce saying they were finally done doing their thing in Indonesia, and they were returning to California, and they intended to take Lizard. But by now Lizard and I have been together a long time. We've grown pretty close.''

"How old was she when you got her?''

"Two.''

Pamela didn't know much about babies. She was an only child, so she'd never had the opportunity to observe younger siblings or nieces and nephews. Even so, it seemed to her that the years between two and five must be significant in a child's development.

"I taught her the alphabet,'' said Joe. "I potty-trained her. I nursed her through the chicken pox. And frankly, I'm not in much of a mood to hand her over to a couple of stuck-up financiers who haven't even seen her in three years.''

"I don't blame you.''

"So, I went to Mary DiNardi—that's my lawyer— and asked how I could go about getting permanent custody of Lizard. And Mary said, 'Joe, look at you. You're thirty years old, you run a bar, you're single and you don't even shave regularly.''' He shot Pamela a sheepish grin. "Meanwhile, Lawton and Joyce have a ten-room house in Hillsborough and a couple million stashed in the bank. The fact that I potty-trained Lizard doesn't count for much with family-court judges. My lawyer said I have to take a flyer on clean-cut living. Specifically, she told me to marry a decent lady." Another flash of a smile, this one curiously seductive. "You wouldn't happen to be decent, would you?"

Pamela shifted uncomfortably, causing the chair's hinges to squeak. She crossed her legs, traced the rim of her glass with her finger and managed a feeble smile. How did one answer such a question? How on earth did one measure decency? Why did the mischievous glint in his eyes make her wish, for a fleeting instant, that she *wasn't* quite so decent?

"It would seem to me," she said, steering clear of his provocative question and his even more provocative grin, "that this child...*Lizard*—" she tried not to shudder at the name "—hasn't really known any family other than you. Why would a judge award custody of her to two total strangers? I would think that after she experienced the trauma of losing her parents, the system wouldn't want to traumatize her again."

"I would think so, too," said Joe, leaning back and balancing one leg across the other knee. The position drew her attention to the faded strip of denim covering his fly. She drank some more wine and was careful to keep her gaze on his face when she lowered her glass. "Thing of it is," he continued, "Lawton and Joyce are rich. They're respectable. They make a fortune pushing papers around. They listen to Bach. They're such fine, fine people." Sarcasm oozed from every syllable.

"Do you think that marrying me would make you look respectable to a judge?"

"Personally, I happen to think I'm just about as respectable as I can stand to be. But Mary DiNardi—who's taking me for two hundred and fifty bucks an hour, so she'd better know what she's talking about—doesn't exactly agree. She says I've got to project stability and maturity and all that kind of thing. And a wife—a nice, neat, well-behaved wife—is just the ticket.''

"What does...*Lizard* think of this?" Pamela wondered whether she'd ever be capable of using the child's nickname without cringing.

"She doesn't know anything about a custody challenge. All she knows is that Lawton and Joyce are these two mysterious people who've been sending her Christmas and birthday cards with funny Indonesian stamps on them. She has no idea some pea-brained judge could rip her out of her home and force her to live with a couple of snobs she's never even talked to. Last time she saw them was probably at her christening or thereabouts. These folks aren't her family. I am—and Kitty and Lois and Birdie and Brick. And my mother when she's in town.''

If Joe Brenner's social circle included characters with names like Birdie and Brick, Pamela supposed it was no wonder he called his niece Lizard.

"Anyway, what I'm looking for here is just a temporary arrangement. A year, tops. I've got a three-bedroom house, so you'd have your own room. If you met someone and fell in love, I'd only ask that you be discreet. You're supposed to be the decent one in this situation.'' He tempered his words with a smile.

"If we had separate bedrooms—" no "if" about it, she thought wryly "—wouldn't that make it obvious that the marriage is a sham?''

"Well, of course, if some social worker stopped by to check us out, we'd have to put on a little lovey-dovey show for her. I don't see that as an insurmountable problem.''

"But Lizard—" *wince* "—would realize something was weird between us, wouldn't she?''

"Number one, Lizard is five years old, and I honestly don't think she has any idea what husbands and wives do behind closed doors. Number two, people down here are pretty hang-loose about things. If a couple wants separate rooms, it's no big deal."

Pamela mulled over what he'd told her, and she wasn't entirely pleased. The separate rooms, the discretion, all the businesslike details of the arrangement suited her fine. But the idea of presenting herself as a perfect wife and mother to a five-year-old... What did she know about raising kids? How were she and Joe going to trick a little girl into believing they were a genuine couple? As scant as Pamela's knowledge of children was, she couldn't shake the understanding that children were a lot harder to fool than family-court judges and social workers.

Beyond that minor misgiving, there was another problem, a much more troubling one: Pamela was in danger.

No matter how much she wanted to elude that danger, she couldn't do it by hiding behind a five-year-old girl. What if—God forbid!—Mick Morrow somehow tracked Pamela down? She didn't want to die—but she wasn't going to save her own life by placing an innocent child in harm's way.

She began to shake her head. "If it's money you're worried about," Joe said, misreading her hesitation, "I've got to tell you, I'm not rich. But we could work something out. I'm willing to support you, put you on my insurance, pay all the expenses—"

"No, it isn't money," she said, cutting him off. She had plenty of money, an embarrassment of money. She'd withdrawn from the bank in Seattle a large chunk of her savings. She hadn't yet opened a local bank account, because bank records were easy to trace. If she could deposit the money as Joe's wife, using the name Pamela Brenner, maybe she would escape detection.

But the child... She couldn't take Joe's name and his hand in marriage when doing so might place his niece in danger.

"If it's the sex thing," Joe continued, "we can work that out any way you want. I'm looking for a little play-acting here. Public displays of affection, nothing more. I'm sure we—"

"No, it's not sex." She stared into his eyes and felt herself tumbling into the blue. When a man with eyes like Joe's talked about sex, she could forget about his earring, his beard, his slovenly apparel. She could forget about almost everything.

But she couldn't forget about Mick Morrow.

"Joe," she said, glancing away to break the spell of his gaze, "there's something you need to know about me before this discussion goes any further."

He leaned forward. Tracing the line of his vision, she noticed that he was staring at her hands. She hadn't re-alized she had furled them into fists so tight her knuckles had turned as white as schoolroom chalk.

She made a concerted effort to relax—and then gave up. There was no way to say what she was about to say and remain calm. "Joe..." She sighed. "Back in Seattle, where I lived before I came here, I testified in court against a hit man."

Joe sat straighter and lifted his eyes to her face. He looked startled, horrified—but also sympathetic. "A hit man?"

"He was convicted of murder based on my testimony. But his conviction was set aside on a technicality. He's free on bail pending a new trial. And—" she sighed again, shuddering the way she did every time she con-

fronted the reality of her current existence ''—he wants
me dead.''

''DEAD?'' THE WORD CAME OUT on a croak. How in the
name of God could a fragile, blond slip of a woman have
wound up on the wrong side of a hit man?

''It's all right,'' she said bravely. She seemed suddenly relaxed, or maybe resigned. ''We haven't signed
any contracts here, Joe. I know you didn't bargain for
anything like this. If you want to retract the offer—''

''Not so fast,'' he said, silencing her. His brain told
him he ought to run like hell from a woman who was
on a murderer's A-list, but his gut told him he should
sit tight and work it through.

He wasn't given to heroics. If a gun-toting mobster
started buzzing the island in a fully armed Apache hel-
icopter, his impulse would be to grab Lizard and split,
and the hell with everyone else. Joe looked out for Nu-
mero Uno—which used to be himself until Lizard came
along and knocked him out of the top slot. He would
sacrifice his own life for the Liz Monster, and he'd do
whatever was necessary to avoid that sacrifice. But he
wasn't about to play the white knight for some silver-
eyed stranger from Seattle who'd been stupid enough to
testify against a professional assassin.

On the other hand, if he didn't marry Pamela while
he had the chance, he might not find anyone better. Su-
perficially, at least, she was everything he needed: con-
servative, personable, reasonably attractive—certainly
not the sort of woman he'd be ashamed to be seen in
public with. Given her current predicament, she was
probably as eager to grab a husband as he was to grab
a wife. She didn't have the luxury of quibbling over the
fine points with him.

And what were the odds that a liquidator from the Great Northwest would track her down to the Florida Keys?

"Okay," he said, leaning forward and staring straight into her troubled eyes. "This guy's in Seattle, right?"

"Yes."

"And he doesn't know where you are?"

"Nobody knows. Not even my parents. I told them I had to get away, and they agreed. I keep in touch with them, of course, through my attorney, who also stays in contact with the police."

"Why didn't the police offer you protection?"

He watched the shifting of her shoulders as she shrugged and decided that if a woman wasn't going to be overly endowed in the mammary region, sexy shoulders were a nice consolation prize. The thin straps of her dress revealed intriguing hollows and delicate ridges in the arrangement of her shoulder blades, collarbones and upper arms. He wondered if her skin would feel as creamy as it looked.

The sound of her voice cut through his half-baked fantasies. "The police didn't seem to think I was in any real danger. I told them I had received a couple of strange phone calls and I'd been followed home from work a few times. They said there was someone keeping an eye on the man I testified against and he hadn't been anywhere near me. I don't know—maybe they were right. But when you look in your rearview mirror and discover that the car behind you is being driven by someone who looks like the man you witnessed shooting someone in cold blood, you tend to get a little nervous."

"It sure wouldn't sit well with me," he agreed, "but if the police say it wasn't him..."

She sighed, then shook her head. "Maybe I *am* worrying about nothing. But...I don't know. I tried hiring a private bodyguard, but frankly, I couldn't stand having him lurking around me all the time. It made me even more paranoid. It's bad enough being followed by one person. I couldn't stand being followed by two. So I decided to leave town until a new trial was scheduled and the hit man was back in custody.''

If the police thought she was safe, how much danger could she possibly be in? Maybe she *was* a touch paranoid, but it would give her a reason to stick around. He could tolerate her minor neuroses as long as they didn't interfere with the big picture—keeping Lizard.

So Pamela Hayes was a little bit nutty. She would fit right in in Key West. ''So,'' he said, feeling a lot less concerned about her story, ''your parents have no idea where you are?''

''For their safety as well as mine, we thought that would be best for the time being.''

''Then I guess we won't invite them to the wedding,'' Joe joked, although merely saying it made him realize that he'd pretty much made up his mind. He needed a wife, and Pamela more or less fit the bill. ''Anything else I need to know?'' he asked. ''Any loan sharks holding your markers? Any preexisting health conditions?''

He watched her hands flutter. Like her shoulders, they were delicate, the fingers slim and graceful, the knuckles smooth enough to pose for hand-lotion ads. The gold bangle bobbed against her wrist, drawing his attention to yet another intriguing bone. He, always a breasts-and-butt man, had never before noticed how alluring a woman's skeletal structure could be.

''Look, Joe,'' she said. ''I didn't know about your niece. Seriously—we can't mix a little girl up in this. I don't even know why I came here....''

"You came to avoid a hit man," he reminded her.

"No—I mean, why I came to your bar to talk to you. Your waitress, Kitty—she seemed so friendly in the laundry room this morning. I don't know anyone in Key West, and she was so nice, and she kept telling me what a great guy you were, how I really ought to meet you, how I was exactly what you were looking for...." A sad-sounding laugh escaped her, and she shook her head.

"I take it you didn't mention to Kitty that you had a goon from Seattle on your tail."

"He's not on my tail," Pamela insisted, though she didn't look totally convinced. "I'm sure he doesn't have any idea where I am at the moment. And Kitty told me she thought you and I could help each other out. She knew I was looking for a new identity and..." Pamela sighed. "My mind just isn't working the way it used to. I used to be so rational. Just yesterday I would have found the idea of marrying a stranger preposterous."

"Now wait a minute," Joe objected. For no good reason, he felt his ego was under attack. "*Preposterous?* You think marrying me is *preposterous?*"

"No," she hastened to assure him. "I think you'd make a fine husband. It's me. I'd make a lousy wife."

He ought to take her at her word. He had Lizard's safety to think of, and marrying a woman with a contract on her head was asking for trouble. But Joe was used to asking for trouble—and acing the answer. And Pamela's linking him, marriage and *preposterous* made him argumentative. "I'll have you know, there are a lot of women who'd jump at the chance to marry me."

"And they don't have hit men chasing them," she pointed out. "For your niece's sake, you really ought to marry one of them."

Joe contemplated the women who'd jump—and for

Lizard's sake, none of them would do. They were flashy, or irresponsible, or pleasantly lax when it came to morality. They were too similar to what Joe had been like before he had Lizard.

Pamela wasn't flashy. She obviously wasn't irresponsible. If she had the courage and integrity to testify against a murderer in a public trial, her morals had to be damn near unimpeachable. She was exactly what he needed for his niece's sake. "Why do you think you'd make a lousy wife?" he asked.

"I'm completely ignorant when it comes to children."

"I didn't know anything about children when Lizard fell into my lap," he admitted. "There I was, busted up over my sister's death, and suddenly I found myself taking care of an obnoxious little twit who had a vocabulary of a hundred words, most of them variations on the word *no*. She thought toilet paper was for tearing into confetti. She refused to eat any food that wasn't pink—we went through a lot of strawberry yogurt in those days. Plus she spent the first three months howling for Mama and Dada, which was a real treat, let me tell you." Aware that he might be coming across as unforgivably self-pitying, he brought his lament to a quick close. "The bottom line is, if I could do it, you can do it. And, I mean, I'll do most of the child care. You'll be just a figurehead, as it were."

She smiled, a real smile, not just one of those anemic, polite smiles she'd been running past him since they'd met. This smile had the effect of widening her face, launching her cheeks skyward and pleating little crinkles into the skin at the corners of her eyes. He wondered what laughter would sound like coming from her.

He wondered about a lot of things—like how she had happened to witness a professional hit in the first place.

What she did for a living, how old she was, what she looked like first thing in the morning, when she was all sleep-tousled and her guard was down.

But now wasn't the time to indulge his curiosity. If he didn't get back behind the Shipwreck's bar soon, Brick's grunts were going to take on blasphemous overtones.

"Tell you what," he said, standing and offering her his hand. "Why don't you come over to my house tomorrow and get a feel for things. Before you agree to anything you ought to meet Princess Liz. We can talk some more...." *And check each other out in broad daylight,* he almost said, although he had the feeling Pamela Hayes wouldn't look any worse in the midday sun than she looked in the white glow of the spotlight above the back door.

"That sounds like a good idea."

"I live on Leon Street. A couple of blocks from the municipal beach. Do you know where that is?"

She reached into the pocket tucked into a side seam of her dress and pulled out a small coin purse. Opening it, she scowled. "I haven't got anything to write your address down on."

"What do you think cocktail napkins are for? Come on inside, and I'll draw you a map." He closed his hand completely around hers, not exactly sure why he felt the impulse to hold her. It wasn't because she was on the verge of becoming his wife. It wasn't simply an act of chivalry, the proper behavior of a gentleman escorting a lady through the rear door of a bar. It had something to do with wanting to reassure her, and himself. If he could touch her, he could trust her. And if she was in trouble, he wanted her to believe she could trust him.

Even though, if push came to shove, he wasn't so sure she could.

CHAPTER TWO

EASY DOES IT, Mick Morrow thought. *Don't make a scene.*

He stepped into the small, clean office and bellied up to a counter decorated with houseplants. On the other side of the counter, two plump, mild-faced, middle-aged women sat across from each other at facing desks, sipping coffee and yammering about an upcoming sale at Nordstrom. On each desk stood an African violet in a clay pot.

The women didn't seem to notice his entrance, so he nudged a plant out of his way. That got their attention. The woman on the left ended her monologue about the costs, both financial and emotional, of keeping her husband in up-to-date neckties, rose from her chair and crossed to the counter. "May I help you?"

He gave her his sweetest Sunday-school smile. "You're the manager here, right?"

"Yes."

"I'm looking for Pamela Hayes. She owns a unit on the top floor."

The woman glanced over her shoulder at her companion, and they exchanged a meaningful raising of eyebrows. Then she turned back to him. "Ms. Hayes does own a unit here, but we're not a missing persons bureau, Mr....?"

He didn't supply his name. "Is she missing?"

"This is the management office. We don't keep tabs on the owners. If someone has a noise complaint or needs a plumbing repair, we take care of it. But if you're looking for someone who happens to own a unit, we can't really help you." She peeked over her shoulder once more, and her buddy gave her an approving nod.

Rage had always been a problem for him, and he engaged in a silent bout with it. The Sunday-school smile remained unaltered, though. He had learned to compensate for his bad temper by being a good actor, never showing his hand until it was time to collect his winnings. "I've been trying to reach Pamela for days," he said smoothly. "I'm beginning to worry that maybe something's wrong. You know, like maybe she's lying on the floor in a pool of blood or something."

The woman grew pale. Another beseeching glance toward her colleague, who stood and approached the counter. "Ms. Hayes is out of town," the second woman said.

Just what he'd expected. If the slut had been lying in a pool of blood on the floor, it would have been because he'd found her.

"Can you tell me where she is? I mean... See, she and I were dating. We had a big fight. I admit I was rotten to her. I want to send her flowers, that's all. I just want to make it up to her."

"Maybe you should contact her family. Really, we can't help you with this."

"You know where she is, though, don't you?"

"No," both women said together.

The rage licked at him, small, hot flames searing the edges of his mind. "But you must be forwarding her mail."

"No," the first woman said. "The post office stopped

delivering her mail about a week ago. I assume they're holding it for her.''

"Or forwarding it directly," the other woman added.

The flames drew closer, grew larger. He pounded his fist against the counter. The two women flinched simultaneously. ''Damn it, someone must know where she is! I've got to find her!'' *Calm down! Don't blow it!* ''I mean, if I can't get a dozen red roses to her right away, she'll never forgive me.''

The first woman moved back to her desk and lifted the phone. ''I'm calling Security,'' she said. ''Please leave now.''

Ass. He shouldn't have punched the counter. If he'd had to hit something, he should have hit one of the women, square in her pinchable double chin. Then the other one might have opened up, spilled the beans, told him where the hell Pamela Hayes had run off to.

Now it was too late. Things were going to get messy if the authorities showed up.

"Okay, okay," he said, holding up his hands in a placating gesture. "Hey, it's just my broken heart talking, okay? I'm upset, is all. I love that girl more than life itself."

"Well, then," the second woman said. The first continued to punch buttons on the phone. ''Why don't you go home and write her a nice letter? I'm sure the post office will forward it to her.''

"Okay, yeah, that's what I'll do," he said, retreating to the door and out. He loped across the chilly chrome-and-marble lobby and out of the building, into the dense June fog. He was in his car, tearing out of the parking lot, before anyone in a uniform could reach the building.

The flames of his anger still nipped at him, crackled and flared. Pamela Hayes had obviously taken a powder.

She hadn't shown up at her office in a full week. Mick was going to have to track her down.

He had to, before the DA put together a new case against him. He had to find that big-eyed, big-mouthed bitch and shut her up before she caused him any more problems. It was her own fault, really. She shouldn't have been where she was when she was, witnessing things that weren't supposed to have witnesses. If only she hadn't been there, he'd be a free man today.

But as long as he wasn't free, neither was she. She'd seen him, she'd spoken against him, and now she was going to pay.

All Mick had to do was find her.

DEEPER AND DEEPER, Pamela thought as she studied the blurred diagram Joe had sketched on a textured napkin at the Shipwreck last night. The ink had bled in spots, and his handwriting left a great deal to be desired. She could find scarcely any resemblance between his drawing and the map she'd obtained from the chamber of commerce six days ago, when she'd cruised the last few weary miles of Route 1 onto the island and comprehended that she had truly, literally, gone as far as she could go.

One part of her considered Jonas Brenner her salvation: marry him and she'd be under his wing. Surely the matron saints of feminism would forgive her for shucking her own last name and submerging her identity within a man's. Once her arrangement with Joe had run its course and she divorced him, she could go back to being Pamela Hayes.

But another part of her couldn't shake the frightening notion that rather than saving herself, she was sinking deeper and deeper into trouble. Her mind conjured up the image of a person in quicksand who, instead of stretching out and floating on the ooze, tried to fight her way out and wound up being sucked down to her death. The woman staring at her from the mirror above the scratched dresser looked an awful lot like someone who was sinking fast.

Sighing, she turned away from her wan reflection and gazed at the neat, stark efficiency apartment that had been her home for the past few days. She suspected that the apartment building had once been a motel; her front door opened onto a second-floor balcony that ran the length of the building to a flight of stairs on either end. The exterior was ticky-tacky tropical—faded pink stucco, wrought-iron railings, rippling roof tiles that were just a bit too orange to be believable. The interior was just plain tacky—carpeting rough enough to file one's nails on, ceilings textured to resemble cottage cheese, a kitchenette as small as a coat closet and furniture constructed of cardboard-thick wood held together with paste.

She wondered what Joe's house looked like, and his furniture. Such things used to matter to her.

Now all that mattered was saving her neck.

She opened the front door, stepped out onto the balcony and glanced toward Kitty's windows. The curtains were drawn. It was nearly eleven o'clock; Joe had told Pamela to arrive at his house in time for lunch. If Kitty was still sleeping, Pamela didn't want to disturb her.

She reentered her own apartment, crossed to the dresser and studied her image in the mirror one last time. The word *drab* sprang to mind.

Most of the clothing she owned had been purchased for work and the cooler climate of Washington State—wools, tweeds, silk blouses and tailored suits. One local shopping trip had harvested the sleeveless shift she'd worn last night and the cotton walking shorts she was wearing now. The cream-colored shell she had on looked too formal, but it would have to do. If Joe had been looking for a babe, he wouldn't have proposed marriage to Pamela.

She gathered up her map, her purse and her cocktail napkin and left the apartment. This time, she noticed, Kitty's curtains were open. She told herself she only wanted a clarification of where Joe lived, but deep inside she knew she really needed a pep talk. If anything, she was edgier today than she'd been last night. Perhaps Kitty could offer some guidance.

Pamela tapped lightly on Kitty's door. "Hold your goddamn horses!" Kitty bellowed from inside.

Pamela's tension increased. She didn't know much about her neighbor, other than that she worked the evening shift at the Shipwreck, that her hair was bleached a radioactive shade of blond and that she had the sort of physical endowments that made women like Pamela feel pathetically scrawny. Yet something about Kitty had put Pamela at ease yesterday morning, when they'd met in the laundry room. As they'd folded their clothing across from each other, on a long, Formica-topped table, Kitty had somehow convinced Pamela that Joe was the greatest thing since french fries, and if Pamela didn't marry him she'd regret it for the rest of her life.

"Marry him?" Pamela had asked, wondering why, if this guy was so great, he needed Kitty to find him a wife.

"He's got a legal situation. Nothing major, nothing criminal. It's just, he's looking for a fine upstanding woman like yourself who'll agree to marry him for a

while. Someone who'll take his name and wear his ring.
Nothing serious.''

Nothing serious? Pamela had thought. Taking a man's
name and wearing his ring sounded pretty serious to her.
So serious she wouldn't consider it. Pamela was definitely not the home-and-hearth type. She was devoted to
her career, and she'd always been an exceedingly private
person. Marriage meant opening up to someone else,
making oneself vulnerable, feeling someone else's fears
and longings as if they were one's own. Pamela simply
wasn't ready to make a commitment like that, and everyone who knew her knew that.

Which meant that if she got married, the likelihood of
her being found, by Mick Morrow or anyone else, might
decrease. Who would hunt for a single-minded, inde-
pendent woman like architect Pamela Hayes in a cozy,
domestic setting? Who would expect to find her doing
her impersonation of a wife?

"Marry him," she'd ruminated once Kitty had run out
of superlatives for Joe.

"Yeah. He'd make one helluva husband. And you
better believe I know a thing or two about marriage.''

Pamela smoothed the cocktail napkin between her
hands and gazed hopefully at the open curtains, longing
for Kitty to give her another inspiring speech before she
paid a call on what might soon become her new home.

At last the door swung open. Kitty filled the doorway
in a colorful silk kimono, a vision of wild platinum hair
and cleavage. Her face broke into a smile. "Oh, Pamela!
I didn't realize it was you. I thought it was this jerk who
tried to pick me up at the bar last night. A real loser,
you know? Swore he was the reincarnation of Ernest
Hemingway, which was reason enough to want to punch

him in the nose. He kept saying he was going to look me up in the phone book and come after me.''

Pamela found nothing amusing about that. Her own experience with Mick Morrow made her suspicious to the point of paranoia about men who threatened to come after women. She stepped inside Kitty's apartment—a mirror-image of hers, only embellished with great quantities of clutter—and closed the door behind her. Then she drew the chain lock. ''Make sure you look through your peephole before you open your door to anyone,'' she instructed Kitty.

Kitty appeared unconcerned. ''The island is full of guys who think they're Ernest Hemingway. I'm used to it.'' She bounded across the room to her unmade bed and did a belly flop onto it, her head propped in her hands and her knees bent so her feet hovered above her rump. She looked like a superannuated teenager at a pajama party, eager to gossip and giggle about boys. ''So, what did you think of Joe?''

''He's…very nice,'' Pamela said, lifting a filmy garment of some sort from a chair and lowering herself to sit. ''He wants me to go to his house today.''

''To meet Lizzie Borden,'' Kitty guessed.

''Lizzie Borden?''

''Okay, his niece hasn't taken a hatchet to anyone yet. She's a maniac, though. Take her with a sense of humor and you'll be fine. I adore that kid.''

A maniacal child, Pamela thought. Alternately referred to as a lower order of vertebrate or America's most famous ax murderer.

''But look, Pamela…'' Kitty tilted her head slightly, her dark eyes narrowing as she appraised Pamela. ''Can we speak frankly? If you're going to marry Joe, you ought to jazz yourself up a little, know what I mean?''

Pamela didn't take criticism from others well—usually because she spent too much of her time and energy criticizing herself. "Jazz myself up," she said warily, trying not to bristle.

"A couple of weeks down here and you'll develop some color, you know? But right now, you look kind of washed out. Here." Kitty sprang from the bed, hauled Pamela out of her chair, and dragged her into the bathroom. A forceful nudge landed her on the toilet seat. "I'm just going to give you a little color, okay? Nothing extreme."

With that, Kitty attacked Pamela's face with a vast array of cosmetic brushes. Choking clouds of tinted powder billowed into the air as Kitty went at her with blusher and eye shadow. Pamela tried in vain to catch a glimpse of herself in the mirror above the seat, but all she saw was the reflection of Kitty's arm wielding her brushes like Jackson Pollock assaulting a canvas.

Pamela hoped she wouldn't look like a Jackson Pollock painting when Kitty was done.

"It's not as if the situation between Jonas and me has anything to do with physical attraction," she protested feebly as Kitty laid down a brush and brandished a mascara wand.

"*Jonas?* Did he ask you to call him that?"

"It's his name." It only just occurred to Pamela that she preferred Jonas to Joe. She liked the Biblical ring of it.

"Gee, he never told me that. I guess he must be serious about you."

"Of course not," Pamela scoffed. "He just wants to marry me."

Kitty stepped back and assessed her handiwork. "Not bad. All you need now is…" She rummaged through a drawer and pulled out a rainbow-striped ribbon. "There you go," she said, arranging it around Pamela's hair. "You ought to do something about those earrings," she muttered, now that Pamela's ears were exposed, along with the plain gold buttons that adorned the lobes. "They're awfully boring. But earrings are one thing I don't lend."

Pamela almost responded that if necessary she could borrow some earrings from Joe. Instead, she rose from the commode and confronted herself in the mirror. The face that stared back at her looked a bit feverish, but that was an improvement over her usual waxy pallor. Kitty stood beside her, beaming proudly at what she'd wrought, making Pamela feel as if she were part of some pagan ritual, the sacrificial virgin who'd been primped by the tribal matriarch before offering herself to the gods so the crops would grow and the local volcano wouldn't erupt.

"So what do you think? You look gorgeous," Kitty said, answering for her.

"Thank you." Pamela didn't agree that she looked gorgeous, but if she said so, Kitty might think she was referring to the makeup job and not the face behind it. "Actually," she said, turning from the mirror and following Kitty out of the cramped room, "I didn't come here for you to attempt to make me pretty. I came to get directions to Jonas's house."

"That bum! He invited you over and he didn't tell you where he lives?"

"He did tell me," Pamela defended him. She pulled out her cocktail napkin and showed the blurry diagram to Kitty. "He gave me this, but I can't make head or tail of it."

Kitty took the napkin, squinted at it, rotated it a hundred and eighty degrees, then shook her head. Without having to be asked, Pamela supplied her with the chamber of commerce map. "Ah, here we go. See, here's Leon Street. You're going to head down to South Street and hang a left, and then you just keep going till you get to Leon Street and make a right. Easy as pie."

"What does his house look like? Have you been there?"

Kitty's laugh was just a tad too knowing. "Sweetie, there isn't a woman on this island who wouldn't want to call that house home."

"What is it, a palace?"

"No, but a prince lives inside. Go get him, Pam. Be the first one to reel him in."

Pamela might be the first, but she wouldn't be the last. This was a marriage with a built-in conclusion. And as for reeling Joe in, the only reason he was biting on her hook was because of Elizabeth. Lizzie Borden. Lizard.

Pamela shrugged back her shoulders and girded herself to meet the maniac. "Okay," she said, tucking an errant strand of hair into her ribbon. "Here goes nothing."

"Here comes the bride," Kitty sang as she ushered Pamela to the door. "You're going to love being married, Pamela. Trust me—I've done it plenty of times myself."

Done what? Pamela wondered as she waved and departed from Kitty's disorderly apartment. Gotten married, or enjoyed the part of marriage she and Joe weren't going to share? Last night he had promised her that she would have her own bedroom. Without separate beds, the deal was off.

Pamela wasn't a prude and she wasn't a virgin. But she wasn't going to get involved any more than she had to with Jonas Brenner. This was a business arrangement. Safety for her, a custody judgment for him. Sex would only complicate matters.

Besides, he was much too grungy to appeal to her in a romantic way. Torn apparel, unshaven cheeks, the mop of hair, the absurdly blue eyes...the taut, lean body, the firm, powerful grip of his hand around hers and that sly, seductive dimple punctuating the corner of his mouth...

Definitely not her type.

She gave a final wave to Kitty, who was watching her from the window with a go-get-'em grin plastered across her face. Then she descended the steps to the parking lot adjacent to the building. The asphalt felt sticky in the late-morning heat; the warm, damp air wrapped around her like a compress. Hers was the only car in the lot with out-of-state plates. She'd have to change the registration.

Right after the wedding, she resolved—assuming she and Joe went through with the marriage. She would get Florida plates and a license under the name Pamela Brenner.

Pamela Brenner. Would that ever sound anything less than bizarre to her?

It's only temporary, she reminded herself, as, after instinctively checking the back seat to see if a hit man was hiding there, she unlocked her car. A gust of scorching air slammed into her when she opened the door, and she gingerly lowered herself onto the steaming seat. The first time she'd gotten into her car after it had baked for a while in the Key West sun, the steering wheel had nearly given her second-degree burns.

Pamela Brenner.

What if she ultimately discovered that she couldn't stand Joe? What if they were incompatible? What if he

expected her to pick up after him, and cook for him, and
iron his shirts, and perform all the other mundane home-
making chores she loathed? Even if he didn't expect her
to be a *real* wife, he might expect her to be a housewife,
a prospect that made facing Mick Morrow almost pal-
atable in comparison.

She ordered herself to calm down. Nothing had been
forged in concrete. She was going to visit Joe's home
and meet his niece, that was all. She was going to pay
a social call on the proprietor of a bar and his ax-
murderer niece.

Allowing herself a fatalistic smile, she turned on the
air conditioner and cursed as fiery air blasted from the
vents. In a minute it cooled down, and after a final
glance at her map, she steered out of the parking lot.

In the week she'd lived in Key West, she'd grown
reasonably familiar with Duval Street, which ran through
the heart of Old Town and seemed to be the commercial
center of the island. The sidewalks were crammed with
souvenir shops, restaurants, bars, art galleries, T-shirt
boutiques, bars, pharmacies and more bars. Perhaps the
overabundance of liquor merchants was in some way
related to the island's population of men who thought
they were Ernest Hemingway.

Stranger than the stores, though, was the landscape
itself. Pamela had visited Southern California plenty of
times; she knew what palm trees were. But here they
didn't seem like lonely oases sprouting in the desert. Key
West was the tropics, everything lush and green and vo-
luptuous—and humid. Hot and humid.

She followed Kitty's directions and navigated into a
residential area of cozy, pretty houses. The neighborhood seemed too homey for someone like Joe, although
as an adoptive father to an orphaned girl he must have

a domestic side to him. She recalled what he'd said last night about abruptly finding himself the primary care-taker of a two-year-old who ate only pink food and sobbed for her parents. There was clearly more to Jonas Brenner than frayed jeans and an earring.

At last she found his home, a sprawling white bungalow on a plant-choked lot. The wide front porch overlooked a shaggy lawn interspersed with a variety of palm species. Flowering bougainvillea crawled up the trellis-like underpinnings of the porch. Slouching wooden chairs sat empty beneath the broad overhang.

Halfway up the pebbled driveway Pamela stopped her car and climbed out. Some sort of tropical bird, cam-ouflaged by the foliage, cawed a greeting.

She wasn't sure what she'd expected, but whatever it had been, this was better. The house had been recently painted. The roof was in good repair. A child's bicycle lay on its side next to the slate front walk. The front door stood open, the screen door veiling the interior of the house from her view.

She could imagine herself living in a house like this. It was certainly big enough, and charming. Although the landscaping was as much in need of a trim as Joe's hair, it was lovely. Yes, she could imagine it....

An arrow whizzed past her head. She shrieked and flattened herself against the notched bark of a royal palm, clinging to the rough surface until her trembling stopped. It took most of her courage to glance at the missile, which lay on the grass a few feet away.

Red plastic, with a suction cup at the end.

Another arrow flew toward her from a cluster of bushes at the side of the house. This one missed her by several yards. She pushed away from the palm and glow-ered at the bushes.

A girl emerged from the shrubbery. She stood about three-and-a-half feet tall, with brownish-red hair braided into two narrow plaits on either side of her face and hanging loose in the back. Gull feathers were woven into the braids. The child had dark eyes, a smudge of a nose, a pouting mouth and rings of grime circling her neck. She wore a yellow T-shirt with bright purple letters across it reading Life's a Beach, and a hula skirt constructed out of shreds of green plastic. Her feet were bare and dirty, and her equally dirty hands clutched a toy archer's bow.

She scowled at Pamela. "You're dead," she announced.

Pamela met the girl's stare. "Do I look dead to you?"

The girl meditated for a minute, then shrugged. "You're ugly," she said.

Pamela knew better than to ask the child if she looked ugly. Her smile, however, felt as plastic as the hula skirt, and she abandoned all pretense of friendliness. "Where's your uncle?"

"He's not here. He went to Birdie's."

"He invited me for lunch."

"Yeah, well, he's at Birdie's. You wanna play?"

No, Pamela did not want to play. Not with a heavily armed savage who called her ugly. "Who is Birdie?"

The girl smirked at Pamela's apparent ignorance. "You know. Birdie. Come on, let's play. I'll be the boo doo chief. You can be the biker." With that, the girl spun around and plunged into the shrubbery.

Pamela took a deep breath and let it out. She didn't want to be the biker. What she wanted was for Jonas Brenner to appear and explain what in God's name was going on.

Her prayers were answered promptly. "Pamela!" His voice sailed toward her from the street.

She turned to see him jogging up the driveway, a bouquet of pale squares drooping from his hand. As he drew nearer, she saw they were loose tea bags.

She shifted her gaze from the tea bags to the man holding them. His grooming had improved considerably overnight. Although his hair was still too long, his chin was clean-shaven, and his apparel—a sky-blue cotton shirt tucked neatly into a belted pair of khakis—was untorn. His eyes were hidden behind a pair of mirror-lensed sunglasses, and his earring was dangly and gold this time, either a heart or a skull, or maybe—she hoped—a peace sign. She couldn't make out the shape.

"Sorry," he said, then smiled. Without the stubble to hide it, his dimple was more pronounced. "I realized you might be a tea drinker and I didn't have any tea bags, so I had to borrow some. Actually, I wanted to borrow the whole box, but Birdie can be funny about stuff." He had reached Pamela's side, and she fell into step next to him as they ambled up the front walk to the porch. "You should have rung the bell. Lizard would have let you in."

"Lizard is outside playing," Pamela told him. "She invited me to join her." *She told me I was ugly.* Honestly, Pamela reproached herself, she shouldn't let a child's opinion mean so much to her. But it did. "Who's Birdie?"

"She's Lizard's main baby-sitter. She lives across the street. You'll meet her eventually," said Joe, holding the screen door open for Pamela and following her into an entry hall. The walls were a muted beige, the oak floor covered with a thick, faded runner rug. The shadows kept the interior air surprisingly cool.

"Lizard, Birdie, Kitty... Is there anyone named Toad I ought to know about?"

Joe threw back his head and laughed. It was such a deep, warm laugh Pamela almost begged him to remove his sunglasses. She wanted to see what happened to his eyes when he dissolved into robust laughter—whether they squinted or sparkled or... No, she didn't want to know anything about his eyes at all.

"I reckon I'm as close as anyone gets to being a toad around here," he said. "We should all count our blessings now that we're about to add a swan to the menagerie."

It took Pamela a full minute to realize he meant that *she* would be the swan. She felt her cheeks grow warm. She hadn't prepared herself for flattery—especially not after Lizard's succinct assessment of her appearance. And Joe's compliment wasn't like the usual line a man would use to beguile a woman. He had already established that he wanted to marry her and that once he did they would sleep in separate beds. Maybe he was trying to soften her up so she would overlook his niece's tactlessness.

Or maybe he really meant she was swanlike.

That was a discomfiting thought. This marriage was going to work only if she knew it was based on nothing more complex than sheer necessity. "Your house is nice," she said to distract herself.

"I'll show you around. Here's the living room." He waved through an arched doorway off the hall. "And through that doorway is the dining room, which leads into the kitchen."

"Everything's so tidy." Given Lizard's appearance and behavior, Pamela would have expected the living room to be strewn with toys—or arrows. But it was an

oddly sedate room, full of old, comfortable-looking furniture brightened with throw pillows and antimacassars
and a few oddities—a brass peacock umbrella stand in
one corner, an unused brown candle shaped like a turkey
on a table, a strange tree-shaped light constructed of ar-
tistically bound fiber-optic threads, a clumsy crayon
drawing of two stick people, one large and one small,
elegantly framed and hanging prominently on a wall.

"I told Lizard if she didn't pick up her things before
you arrived, I'd hang her from the ceiling fan by her
toes and turn the fan on high speed. Apparently that was
the wrong thing to say," he added, at last removing his
sunglasses and treating Pamela to a flash of glittering
blue. "She pleaded with me for half the morning to tie
her to the fan. She said she wanted to see if she could
vomit in a perfect circle on the rug. The thing about
Lizard," he went on, leading Pamela back into the hall
and up the stairs, "is she's as gross as any boy. There's
not a prissy bone in her body. I like to think she's lib-
erated."

"Does she vomit much?" Pamela asked delicately.

"Rarely." Joe tossed her an easy smile. "I'll be in
charge of all upset stomachs. Don't worry about it." The
upstairs hall was also lined with a faded runner rug. Joe
gestured toward a half-open door. "That's Lizard's
room. I wouldn't look inside if I were you. It's a night-
mare scene. My room's way down at the end of the hall.
And your room would be here," he said, U-turning and
heading to the opposite end of the hall.

Despite the sloping ceiling beneath the eaves, the bedroom he led her into was bright and airy, the walls pa-
pered in a sunshine-yellow pattern, the double bed neatly
made and the few pieces of furniture polished to a high
gleam. The mirror above the dresser wasn't warped, and

the dresser itself was constructed of solid maple, not particleboard. The rug covering the floor was the color of honey.

She closed her eyes and visualized the bedroom in her sleek condominium back home in Seattle, with its cool parquet floors, its marble master bathroom and its floor-to-ceiling windows. She pictured her platform bed, the simple lines of the room's decor—a hybrid of Shaker and Asian styles—and the enormous dimensions of her closet. Opening her eyes, she saw the exact opposite of the exquisitely designed bedroom she'd left behind when she'd fled for her life.

"This is beautiful," she said.

"I think you'll find it pretty quiet. The windows overlook the backyard, so you won't get much street noise. If it's too hot for you, I can install a window AC unit. But with all the windows open, you'll probably get a nice breeze in here." He watched her expectantly, as if not quite convinced she liked the room.

She turned and smiled. "Really, it's fine."

He returned her smile. She wished he would laugh again, another big, rousing, heartfelt laugh. In spite of his smile, his eyes were serious, the blue of his irises layered in shadow. He seemed as nervous today as she'd felt last night.

She was nervous, too. Even though they seemed to have cleared a hurdle, they hadn't finished running the course yet. Too many things could still go wrong. She could still discover Joe was a slob, a wastrel, demanding or moody or any number of other unpleasant things.

And then there was his lunatic niece, armed and dangerous.

Yet her anxiety waned when she stood with him in the sun-filled room that would be hers if she agreed to marry him. She thought about what she'd seen of the house—the massive, well-used furnishings, the old-fashioned arrangement of the rooms, the verdant yard, all of it the antithesis of her condo back home. She considered the comforting order of the living room, the small, personal touches, the framed crayon drawing of a man and a child side by side, holding hands. She surveyed the room that would be hers and contemplated the long hallway that connected her room to Joe's.

How many steps loomed between the two rooms? she wondered. How many paces separated a husband and a wife?

Silly thought. Ridiculous thought. No one would be pacing anywhere. That was the way she wanted it, the way they both wanted it. If she and Joe got married, that was the way it would be.

"It's a very nice room," she said one final time, then edged past him and out the door, ready to face the next hurdle: his niece.

CHAPTER THREE

A MILD BREEZE WAFTED through the screened porch as
they sat around the table. Lois, one of the barmaids at
the Shipwreck, boasted of having read everything Martha Stewart had ever written, and she'd suggested to Joe
that they eat lunch on the porch instead of in the dining
room—"Too stodgy," she'd said. As for the kitchen—
"Too familiar. The porch is just right. Casual elegance.
Even kinda romantic." Lois had also suggested that Joe
festoon the house with cut flowers, set the table with
cloth napkins rolled and tied with string as if they were
diplomas, and serve deviled eggs and endive salad in a
vinaigrette for lunch. Some of her suggestions were better than others.

Canned tuna fell within his limited culinary capabili-
ties, so tuna, sliced tomatoes and a loaf of seven-grain
bread was the menu he went with. He knew some
women preferred green, crunchy things for lunch, but as
eager as he was to make a good impression on Pamela,
he wasn't going to impress her at the expense of his own
stomach.

Besides, Lizard considered salads toxic. Not that that
mattered much; nowadays, the only thing she would consider eating for lunch was peanut butter and mashed banana on a bagel, accompanied by a glass of milk flavored
with enough strawberry syrup to turn it shocking pink.

She was seated across the table from him, gnawing

on her bagel and glaring at Pamela, who sipped her water-on-the-rocks and pretended Lizard's flagrant rudeness wasn't getting to her. Joe was tempted to haul the brat out of her chair and throttle her.

Instead, like Pamela, he pretended not to notice her testy mood. "So, does the house meet with your approval?" he asked Pamela.

"It's lovely. It's larger than I expected. Have you lived here long?"

"Ever since Lizzie came to live with me. Before that I lived on a houseboat."

"A houseboat?" Pamela looked astonished.

He stifled a reflexive sigh. Man, but he'd loved that houseboat. He'd loved the smell of the gulf surrounding him, clinging to him, and the way the timbers creaked and the ropes clanked and the wind whispered its secrets to him. Most of all, he'd loved lying in bed and being rocked by the waves, caressed by the tide. Sometimes he'd liked that even more than the usual rocking and caressing that went on in his bed.

He supposed it all depended on who—or what—one was being rocked and caressed by. For not the first time, he wondered how Pamela would stack up as a bedmate. Better than the gulf tides?

He would never know. And he ought to quit thinking about it. "I couldn't continue living on the boat with a rowdy little toddler," he explained. "She could have toddled overboard."

"I'm not rowdy," Lizard protested, then took another lusty bite out of her bagel.

"Sweetheart, you are the definition of rowdy. Anyway—" he turned back to Pamela "—the fellow who owned this house had just been divorced and was antsy to remove himself from the scene of his folly. He wanted to sail away from all his troubles, and I wanted to put some terra firma under Lizard's feet. So he and I swapped homes, with a bit of cash thrown in to make up the difference.''

''I don't need anything under my feet,'' Lizard announced, then held her half-eaten bagel above her chin, hiding her mouth behind the semicircular sandwich. ''Look,'' she said. ''I'm smiling.''

''Don't play with your food.''

''I'm not playing. I'm smiling.'' She turned her bagel grin to Pamela. Her voice emerged from behind the sandwich: ''You like our house?''

''I do indeed,'' Pamela said.

''You gonna move into the spare room upstairs?''

''Maybe.''

Lizard's big, dark gaze slid back to Joe. ''What if I don't like her?''

''Now, Lizard—''

''No, that's all right,'' Pamela interrupted, her hand reaching across the table to pat his arm. Her touch was brief but consoling, her fingers cool and soft against his skin, like silk ribbons. Before he could react, she retreated, shifting in her seat so she could address Lizard directly. ''You don't have to like me, Lizard. And I don't have to like you. All we have to do is get along.''

Lizard sized her up. ''You gonna marry my uncle?''

She shot Joe a look even more fleeting than her touch. Then she turned back to Lizard. ''Maybe.''

''Does that mean you love him?''

''It means he and I think we can make a life together.''

''My mommy loved my daddy.''

Pamela had been batting a thousand up until then, but Lizard's fastball whipped past her for a strike. She fell back in her seat and glanced toward Joe, evidently expecting him to step up to the plate and pinch-hit for her.

Not knowing what else to say, he opted for the truth. "Yes, Liz. Your mommy and daddy loved each other."

"Is that the way you love *her?*" Lizard asked, tilting her head toward Pamela, who had somehow managed to twist her napkin tighter than a nautical rope.

"No two people ever love each other the way two other people do," he said, relying on vague platitudes. "Besides, Pamela and I haven't known each other that long. But I think she'll be a nice addition to the household, don't you?"

"I think," Lizard said with titanic self-importance, "she doesn't eat enough."

Joe had noticed that, too. Maybe Pamela didn't like tuna. Maybe she wanted green, crunchy things.

"It's the heat," Pamela told Lizard. "I'm not used to such hot weather. It takes my appetite away."

Lizard slurped her milk, then squirmed into a kneeling position on her chair. "What do you do?"

"I beg your pardon?"

"What do you do? Like Megan—she's sometimes my best friend when she isn't being a dope—her mother is a county at the Casa Marina."

"An accountant," Joe translated, secretly pleased that Lizard had asked Pamela what he himself had wanted to ask.

"Or like Birdie? She's a boo doo chief."

Pamela sent a bewildered look Joe's way. "Voodoo," he mumbled, recalling that he'd already identified Birdie as Lizard's baby-sitter. Birdie had immigrated from Haiti back in the seventies, and the older she got, the quirkier she got. She made puffy fabric dolls and used them for pincushions, and she spent hours with Lizard in the backyard, mixing dirt from the garden and water from the hose, a sprig of this and a leaf of that, and chanting mumbo jumbo. Joe didn't believe her routines accomplished anything more useful than keeping Lizard entertained—which, granted, was no small feat.

Pamela nodded uncertainly, then turned back to Lizard. "I'm an architect," she said.

Joe swore under his breath. Sure, he'd wanted the woman he married to make a positive impression on anyone who had the power to take Lizard away from him. He'd wanted his wife to be educated and affluent and well put together and all that. But he didn't want her to be a hotshot. He didn't want to be married to an uppity yuppie who would pontificate on Corinthian columns and Frank Lloyd Wright's genius at the drop of a hat.

An architect. Jeez.

He cautioned himself not to panic. For one thing, there wasn't much an architect could do in Key West, professionally speaking—not without a commission and some heavy-duty financial backing, neither of which Pamela was likely to have in her current predicament. For another thing, once she married Joe—her savior, her protector—she would be beholden to him, wouldn't she? She couldn't put on airs, not when her neck was on the block.

Okay. He could handle being married to an architect. As long as she didn't act like an architect.

"What's an ock-attack?" Lizard asked.

"It's someone who designs buildings," Joe told her.

"Like with Lego?"

"Sure."

"I got lots of Legos. I guess I'm an ock-attack, too." Lizard dropped her half-eaten sandwich onto her plate and shoved back her chair. "If you want to eat the rest of my bagel, go ahead. I'm done," she announced, rising and heading for the door out to the yard.

Joe reached out and snagged her wrist. "Hey, pal, what do you say?"

"May-I-be-excused," she recited as if it were a single word, not a question. She slipped out of his grasp and raced outside.

Pamela watched through the screened walls as Lizard bounded across the backyard, tramping haphazardly through a scraggly herb garden and vanishing into the denser shrubs beyond. Then Pamela lifted her glass and sipped her water. Her eyes were hard and silver, like the ice cubes clinking in her glass.

The silence grew as heavy as the thick, warm air. Joe felt obliged to say something. "Lizard has a way to go when it comes to manners," he explained with what he hoped was an endearing smile. "She tends to confuse bluntness with honesty."

"That's all right," Pamela said, though she didn't look all right. She looked pale and fragile and uncomfortable—which, under the circumstances, he should have expected.

Even so, he wanted to vanquish the worry that shadowed her eyes and pinched her lips. "Really, she's a great kid. A little mouthy, but..."

"She said I was ugly," Pamela announced.

Joe opened his mouth and then shut it. Definitely the brat deserved a throttling. "When did she say that?"

Pamela seemed embarrassed all of a sudden. "Oh, I know she didn't mean anything by it. I don't know why I mentioned it—"

"You are *not* ugly."

"As you said, she's very honest."

"I didn't say that. She's a little beast, and she'll do anything to get a rise out of people. Please." He wanted to grab hold of Pamela, hug her, reassure her. "Trust me. You're not ugly."

"Thank you," she said stiffly.

Did she think he was just handing her a line? Trying to preserve her ego? Should he haul her into his arms and kiss her, ravish those pursed lips of hers until she realized her appearance wasn't a turnoff?

He swallowed a wry laugh. If he tried to kiss her she'd probably slap his face, or kick him someplace lower. One wrong move on his part, and she'd decide she was better off dealing with her Seattle assassin than marrying Joe.

"You know what?" he said, trying a new tack. "I think Lizzie's biggest problem is that she doesn't have a female role model. She needs someone to show her the proper courtesies. I try—it took me two years to train her to ask to be excused before she bolted from the table, and she still doesn't always remember. Maybe she needs a woman in her life."

"She has Birdie," Pamela pointed out.

"The boo doo chief." Joe rolled his eyes and laughed.

"And Kitty. Kitty told me she adores Lizard."

"Yeah, well…Kitty's a great lady, to say nothing of the best waitress I've ever had. But role-modeling isn't her forte. Are you sure you don't want some more to eat? Should I make some coffee, or tea?"

"After all the trouble you went to to get those tea bags, I suppose I should have tea." The smile Pamela gave him was brittle.

Things were falling apart, and Joe was having trouble finding the crack and repairing it. Lizard had done her part, sure. And he himself was still unsettled by the news that Pamela was a member of a highly esteemed profession, a good two thousand rungs up the ladder from bar owner. But more than that was wrong. There was an undercurrent of uneasiness, a tension between Pamela and him that he needed to fix before the situation was broken beyond repair.

He had to touch her. No kisses, no graphic proof that she wasn't ugly, but he had to connect with her in some friendly way. If she misread him, if she slapped and kicked and otherwise gave vent to her rage at his taking even the mildest of liberties, well, so be it. If this engagement was doomed, better to find out now, while he still had a little time to hunt down a wife on the mainland before his in-laws showed up and staked their claim on Lizard.

It was unlike him to make such a big deal out of taking a woman's hand. He'd held her hand last night at the Shipwreck, and no thunderbolts had descended from the heavens. But now that his niece—the beast, the monster, the troublemaker *extraordinaire*—had introduced the subject of Pamela's attractiveness, to say nothing of love...

The hell with it. He stopped dissecting his impulses, eased Pamela's hand free from her tortured napkin and sandwiched it between his palms.

Despite the heat, her fingers were as icy as her eyes. If she'd had less poise, she no doubt would have been trembling.

"Pamela." He tightened his hold on her, hoping to warm her up, thaw her out. "I think we can make this marriage work, as long as we don't lose track of what's important. Okay? The thing isn't perfect, but we can make it work."

She flicked her tongue against her lips to moisten

them. Observing the damp pink tip as it circled her mouth made him far more aware of her lack of ugliness than he wanted to be. He lowered his gaze to her chest to remind himself that her body wasn't his type, but somehow, in her demure silk shell, the modest dimensions of her chest looked right. A small bosom became her. He imagined her breasts would be like ripe peaches—perfectly round, firm and sweet....

He banished the image with a quick shake of his head. "If you're having problems," he continued, his voice as tame as his thoughts had been wicked, "now's the time to make them known."

"Well..." She flexed her fingers against his palm, and he was visited by more uninvited thoughts: her fingers flexing against his naked back. Her slim, neat, nude body pressed beneath his. In his bed on the houseboat, rocking, rocking... "I think we ought to spell some things out first," she said, wrenching him from his fantasy.

"What things?" No rocking. No bed. No nude bodies.

He felt her fingers move again—not as if she wanted to escape his grip, though. He loosened his hold slightly, but she didn't slide her hand out from between his. Her eyes looked a little less sleepy. "Exactly how much of a role model would you expect me to be?"

Lizard. Damn the kid. Why couldn't she have behaved better with Pamela? "Forget Liz's big mouth," he insisted, cramming his voice with earnest emotion. "You aren't ugly."

At that Pamela did slide her hand free. She inched her chair back, pivoting it to face him. "I really don't care whether she thinks I'm a gorgon," she said. "I'm more concerned with how much of a mommy you expect me to be. I told you last night, I'm not terribly maternal. I don't derive pleasure from baking cookies and playing with dolls.''

"Lizard isn't into dolls, either," Joe assured her. "She's big on action-adventure games."

Pamela nodded. "Boo doo and bikers."

"Yeah, that kind of thing."

"Well, I'm not big on boo doo and bikers. Understand, Jonas, what my life was like before I came to Key West. I lived in a condominium full of expensive furniture and breakable objects. I listened to classical music. I went to work, and after work I went out to dinner or to the theater with friends. I'm not used to clearing my schedule with a baby-sitter before I make plans. I'm not used to tripping over toy arrows."

A few particulars leapt into sharp relief: she went out with friends. Boyfriends? Dates? Had she left a lover behind when she'd fled from Seattle? Was she going to cry herself to sleep every night in her bed at the opposite end of the hall from his?

And *Jonas*. Why had she called him that? Was she trying to maintain a greater degree of formality in their relationship? Was she trying to distance herself from him? "Most people call me Joe," he reminded her warily.

"I like Jonas. It's an unusual name."

Okay. He'd take his compliments where he could get them. "Then call me Jonas. Can I call you Pam?"

"Nobody calls me Pam," she blurted out. Then a slow smile crept across her mouth. "Sure. Pam would be fine."

He supposed that meant she hadn't ruled out their possible marriage. It also meant that she was allowing Joe to call her what no one else called her. Did she consider him unique? Or was she just pretending that who she was in Key West bore no relationship to who she'd been in Seattle?

Why in God's name was he analyzing every little detail? He ought to just push the negotiations forward, get the final okay from her and tie this sucker up. "All right," he said, wishing he could take her hand again. "As far as maternal responsibilities, no sweat. Birdie takes care of Lizard. There are plenty of bakeries in town if any of us develops a craving for homemade cookies. And I'm around most days. I've got two other bartenders working for me, and we rotate shifts, but I'm usually around the house through midafternoon, so I can take care of most stuff. Next September Lizard will start kindergarten, so child care will be even less of a problem."

"Then what am I supposed to do during the day?"

He shrugged. "That's up to you. Maybe there's an architectural firm hiring on the island."

She scowled. "No. I can't do that. I'm trying to make it impossible for anyone to find me. The architectural world isn't so big. If a firm hired me down here, someone might hear about it someplace else." She shook her head. "No, I definitely can't go back to work right now. I can't pursue jobs that would draw attention to me."

He resolved to stop resenting her fancy career. How could he not feel sorry for someone who'd had to sacrifice her job—and so much more—because some gangster had slipped through the cracks? "You can do whatever you want," he said gently. "I'd only ask that if a social services lady comes to call, you try to act domestic."

"I'm never going to be mistaken for June Cleaver."

"Oh, I don't know about that," he teased. "Maybe if you wore a string of pearls and a starchy dress—"

"And baked cookies." Pamela sighed. "What about cleaning the house? Who's responsible for that?"

"Lizard," he deadpanned. "Can't you tell?"

"Seriously, Jonas—are you going to expect me to vacuum and dust and—"

"How about we all pitch in. You make a mess, you clean it up. I make a mess, I clean it up. Lizard makes a mess, so what's new?"

She fought against a grin and lost. "Are you sure you want me to marry you?"

"We need each other, Pam," he said. That sounded melodramatic, but it was true. "I think you can help me convince the social workers that Lizard's got a good home here. That's all I'm asking of you."

She moistened her lips once more and averted her eyes, as if what she was about to say was extremely difficult. "What about money?"

"What about it?"

"I can contribute something toward room and board. Most of my money is tied up in a bank in Seattle, and getting it out of there without alerting half the world to my whereabouts won't be easy. But..."

Typical yuppie attitude—distilling everything down to dollars and cents. "I'm asking you to marry me, okay? You're going to be my wife, not my tenant."

She lifted her gaze back to him. Her eyes were as moist as her lips. Oh, God. He didn't want her to start crying. Especially over something as trivial as money.

But before he could think of what magical words he could say to cheer her up, she spoke. "I don't want to take advantage of you, Jonas. You're being so generous. I think I ought to pay something...." A tear skittered down her cheek.

"The hell with generous. You're doing me a favor."

Why was she crying? It couldn't be money, and it sure as hell couldn't be how generous he was, because he really wasn't that generous at all. He'd asked her to marry him for a purely selfish reason: because he wanted Lizard.

Something else was bothering her, something he couldn't begin to fathom. He felt utterly helpless watching her dab at her cheeks with her tattered paper napkin.

"What if he finds me? What if he tracks me down?"

The assassin. "He won't track you down," Joe promised, although he had no way in hell of guaranteeing that. But the proper manly response to a woman's distress was to swear she was perfectly safe with him, and when a woman started crying, a man had little choice but to be properly manly. "How could he possibly find you? You're just going to be a quiet little housewife in the Keys, right? Mrs. Jonas Brenner."

"Because if my marrying you endangered your niece in any way whatsoever, I..." She let out a shaky sigh. "I couldn't live with myself if anything happened to her."

If anything happened to Lizard, Joe couldn't live with himself, either. The whole reason he was going through this charade was to prevent something from happening to her. Not that his in-laws were as bad as hit men, but he simply couldn't believe living with them in their ritzy-glitzy California home would be good for her.

All night long he'd thought about it. He'd weighed the pros and cons, the risk of marrying Pamela versus the risk of remaining a bachelor, or marrying the wrong woman. He'd considered everything Pamela had told him at the Shipwreck last night. And he'd concluded she wasn't in all that much danger. The cops in Seattle were keeping tabs on the hit man, right? They'd know if he left the state. Besides, a gangster couldn't turn up in Key West without everybody knowing about it. It was a small place. Everyone knew everyone—which was why he hadn't been able to find a wife among the locals.

And if Pamela Hayes the architect transformed into Pam Brenner the little woman, how would anyone at the opposite end of the continent track her down?

Except for her weird entanglement with a professional criminal, Pam was perfect. Joe wanted to marry her. And he wasn't going to let her apprehension stand in his way.

"Lizzie's going to be fine," he promised. "We're going to make a great little family, Pam."

"I hate..." Her voice cracked, and she bit her lip and dabbed at her cheeks once more. "I hate having to impose on anyone."

"Who's imposing on whom? You're doing me a favor, remember?"

She began to weep freely. "I hate crying. I hate being afraid like this. I used to dream of getting married, Jonas—all little girls dream of big white weddings. Except maybe Lizard..." She sniffled. "And instead, here I am, inflicting my danger on her. If he finds me...if he finds me..."

That did it. Joe stood, gathered Pamela's hands in his and lifted her out of her chair. Then he closed his arms around her.

She was thin but not skinny. He felt the sleek padding of her skin over her shoulder blades, the surprising softness of her narrow waist. She sobbed into his shoulder, and a strange sense of power stole over him.

She would be his wife, and he would protect her. "Everything's going to be all right," he whispered. "The biggest danger you'll face if you marry me is that Lizard might drive you insane."

He felt her smile, her cheek moving against his shirt, her hands timidly rising to his sides. "I guess I didn't really want a big white wedding, after all."

"Not this time," he said. "After everything's all squared away, and you go for the real thing, you can make it as big and white as you want. Okay?"

She pulled back and gazed up at him. Her eyes were wet, as if all the ice had melted. "Are you sure, Jonas? Are you really sure this is going to work out?"

"I'm sure." And the pope was Jewish. But what else could he say? If he revealed he was as dubious about the whole thing as she was, he'd lose her—and Lizard, too. He'd wind up with nothing but sorrow.

Declaring his certainty seemed like the right thing to do. With a tenderness he'd thought had been reserved only for Lizard, he wiped the last of Pamela's tears from her cheeks, brushed a pale strand of her hair away from her face, and told himself that even if he didn't get to indulge in the fun parts of being a husband, he'd do his damnedest to hide his misgivings from his wife-to-be.

That, after all, was what husbands were supposed to do.

CHAPTER FOUR

"TONY? IT'S MICK Morrow."

"Mick!" Tony's voice boomed through the telephone. "What are you up to? I've got to file a report on you."

"Another report?"

"Hey, you're my job these days, Mick. I'm supposed to submit a daily record of your comings and goings. I didn't know I had such a flair for fiction. They don't teach creative writing in the police academy, you know."

"What have you said about me?"

"According to my reports, you live the most boring life in the world. You go to the supermarket, you go to the post office, you go to the pizza place for take-out. You're a model citizen, Mick."

"And you're a model cop."

"Hey, I admire you, Mick. The way you beat that murder rap—you really have Lady Luck in your bed."

Mick forced himself to smile. He hated small talk, but he knew he had to suffer through it before he could get down to the business at hand. Tony was a small-talk kind of guy.

"I mean, the way you manage things, she's just spreading her legs for you," Tony went on, obviously taken with his metaphor.

Patience, Mick ordered himself as he gazed around

his modest kitchen, a room full of unoriginal pine furniture and built-ins, with white blinds at the window and
muffin crumbs on the counter. He made a lot of money
doing what he did, but he was too smart to spend it all
in one place. His apartment's decor was the residential
equivalent of a plain brown wrapper, the sort of home
that shouted, "No wife, no kids, no pets, no attach-
ments." That pretty well summed up Mick's life.

"You and I both know I didn't beat the rap," he reminded Tony. "I'm still under indictment. They tossed
out the verdict on a technicality."

"Yeah, right. One of the jurors went to nursery school
with the widow of the guy that got murdered. And that
never came out until after the verdict was handed
down."

"Don't blame me," Mick said, all innocence. "The
DA didn't do a good job of interrogating the jurors."

"You'd think that juror would have disqualified himself."

"Maybe he figured it wasn't worth mentioning until
it was too late. Not that I'm saying I had anything to do
with it, even though the whole thing bought me a new
trial. That's the American system of justice, Tony."

"You're clever, Mick. Very clever."

Enough chitchat. "Listen, Tony, I've got a problem.
They're planning to retry me, you know that. You also
know the district attorney hasn't got much against me,
other than the word of that woman."

"Pamela Hayes."

"She's left town, Tony."

"How do you know that?"

"I know it," Mick said tersely. He wasn't about to
tell the cop who was supposed to be keeping an eye on
him all the things he'd been up to while the cop *wasn't*

keeping an eye on him. "She's disappeared, Tony. And you know damned well she's going to reappear the minute they put together a new trial for me. The broad's going to show up in time to testify against me again. You see what I'm saying, Tony?"

"I know, Mick, but—"

"She's their whole case. Nobody else saw the hit go down. No evidence was found at the scene, other than a slug in the guy's body. But this Hayes broad swears it was me she saw doing the job."

"And she's taken a powder?"

"Vanished into thin air."

"What else have you got on her?"

Mick pulled out his notes. His lawyer had done a lot of research before the first trial—a lot of frustrating research. Pamela Hayes had proved to be what in legal circles was referred to as an unimpeachable witness. "She's thirty years old. The only child of Ronald and Margaret Hayes of Kirkland. Never been married."

"You wouldn't by any chance have her driver's license number, would you?"

Mick snorted. Tony was the cop here; he was the one who had access to all the data. "No, Tony. But I do know she worked for Murtaugh Associates as an architect. Did her undergraduate work at Stanford, graduate studies at UW. She's skinny and blond—or at least she was during my first trial. She could be a brunette now, for all I know.

"I visited her old address and they told me she was out of town. Got real antsy when I tried to find out where she was, but if something happened to her, me and my lawyer would know about it."

"Here I am, supposed to be tracking you, and now you want me to track her."

"Carefully, Tony. Not so anyone would find out."

"I'll see what I can do," Tony promised. "God gave us computers for a reason, didn't he."

Sure, Mick thought. *And God gave us crooked cops like Tony for a reason—to make life a little easier for guys like Mick.* "Whatever you can find will be greatly appreciated."

"Meaning, we'll be celebrating Christmas the usual way?"

Mick pulled a face. "Of course, Tony," he said, laboring hard to filter the irritation out of his voice. Mick always honored the holiday by donating a huge sum of money to Tony's favorite charity: the Tony fund. These days it wasn't easy to own your very own personal police officer. Too many honest cops screwed up Mick's way of doing business.

But Tony had his price. And especially now, when a second murder trial loomed ominously on the horizon, Mick considered his associate worth every penny.

"I DON'T KNOW," Mary said.

She was seated next to Joe at the table on the screened porch. Through the screen they could observe Lizard and Pamela in the backyard doing what Joe hoped was some extremely quick bonding. Pamela, as usual, was dressed too formally, in a linen shirt and pleated slacks and those gold-button earrings that seemed like the sort of jewelry best suited for a funeral. Lizard, as usual, was dressed like a savage, wearing a pair of bib overalls with the legs cut off and multicolored ink scribblings all over them, and under the overalls the top half of her Bart Simpson pajamas. She scampered barefoot through the herb garden, identifying various plants to Pamela, who seemed alternately interested and dismayed.

Sighing, Joe turned to glance at Mary DiNardi. It occurred to him that Pamela looked more like a lawyer than his own lawyer did. Mary had shown up at his house an hour ago, dressed in a Hawaiian-print shirt and khaki shorts and carrying a canvas tote with several folders of documents in it. He happened to know Mary owned a couple of suits—he'd seen her in one, once—and a leather briefcase that she saved for court appearances. But any lawyer who made house calls certainly couldn't be expected to resemble a Wall Street wheeler-dealer, or even an architect from Seattle.

Mary, not Pamela, was the expert when it came to child custody hearings—and she was the one who'd told him he had to clean up his act and present himself as a proper family man before his in-laws attempted to spirit Lizard away.

"What don't you know?" he asked.

"Whether you and Ms. Hayes can make this marriage work."

Joe turned back to watch his niece and his bride-to-be. It wasn't dismay he read in Pamela's face, he decided: it was disgust. Evidently she had an aversion to little girls with mud caulking the cracks between their toes, graffiti on their butts and the ability to lecture their elders on the difference between fennel and anise.

So what if Pamela didn't like Lizard? Joe had never intended the marriage to work, except as a charade. When it was time for him to get married for real, it would be to a woman who was loose and sultry and buxom, a woman who thought muddy feet were just fine.

"It was your idea," he reminded Mary. "You told me I had to settle down if I wanted to convince the courts to let me keep Liz. You know as well as I do that most of the single women on the island aren't settling-down material. Or else they're into multiple settlings, like Kitty.''

"In other words," Mary said skeptically, "there's not a single local woman you could marry, even temporarily."

"I would have picked you," Joe said with an ingratiating smile, "but Frank got to you first."

Mary grinned. "Even if he hadn't, I would have turned you down. The last thing I want is children, whether my own or someone else's. And if you ask me—" she directed her gaze through the screen and watched as Pamela picked a gingerly path through the rows of sprouts, her arms akimbo and her nose twitching in distast "—your fiancée doesn't seem too enamored of children, either."

"She said she was willing to give it her best shot. That's the most anyone entering a marriage can do," Joe said as if he were some sort of expert on the subject. "All of which is academic, anyway. I don't have time to waste. I've got to get this marriage up and running before the Prescotts make the scene."

"Which should be sometime in early August," Mary reported, riffling through the folder of papers she'd pulled from her tote. "Your in-laws want to move Liz to California so she can get settled in by the end of the summer. They want her to be fully at home in their house before she starts kindergarten."

Joe grimaced.

"I've written to their attorney that you aren't going to relinquish custody," Mary said, separating a paper from the stack. "This communication from their attorney arrived yesterday."

Joe took the letter. Beneath an intimidating letterhead appeared several paragraphs of neat type, most of which he was able to translate from jargon into English. The gist of it was, the Prescotts intended to fight him for custody. They considered him unfit as a parent, and they would do whatever was necessary to remove the Liz Kid from the pernicious influence of the Brenner half of her family.

The letter only confirmed what he'd already known, but it ticked him off, anyway. "What a crock," he grumbled, tossing the sheet onto the table. "They're so damned eager to take Lizard, but they couldn't spare a thought for her well-being while they were raking in the profits in Indonesia."

"Their position is that although they wanted Lizard right from the start, they felt it was in her best interest to remain in the United States."

"Her best interest." He snorted. "It was in her best interest to stay with someone who was willing to turn his life inside out for her. They weren't willing to do that. I was."

Mary patted his shoulder. "I'll make sure that argument gets entered into the record."

But Joe was on a roll, and he wasn't going to let Mary's assurances silence him. "They were traipsing around the Far East, making a bundle on their development deals while I was rocking Lizard back to sleep when she woke up in the middle of the night screaming for her mother. They were attending formal dinners at the American Embassy in Jakarta while I was teaching Liz how to pee in the potty and chew with her mouth closed. Don't tell me they're better parents than I am."

"Relax, Joe. I'm not telling you that."

"Of course I'm the better parent. But it's not enough, is it. I've got to have a wife by my side. We both know that if I appear before the court as a bachelor, I haven't got a prayer.''

"I'll try not to take that as a commentary on your faith in my abilities,'' Mary muttered. "There's no question about it, Joe—you do need to present yourself as square as a chessboard.''

"Okay. So if Pam's so perfectly square, how come you think my marrying her won't work?''

Mary waved her hand toward the backyard, where Pamela stood rigidly, her expression one of vague horror, while Lizard scampered in circles around her, yammering about sage as it pertained to assorted voodoo rituals. "Perhaps the expression 'fish out of water' means something to you.''

"She'll learn to swim.''

"Look at her. She's dressed like a northerner.''

"She *is* a northerner.''

"She's got a manicure.''

"Your nails could use a little TLC, too,'' Joe snapped. Mary had the hands of a forty-year-old—which made sense, since she *was* forty—but the fingernails of an eight-year-old. She'd bitten them down to nothing, a bad habit she'd reacquired after she'd quit smoking a year ago.

"Get real, Joe. What do you think people around here are going to say when you suddenly show up with a woman like Pamela Hayes on your arm? They're going to know it's a sham.''

He clasped his hand over his heart and gave Mary his most sincere smile. "They're going to think I've turned over a new leaf.'' Leaning back in his chair, he extended his legs, too restless to sit still but unwilling to let Mary see how close to the bull's-eye her darts were hitting. "As wives go,'' he said, "Pamela's not bad. What makes you think a woman like her would never be my type?''

Mary's scowl spoke volumes.

He shrugged. ''Before Lizard fell into my lap, the very concept of a wife was beyond my comprehension. But I've changed. Surely you can see that.''

Mary leaned forward and glowered at him. ''It doesn't matter what I can or can't see. All that matters is what a judge is going to see, and the court-appointed advocate for Lizard. What they're going to see, Joe, is a Key West lowlife bar owner—''

''A small-business entrepreneur,'' he corrected her.

''With a woman who's much too classy for him.''

''Maybe she finds lowlife bar owners irresistible.''

''As the saying goes, 'Tell it to the judge.'''

''And anyway, I'm not a lowlife,'' Joe argued. ''I haven't partied hearty in three years. I work my tail off and pay my bills. I've got a car. I've got a Visa card. I've got a mortgage.''

''Have you got a necktie?''

''I'll buy one,'' he promised.

''You'll need one.'' Mary slid her folder back into her tote. ''If you want to marry that woman, I wish you the best of luck.''

''Gee, thanks, Mary,'' Joe grumbled. ''If that's going to be your attitude, I may not invite you to the wedding.''

''If you want a wedding present from me,'' Mary warned, rising to her feet, ''you'd *better* invite me.''

Chuckling, Joe stood as well. ''What the hell, then— I'll invite you. I definitely want a present from you. Something really bridal. Sterling silver napkin rings, okay? Or matching champagne flutes tied in white satin ribbon.''

"Watch your step, Brenner, or I'll buy you a marital aid."

"Aagh!" Joe made a strangled sound. "Do that and I'll find myself another lawyer."

Mary smiled smugly and hoisted the straps of her tote onto her shoulder. "You need me more than I need you, honey. Do me a favor—" she inclined her head toward Pamela "—and try not to hurt her, okay? She doesn't deserve what you're going to do to her."

Before Joe could think of a clever retort, Mary was gone.

He should have accompanied her around the house to her bicycle, but her parting words had shaken loose his tenuous grip on etiquette. What did Mary think he was going to do to Pamela? What terrible thing that Pamela didn't deserve?

He was providing the woman with a new identity, far from a criminal who might or might not be out to get her. He was giving her a home and the use of his name for as long as she needed them. He was paying her expenses and offering her a credible excuse to remain on the island.

Why would Mary think that Joe was going to hurt Pamela?

Sure, she wasn't his type. Sure, anyone who knew him well might have trouble believing he'd turned over a new leaf. But...

But he still remembered the way she'd felt in his arms yesterday, her tears dampening his shirt, her body slim and taut against his. He still remembered the sheer dread that turned her eyes as pale as zinc, the fear that made her turn to Joe, of all people, for solace.

He still remembered the way she'd called him Jonas. He stroked the day-old stubble of his beard, wondering if being Pamela's husband meant he would have to shave on a daily basis. Hell, marriage was supposed to be about compromise. If he had to shave every day, he would. The truth was, he was doing it—shaving, getting married, compromising—for Lizard, not for Pamela.

He pushed open the screen door and descended the back steps to the yard. Pamela was standing beside the scruffy patch of garden, her hands on her hips and her eyes wary. Lizard, up to her elbows in dirt, was babbling. "See this? It's a weed. Birdie says a weed is just a plant that didn't get enough love."

"A weed is a plant that isn't happy unless it's choking all the other plants to death," Joe asserted.

Lizard peered up at him and wrinkled her nose in disdain. "That shows what you know," she scoffed. "Birdie says half the people in the world are weeds. They just need a little love."

"I'll go along with the first part—half the people in the world are weeds. Maybe three-quarters." Joe glanced at Pamela, hoping to find an ally. Pamela remained impassive, her gaze darting back and forth between uncle and niece. "So, Pam, has Lizzie told you everything you ever wanted to know about chives?"

Pamela managed a feeble smile. "What did your lawyer have to say?"

"She thinks we're perfect for each other," he lied.

Pamela frowned. "If she really said that, I think you ought to consider looking for a smarter lawyer."

Joe laughed. The corners of Pamela's lips twitched upward, as if she wanted to smile but she didn't find anything amusing in the situation. If Joe allowed himself to think about it, he wouldn't find it all that amusing, either.

He watched Lizard race to the side of the house and

return dragging the hose. "I'm gonna water," she said less than a second before she aimed the nozzle half at the garden and half at Joe's feet and squeezed the lever.

Joe didn't care about getting his sneakers wet. He did care about getting Pamela's pristine outfit splattered, however. Grabbing her arm, he yanked her out of the way.

She stumbled against him, then shook free of his clasp and took another step back. Her brows dipped in a frown as she watched Lizard wield the hose as if she were wrestling a boa constrictor. The hose seemed to be winning the tussle. Silvery arcs of water doused the rhododendrons, the king palms and the rear shingles of the house.

Joe scrutinized Pamela's sour expression and heard Mary's voice echo in his skull: *A fish out of water.* Although, if Pamela stuck around in the back yard much longer, she would most definitely get wet.

He heard Mary's voice again, haunting, warning: *She doesn't deserve what you're going to do to her.* What he was going to do, assuming Pamela married him, was saddle her with an obstreperous little girl with a soft spot in her heart for weeds. And maybe she didn't deserve that.

"You hate Lizard, don't you?" he said, so Pamela wouldn't have to say it.

Pamela meticulously dusted a few flecks of dirt from her hands. "No, I don't hate her."

"But the idea of living with her makes you want to run howling into the night."

"She needs a little guidance," Pamela said. "And a lot of soap. But I can tolerate her."

Tolerate? It was one thing for Joe to joke about his niece's feral proclivities, and quite another for Pamela to imply that Lizard was to be tolerated, like bad weather or a booster shot. *Tolerate.* Architect Hayes ought to realize that marrying her was the ultimate act of tolerance on Joe's part.

He wasn't going to get into a competition with her over who was being forced to tolerate more than whom. What mattered was that his in-laws were planning to fight Joe's custody claim, and he had to get his act together pronto.

Turning his back on the havoc Lizard was wreaking with the garden hose, he faced Pamela. She stared past him at Lizard, but Joe took her hands in his, urging her to look at him. Her hands felt cool, and once again he was astonished by how slender and silky they felt.

"Pam," he said, gazing directly into her metallic eyes, wishing they would thaw for him—not melt into tears the way they had yesterday, but show some warmth, some receptivity. "I've got to be down at the Shipwreck in about half an hour, so we really ought to work some stuff out. You've spent two afternoons at the house, and maybe that's not enough time to get a feel for things. But time isn't something we've got a whole lot of. Do you think we can make a go of it?"

Either she was blushing or the sun had added some color to her face during the hour she'd spent in the yard with Lizard. Her eyes, if not exactly warm, sparkled with ironic humor. "Is this a proposal?"

He smiled wryly. "If you've got to ask, I guess I haven't done a very good job of it. You want me to get down on my knees?"

"No—the ground is too muddy. It's a wonder Lizard hasn't washed away the entire yard with that hose." She slipped her hands free of his and crossed her arms, although it looked as if she were actually hugging herself.

"Okay, so..." He hated to pressure her, but he was under a bit of pressure himself. "Do you want to go forward with this marriage setup?"

She managed a limp smile. "No better ideas have presented themselves, Jonas. I guess we may as well."

"Great." He had to force enthusiasm into his tone. If only she'd sounded a little less resigned, a little more excited...

Why would she? He was as excited about the prospect of marrying Pamela Hayes as he'd be about scheduling a dental appointment. He knew it was good for him, he knew it was necessary, he knew it would make his life better in the long run, but really, a guy didn't kick up his heels and shout for joy at the thought of getting his ivories professionally cleaned and flossed.

He might have only been imagining it, but Pamela seemed to tighten her grip on herself. "What sort of time frame are we looking at?" she asked.

"The sooner, the better. I'm friends with a semiretired judge up on Big Pine Key. I think we can get him to do the honors. You didn't want a church wedding, did you?" Cripes, they hadn't even discussed religion. For all he knew, Pamela could belong to a cult or something.

"I think a church wedding would be a bit hypocritical under the circumstances. Can we drive up to Big Pine Key and have the judge take care of the paperwork there?"

"Well, actually, I'd like to make it a little more public than that. If we want to convince the family court that it's a real marriage, we shouldn't be too secretive about the wedding. What I was thinking, if it's all right with you, is maybe closing the Shipwreck to outsiders on—let's say, Monday afternoon—and inviting some folks over and hosting a small party. My treat, of course. All you've got to do is show up and say 'I do.'"

If she hugged herself any tighter, she'd suffocate. Her smile glistened with pain. But he wasn't going to have the chance to comfort her; her eyes were as dry as cold ash. Would she have preferred for him to sugarcoat the deal? Make it sound like something genuine, something that came from his heart? He was offering to pay for the bash. She didn't have a right to expect more.

She gazed past him once more, at Lizard—who, from the sound of her whooping, was doing some sort of Seminole fertility dance around the herb garden. *For her,* Joe wanted to say. *This isn't for me. It's for her.*

And for Pamela, too. For the sake of keeping her head attached to her body, with no significant holes shot through her vital organs. This marriage was for her good as well as his, and if she didn't like it, she could get the hell off his property and—

"Are you sure you wouldn't like me to chip in toward the party?"

His anger vanished before it had a chance to build up much steam. If that was as close as she could come to a yes, it was close enough. "Forget it. My treat."

"Okay." Her voice was drier than her eyes. Even her skin was dry. She should have been sweating in the humid heat, but she was brisk and crisp, all business, every messy emotion neatly tucked away.

He told himself that was good. He told himself it was better that she refuse to let her feelings out the way she had yesterday. He told himself that this marriage was going to serve the function he needed it to serve. A cool customer like Pamela Hayes was going to blow his in-laws' arguments to smithereens. Everything was going to work out perfectly.

Even so... As Pamela broke from him and picked a careful path through the puddles to Lizard, calling, "Liz, it looks like your uncle and I are going to get married," Joe couldn't stifle a twinge of...wistfulness? Regret? He wasn't sure exactly what he was feeling.

Except that it seemed an awful lot like longing.

A BRIDE NEEDED HER MOTHER at a time like this.

Sighing, Pamela leaned back into the pillows. She was stretched out on her bed in the dreary furnished room that was destined to be her address for only a few more days. Her eyes burned, and she closed them against the too-bright light of the bedside lamp. She wanted to believe her tears were a result of frustration or even exhaustion. But she knew they weren't.

Although it made no sense, she believed Jonas Brenner was the cause of her weepiness.

She couldn't begin to fathom what it was about him that made her want to cry. Marrying him was far from the most arduous task she had ever faced in her life. Living in the charming room at the end of the upstairs hall in his house would be a pleasure after the week she'd spent at the ticky-tacky apartment complex. Lizard was a brat, but an intriguing one—and without her work, Pamela needed something to occupy her mind. Lizard would surely fit the bill.

So why were tears seeping through her lashes and skittering down her cheeks? Why was it that she could witness a cold-blooded murder, survive the ordeal of testifying against a killer in court, comprehend that she was in danger and flee for her life without shedding a single tear—and now all of a sudden, when salvation seemed at hand, she was as touchy as a twelve-year-old besieged by puberty?

Perhaps all brides went through this. Premarriage jitters. Second thoughts. Abject dread. Wedding-bell blues. Third and fourth and fifth thoughts.

If only she could talk to her mother and ask whether it was normal to experience this strange blend of melancholia and exhilaration as she contemplated the step she was about to take. Had her mother been this anxious on the eve of her wedding?

Of course not. Her mother had been a sweet young thing, and madly in love with the man she was about to marry. She'd known him for two years, had a long, properly public engagement, become a part of his family and welcomed him into hers.

None of which described Pamela's situation.

She fingered the telephone on her nightstand, then shoved it away. Her lawyer had warned her, for the safety of her parents, not to try to contact them directly. She could convey messages through him. "It's easy enough for Mick Morrow to find your parents, if you honestly believe he's after you," her attorney had pointed out. "Don't put them in a position where they have to conceal information about you. They're safer if they don't know anything."

What would her mother say if Pamela called with the news of her betrothal?

She'd be miserable, Pamela realized. Miserable because she wouldn't be able to attend the nuptials. Even more miserable because she would understand what a desperate step this was.

She would argue that Pamela could change her name and her identity without getting married. And Pamela would reason that getting married would make a name change seem more natural, and that it would be the last thing Mick Morrow would expect her to do. She was supposed to be a high-powered professional woman, not a mousy little hausfrau.

Her father would dwell on the practicalities. He would want to know what financial arrangements had been made, what contingencies had been planned for. But her mother would focus on matters of the heart. "How can you do this?" she would wail. "You don't even love him!"

And Pamela would have no way to refute that.

She felt a steady stream of tears leak down her cheeks. She pictured the hose Lizard had wielded like a mad fire fighter that afternoon in the garden. Her eyes gushed just as freely.

To her amazement, a chuckle slipped through her sobs. Lizard was a pint-size lunatic, but how could one not laugh at a little girl spouting arcana about mint and sage? Especially a little girl in a pajama top and jeans that apparently doubled as a doodle pad. Pamela recalled the solemn expression on Lizard's face as the little girl told her, "It's called *foodilizer* because plants eat it," and "Earthworms are good 'cuz they stick air in the ground, and also 'cuz they're slimy."

Jonas had looked solemn, too—in a very different way. As Pamela had listened to Lizard's dissertation on herbs, all the while trying to remain clean and dry while the wild child dug in the dirt and sprayed it with water, one part of her mind had remained firmly with Jonas on the porch with his lawyer, going through papers and planning strategies.

She didn't know what to make of him. Yesterday, he'd been surprisingly tender and protective, letting her humiliate herself by crying in his arms. Once she'd gotten control of herself, he'd nobly acted as if she hadn't fallen apart, as if she hadn't blubbered and leaned on him and all in all behaved like the one thing she never wanted to be: a helpless female. When he'd suggested that she return for lunch today, she was afraid he would remind her of the fool she'd made of herself, but he hadn't.

Still, it troubled her to think he had seen her at her weakest. What if he only kept all his promises until they were legally a couple and then took advantage of her— not financially or even sexually, but emotionally. He knew how frightened she was, and how much she hated to be frightened. He knew what a strain she was under. Yet she had to trust him. She'd run out of options.

She shoved away from the bed, crossed to the door and stepped outside. The night sky was dark, laced with pale clouds. A tropical breeze floated across the parking lot, thick with the perfume of the ocean.

Three days. Three days until she would be Jonas Brenner's wife. Three days to erase all her notions of white weddings, of the grand organ at the Presbyterian church her family had belonged to since before she was born, of her father proudly bearing her down the satin-covered aisle to deliver her to the man of her dreams— someone tall, dark and handsome, with a wall full of framed diplomas and a notable absence of jewelry on his ears. Three days to replace her fantasies of a reception dinner at her parents' country club with the reality that awaited her: a grunge-fest at the Shipwreck.

Three days to come to her senses.

At this point, though, she wasn't sure whether coming to her senses meant going through with the marriage or climbing into her car and hitting the road, searching for a new hiding place, a refuge, a haven not only from Mick Morrow but from Jonas Brenner and all the trouble he might well turn out to be.

CHAPTER FIVE

"LET'S SEE, NOW. You've got something old—" Kitty gestured toward the gold locket strung on a chain around Pamela's neck. "And something new—" She tapped the white satin headband around which Pamela's pale blond hair was arranged. Two more dabs with a cosmetic brush in the vicinity of Pamela's eyes, and then Kitty hauled Pamela off the toilet seat and guided her to the mirror above the sink so Pamela could see for herself the lush blue eye shadow Kitty had applied. "Something borrowed *and* something blue," she said, snapping shut the cake of shadow and beaming proudly at her handiwork.

Pamela stared at the borrowed blue makeup, wondering whether two of the traditional bridal requirements could be met with a single item. Not that such details mattered. This wedding was a farce. Kitty knew it as well as Pamela did.

"I should have bought a new dress," she grumbled, scrutinizing the sleeveless white shift that emphasized the ruler-straight lines of her physique. "This thing looks like an oversize undershirt."

"It looks wonderful," Kitty assured her, preening beside her in a strapless flowered sundress. "Anyway, it's white. How do I look?"

"Spectacular," Pamela said, meaning it. Kitty's cleavage bisected her sun-bronzed upper chest. The flare of her dress emphasized her narrow waist. Her bright blond hair glowed. Pamela wondered whether anyone would even notice the bride standing in the shadow of her bridesmaid's resplendence.

"I'm so excited!" Kitty squealed. "I've been married four times, but I've never been a maid of honor. Ever hear the expression 'Never a bridesmaid, always a bride'?" When Pamela didn't smile, Kitty slid her arm around Pamela's narrow shoulders and gave her a comforting squeeze. "Trust me, Pamela—this is going to be the party of the summer. A major blast. You're going to have a great time."

Pamela had never thought of weddings in terms of blasts, major or otherwise. She'd certainly never thought of her own wedding that way. A wedding ought to be a solemn occasion. Relinquishing one's freedom shouldn't be taken lightly.

Of course, Pamela had relinquished her freedom the moment she'd telephoned the police and announced that she'd witnessed a murder. Compared to that, marrying Jonas Brenner was hardly significant.

"You did say he cleaned up the Shipwreck," she half asked.

"We all did—Lois, Brick, me and a few others. You're not going to recognize the place." She marched Pamela into the bedroom, deftly navigating through the clutter, and lifted two bouquets from her unmade bed. Gardenias, Pamela noted wryly. Not exactly the sort of blossom she associated with weddings. When she thought of gardenias she thought of sultry southern weather and fading southern belles, and...

Sex. Gardenias implied eroticism, something hot and steamy and private.

With a weak smile, she accepted her bouquet from Kitty and followed her out of the flat. The late-afternoon air was sweltering. Pamela felt as if she were wading through sludge as she descended the stairs to the parking lot. By the time she reached Kitty's ancient VW Beetle, she was drenched with sweat.

She settled onto the passenger seat and cranked down the window. Her palms were soaked, and she let the bouquet rest in her lap so she wouldn't accidentally drop it onto the floor, which was littered with fast-food wrappers, bent straws and sand.

"Nuptial jitters," Kitty said sympathetically as she coaxed the engine to life. "I had them before my first and third weddings. Don't worry—a couple of beers and you'll be feeling fine."

Pamela eyed Kitty warily. "Jonas promised he'd have champagne."

"Oh, yeah, sure, if you like that stuff. Me, I find it gives me a roaring headache. Plus, it's too sweet. Tastes like soda pop."

Pamela considered explaining vintages to Kitty, and the difference between sec and brut, but decided it wasn't worth the effort. No doubt the champagne Joe would serve at a place like the Shipwreck would be just what Kitty predicted—sweet and guaranteed to cause a crippling hangover.

The drive took only five minutes. Emerging from the car, Pamela heard a cacophony of voices through the Shipwreck's screened front door, on which was hung a sign that read Closed for Private Party. Judging by the noise, Pamela doubted the party was all that private. It sounded as if Joe had invited the island's entire population to this shindig.

Before Pamela could either march bravely into the bar or come to her senses and flee, Kitty grabbed her arm and ushered her around the building, up an alley and into the small back lot where Jonas had offered his hand in marriage less than a week ago. "You can't go in the front door," Kitty reminded her. "No one can see the bride before the wedding."

"What are we going to do? Stand out here roasting in the sun?"

Kitty ignored the exasperation in Pamela's tone. "I'll sneak you into Joe's office. Hang on." She opened the back door a crack, releasing a blast of boisterous voices. It sounded as if the party was already well under way.

Pamela glanced at her watch. Four-forty-seven. The ceremony was supposed to start at five o'clock. Jonas had taken charge of the invitations, and Pamela had no idea what time he'd told people to arrive. In Seattle, wedding guests generally came at the hour the service was scheduled to begin—and early arrivals were *not* served liquor.

Who cares? she muttered inwardly as, baking in the merciless heat, she waited for Kitty to sneak her into the office. Who cared if her wedding guests were three sheets to the wind? Who cared if she was getting married in a seedy bar, surrounded by strangers?

To her surprise, Pamela realized that *she* cared. If she'd resolved to get married, she should have asserted herself a bit about the particulars: a chapel, not a bar. A morning service followed by a brunch for a few close friends—although in Pamela's case, the only locals who could pass for friends, and not close ones, at that—were Joe, Kitty and Lizard. But the event should have had at least a modicum of class.

Tears dampened her lashes. She hastily wiped her eyes before Kitty returned to the back lot to fetch her. "Come on," Kitty whispered, as if anyone could have heard her over the din in the main barroom.

Pamela let Kitty lead her inside, down the back hall and through a door. Jonas's office was a small room taken up with an old chipped desk, an even older-looking swivel chair, a tattered sofa and a few file cabinets. Crayon drawings decorated the walls, and a cardboard carton in a corner held assorted toys. Pamela peeked inside and saw a tricorn hat, a rubber knife and what appeared to be a cheesily constructed prosthetic hook.

"That's Lizard's stuff," Kitty explained. When Pamela dared to pick up the plastic hook, Kitty added, "That's part of her pirate costume. You should see her when she gets all decked out—the eye patch, the peg leg, the gun.... It's adorable."

I can imagine, Pamela thought wryly. "Why does she store her toys in Jonas's office?"

"So she'll have something to play with when she's hanging out here."

"*Here?* What on earth would a little girl be doing in a bar?"

"Well, it's not like she's knocking back a few," Kitty said. "But if Joe has a baby-sitting snafu or something, he brings her along with him. She used to spend lots of time here when she was younger. He had a little port-a-crib set up in here for her to sleep in. Although sometimes it was hard to get her down with the jukebox going, or if there was an especially rowdy crowd, so we'd bring her into the main room—"

"The bar?" Pamela couldn't believe it. An innocent, defenseless little girl spending her evenings in a bar?

Then again, innocent and defenseless weren't appropriate words to describe Lizard. In a brawl among a group of drunken brutes, Pamela would bet on Lizard to land the most punches.

"Everybody in the bar loves her. Me and Lois, even Brick. And the customers. And Joe, of course, most of all. It's not like he wants to bring her here, but he's got to earn a living and he can't just leave her home alone. His mom was supposed to be Lizard's baby-sitter, but sometimes she didn't come through. Great lady, but less than a hundred percent dependable. And now she's off in Mexico digging up bones—"

"Bones?"

"That's the rumor." Kitty swung out the door, calling over her shoulder, "I'm gonna see if we're ready to roll."

Pamela sighed. She wasn't ready to roll. She wondered if it was too late to bail out of this charade. Surely people had been stranded at the altar with far less cause. And there wasn't even an altar at the Shipwreck.

But if she didn't marry Joe, where would she go? She was tired of running, and she'd literally reached the end of the road. Even if Joe's child-rearing strategies were a bit unorthodox, he deserved to keep his niece. And Pamela wasn't a quitter. She followed through on things, finished what she started and obeyed the dictates of her conscience. Right now, her conscience was telling her she couldn't jilt Jonas Brenner.

Kitty returned to the office, smiling brightly. "It's show time," she announced. "Brick's got the boom box set up, the judge is here, and you're about to tie the knot."

Swallowing a lump of emotion—part rue, part dread, part sheer panic—Pamela straightened her shoulders and joined Kitty at the door. They tiptoed out into the hall as a tinny rendering of "The Wedding March" resounded through the small speakers of a portable stereo atop the jukebox.

As Kitty had promised, the barroom had been spruced up. The tables, pushed to the perimeter of the room, were all draped in white paper tablecloths, and white satin ribbons had been looped over the exposed rafters and the steering-wheel clock. A strip of what appeared to be unbleached muslin lay along the length of the room. Although chairs had been arranged on either side of the runner, most of the guests were standing, peering toward the front of the room, where a silver-haired man in a straw hat and a dapper seersucker suit stood before a table that was bedecked with flowers. Pamela assumed he was the judge.

Lizard abruptly appeared at the rear edge of the bar, near where Pamela and Kitty were standing. Nudged by a wizened, dark-skinned woman in a caftan trimmed with feathers, Lizard started down the muslin runner. She wore a cotton sunsuit with a pretty floral pattern— not a dress, but infinitely more respectable than a plastic hula skirt or pajamas. Her hair was half braided, half loose, and she carried a bouquet of peacock and gull feathers.

Pamela couldn't see her face, a fact for which she was grateful. She knew Lizard didn't care much for her. Lizard's reluctant shuffle down the aisle, her feathers fluttering and her steps making clicking sounds as her rubber sandals slapped the bare soles of her feet, told Pamela all she needed to know about the child's opinion of her uncle's wedding.

She shifted her gaze from Lizard to the wedding guests. Perhaps they'd been whooping it up before, but now they were still and nearly silent, respecting the sanctity of the occasion. It looked to Pamela as if at least a hundred people were crammed into the room. In her plain white cotton shift, she seemed to be the most elegantly dressed person present.

It isn't really a wedding, she told herself, but the thought rang false in her soul. A thousand-dollar wedding dress, engraved invitations, a live organist and a sun-filled church weren't what made a wedding. When she stared down the long, wrinkled strip of muslin to the judge at the other end, she knew this *was* a wedding. *Her* wedding.

The comprehension staggered her. She reached out to grab Kitty, but she was too late; her matron of honor was already sauntering down the aisle, flashing her smile to the left and to the right and occasionally acknowledging a familiar face with a cheerful wave. Pamela remained alone at the rear of the barroom, gathering her wits and praying that going through with this marriage wasn't an even bigger mistake than testifying against Mick Morrow.

From the front of the bar, Kitty turned and beckoned Pamela with a crook of her finger. Pamela felt the assembled guests turn en masse to stare at her. She was sure the hushed murmurs she heard as she took her first step onto the runner were not comments about the beautiful bride, but rather Joe's friends whispering, "Who the hell is she? Where did he find her?"

Once again she had to resist the urge to bolt. Holding her head high, squeezing her gardenia bouquet, she walked sedately down the aisle, refusing to glance to either side, refusing to admit that she felt queasy. She concentrated on the judge's benign smile and counted her steps, maintaining a slow, courtly pace.

The late-afternoon sunlight sifted through the windows, casting the front of the room in a golden glow.

When she was nearly at her destination, Joe stepped forward to greet her.

Pamela froze. Not from fear, not from panic, but from the shock of her response to him. He looked tall, relaxed and absolutely sure of himself. His hair was brushed back from his face, his cheeks were clean-shaven, and his glorious blue eyes seemed to connect with her, communicating that this was okay, everything was going to be okay, she was going to make it to the end of the muslin runner without losing her lunch. He wasn't quite smiling, but she noticed his dimple.

Clad in a white linen blazer, a brightly patterned shirt and cotton slacks, with an orchid pinned to his lapel, he was put together as informally as she was. But he looked...if not like a husband, at least like a man who didn't regret having chosen Pamela for his wife.

He also looked extraordinarily handsome.

Pamela recalled her first impression of him—that he looked like a bum. Not all that much had changed since then. His hair was still way too long, the laughter in his eyes still teasing, and of course he had a hole through his ear. And yet... It wasn't just because none of his apparel was obviously torn, or because he had suddenly transformed into a model out of *GQ*, but in the instant her gaze locked with his, Pamela honestly believed marrying him was the right thing to do.

Joe extended his hand and she took it. He closed his fingers around hers, snug but not tight, just a gentle squeeze of reassurance. Yet his eyes changed somehow, darkening slightly. He almost looked...glad.

Glad that he was improving his chances of winning permanent custody of Lizard, Pamela rationalized. Glad that Pamela had come through, that she wasn't an embarrassment to him, that she would help him to convince the family court of his stability as a parent figure. It was nothing more complicated than that.

Yet as he turned her to face the judge, he didn't let go of her hand. His fingers remained woven loosely through hers, as if he and she were taking a stroll along the beach rather than standing side by side in front of the man who was going to join them legally together.

The judge cleared his throat and smiled. "Ladies and gentlemen," he drawled, speaking past Joe and Pamela to address the entire room, "we're assembled here today to witness the marriage of Joe Brenner and Pamela Hayes. Now, you all know Joe. He's one heck of a fine fellow. Generous as the day is long—and right about now, the days are pretty long. Joe always fills the glass up to the rim. He always listens to a tale of woe, and he always laughs at a joke, no matter how poorly you tell it. I don't have to tell you what kind of a guy he is."

This assessment was greeted with a quiet chorus of assent. Pamela shot Joe a quick look. He was grinning and rolling his eyes in embarrassment.

"Pamela, on the other hand, is new to the island. I've never met her, and I reckon most of you haven't, either. But she seems a charming young lady, and I'll tell you this—if Joe loves her, she's aces in my book, and I think we can all count her as a friend."

"Hear, hear!" someone at the back of the room shouted.

"Today we're here to unite these two special people in matrimony. I know Joe's got a lot of refreshment on hand for the celebration, so let's get on with it. Is there anyone present who would speak against Joe and Pamela getting hitched?"

Pamela eyed Lizard cautiously. Lizard slid her left foot out of the rubber sandal and used it to scratch the back of her right calf. Pamela noted that Lizard's toenails had been painted purple. She also noted that Lizard was making a great effort not to look at her. She stared at her feet, at the door, at Kitty, at her feathers and her uncle. Anywhere but at Pamela.

"Well, then," the judge continued. "Pamela, do you take Jonas Brenner to be your lawfully wedded husband through the good times and the bad, the ups and downs, the high tides and low, the calm days and the hurricanes, to make this marriage a thing of joy and beauty?"

Not exactly the standard lines, but Pamela had to admit she liked them. They fit what she and Joe were entering into, and the judge hadn't mentioned "till death do us part." She wondered whether Joe had told him this marriage was going to be parted by a divorce decree as soon as Joe had permanent custody of Lizard and Pamela had proof that Mick Morrow was behind bars to stay.

Whether the judge knew or not, Pamela found it easy to affirm the vow as he'd stated it. "I do," she said.

Joe squeezed her hand again, and she smiled at him shyly.

"Joe," the judge said, "do you promise to take Pamela as your lawfully wedded wife, to honor and respect, to talk to and to listen to, to share the burdens and the blessings of each day with, to partner through the dance of life?"

"I do," Joe said. The smile he gave Pamela wasn't remotely timid. He looked downright pleased.

"The ring," the judge cued him.

A ring? Pamela cringed inwardly. She hadn't bought him a ring—she hadn't even thought of it. Surely if Joe hadn't gotten a ring for her, he would have told the judge to skip this part. She hoped he wouldn't make her wear something cheap and brassy. A wedding band was a sacred symbol. A fake one would be a travesty.

To her amazement, Joe pulled a real ring from his pocket, a thick band of hammered gold. He slipped it onto her ring finger. Cool and heavy, it fit perfectly.

"Joe—"

"Shh," he silenced her, still grinning.

"By the authority vested in me by the state of Florida," the judge concluded, "I now pronounce you husband and wife. You may kiss the bride—and *you*," he invited Pamela with a wink, "may kiss the groom."

Joe had explained the necessity of pretending in public that theirs was a love match. Obediently, she leaned toward Joe, closed her eyes and puckered her lips, bracing herself for the feel of his mouth on hers.

His kiss was light, sweet, a tender brush of his lips that left her feeling oddly frustrated. But before she could lean into him, before she could submerge herself more deeply in this pretense of affection, the crowd began to hoot and cheer and demand drinks, and Joe broke away from her to step into his role as the host. "We've got plenty of food and libation, folks," he shouted above the celebratory cheering. "Brick, Kitty, let's get some glasses filled."

"Hey, groom," Kitty chastised him as he started toward the bar. "You're not supposed to be working tonight. You've got a bride to take care of. Don't the bride and groom have to have the first dance?"

Brick grunted in confirmation.

Joe turned to Pamela with a smile. "Okay, then. Someone punch some buttons on that jukebox. It's rigged—no coins necessary."

A group of guests huddled over the jukebox, arguing about which song would be most suitable under the circumstances. Others rolled up the muslin and shoved the chairs toward the walls, clearing a dance floor at the center of the room. Pamela eyed Joe, wondering whether they were going to be treated to a slow, sensuous dance—and wondering why she wasn't alarmed by the likelihood that they would be.

The crowd simmered down as a sinuous bass line filled the air. "Stand by Me." Pamela recognized it even before Ben E. King's soulful voice began crooning. Joe seemed delighted by the choice as he drew her onto the improvised dance floor, into his arms. "How are you doing?" he asked.

He was holding her decorously, one hand resting at the small of her back and the other folded around her hand. His eyes sparkled, and his smile took on a wistfulness as he gazed at her.

"I'm fine."

"Good." He urged her closer, and she relaxed into the rhythm of the song. "Do you think we've convinced the world that we're in love?" Although his smile remained enigmatic, his voice was tinged with laughter.

"Actually," she chided softly, "you went above and beyond. Why did you get such a fancy ring?"

"It's not so fancy. Just plain gold. If it isn't comfortable, we can take it back and get the size adjusted."

"It's very comfortable," Pamela told him, refusing to admit to herself that its very comfortableness made her *un*comfortable. The ring shouldn't have felt so natural on her finger. It shouldn't have felt as if it belonged there. "But you obviously spent a lot of money on it, and—"

"There you go with the money again," he muttered, although his tone lacked any real anger. "What sort of guy would I be if I'd given you something from a

Cracker Jack box? You're my wife. You deserve a nice ring." He pulled her even closer, until her cheek was resting against the soft linen of his blazer. "Lord knows you're going to earn it."

She leaned back and glared at him. "That sounds ominous."

He grinned. "You look real nice, by the way."

She faltered for a moment, then managed a smile. Joe hadn't seen her since the afternoon he'd introduced her to his lawyer, three days ago. The lawyer had treated her cordially—yet Pamela had hardly found her reassuring. In fact, the meeting had made her retreat, giving Joe a chance to rethink his decision.

If he'd rethought it, his decision had remained the same. Pamela had talked to Joe several times on the telephone since then, but he had been busy organizing the wedding and preparing Lizard for the event, and she had been busy coping with Kitty's exuberance, which tended to manifest itself in protracted shopping excursions.

Perhaps, during the three days they'd been apart, Joe had forgotten what Pamela looked like. Perhaps he'd remembered her to be homelier than she actually was, so today, all spruced up with something-borrowed, something-blue cosmetics, she looked better than he'd recollected.

Or else he was just being cordial, like his attorney.

He must have read the skepticism in her frown, because he elaborated. "I like your hair pulled back like that. It shows off more of your face."

"Kitty wanted me to wear a veil. We spent two hours at Sears yesterday, bickering over swatches of white lace."

"You don't need a veil." He tucked her head back against his shoulder once more. "You look great."

Okay. He was in a complimentary mood. "You don't look so bad yourself," she said, returning the favor.

"Wait till you've downed a few glasses of bubbly. I'll look even better."

She laughed. So did he. His chest vibrated against her chin, and his arms drew her closer still. Through the jukebox speakers, the singer pleaded with his darling to stand by him.

That would be their song, Pamela decided. Not a song of love, but a song of mutual support. That was what this marriage was truly about: standing by each other.

LIZARD WAS IN RARE FORM, Joe noticed. She was perched atop the bar, swinging her bare feet, her peacock feathers sticking out of the waistband of her shorts and a sea gull feather wedged behind each ear. She was eating everything she could get her hands on, even though the only pink foodstuff being served was strawberry margaritas. She'd already drunk one margarita—minus the tequila—and Joe had since limited her to ginger ale. "It looks like champagne," he pointed out.

As far as food went, he'd gone for quantity over quality: cold cuts, sliced cheese, fresh rolls and rye bread, pickles and mustard. Lois had insisted that he stock up on those little toothpicks with the colored plastic tassels on them—because Martha Stewart would have done it that way—and she'd banned onions from the premises. "You eat onions and your bride won't want to kiss you," she'd declared.

He hadn't expected to be so eager for Pamela to want to kiss him. But when he'd seen her walking down the aisle, slim and statuesque in her white sheath, with her hair pulled back and her chin held high, he'd been really glad he'd listened to Lois about the onions.

Dancing with her wasn't the first time he'd ever held her. He knew she was thin. He knew that when he closed his arms around her he wouldn't feel pillows of bosom cushioning his chest. Yet her body felt good. Her height worked well with his; their hips lined up in an unintentionally sensual way. When Ben E. King wailed "darling, darling," Joe realized how very much he wanted Pamela standing by him.

Without having to budget their spare change, his guests kept the jukebox playing nonstop—and at least once every fifteen minutes, someone would select "Stand by Me" and the entire assembly would stomp their feet and clap their hands and demand that Joe take his new wife for another spin around the dance floor. He and Pam would put up a token protest, and then they'd concede defeat and dance—each time a little closer, each time a little slower.

But that one kiss to seal the marriage was probably all he'd get from her. This marriage wasn't about sex. And the better Pamela felt in his arms, the more diligent he'd have to be about remembering that.

"Hey, Joe-baby!" Peter Hyland bellowed as Joe and Pamela separated after their seventh dance. Peter managed a marina in town. He and Joe had gone to high school together.

"Peter. Have you met Pam yet?"

Peter took Pamela's hand, bowed and kissed her knuckles. *"Enchanté,"* he said, then straightened up. "You got yourself a winner, Joey. Who woulda thought?"

"There, there," clucked Peter's wife Margie, who had moseyed over with a couple of turkey sandwiches. "It's not that no one ever expected you to take the plunge, Joe. It's that for so long now, Elizabeth has been the only woman in your life.''

''Well, now Lizzie and I have a woman in our lives.''

''Lizzie could use someone in her life. She's threatening to dive headfirst into the cake if you don't start serving it immediately.''

Joe groaned and excused himself. Letting go of Pamela's hand filled him with a vague sense of loss. He'd been holding it for most of the evening. He'd justified it with the thought that he didn't want to lose her in the crush of his effusive friends, none of whom she knew. But the truth was, he'd held her hand because it felt right. She was Mrs. Jonas Brenner, and he wanted to hold her.

But Lizard needed attention, and that was his job, not Pam's. Wading through the crowd to the bar, he spotted the kid hovering over the tiered white cake Lois and her mother had baked as a wedding present. ''Lizard, stop drooling on the frosting,'' he reproached her, looping his arms around her waist and swinging her off the bar.

''I'm *starved,*'' Lizard whined. ''Birdie said I could have cake.''

''Did she say you could have cake this very instant?''

''Yeah.''

Liar, Joe thought, but he was in too good a mood to give Liz a hard time. ''All right, then. I know better than to mess with a voodoo chief. Cake time it is.''

Brick placed a knife in his right hand. Kitty placed Pamela's right hand in his left. Lois yelled that someone had better turn the damned jukebox off, because the bride and groom were going to cut the cake.

Revelry ensued—cheers, applause, whistles and a boisterous chorus of ''The bride cuts the cake,'' to the tune of "The Farmer in the Dell." Pamela looked abashed; Joe imagined she was used to far classier receptions. Her cheeks glowing pink, she slid the blade through the top tier of the cake, cutting a neat wedge. As she lifted it onto a plate, she whispered, "If you smear this on my face, I'm having the marriage annulled tomorrow."

Joe had been to a few weddings where the bride and groom had shoved wedding cake into each other's mouths. While he could see the slapstick humor in it, he had to agree it was kind of tasteless. "I'll be neat," he promised as he took the plate and a fork. He daintily broke off a small piece of cake and slipped it between her lips.

Her eyes grew round. "Whoa! It's rum cake!"

"In that case, cut me a piece."

She laughed and cut a second wedge for him.

Birdie sidled up to him. She had helped Lizard with her outfit that afternoon, making Joe think of the old saying about birds of a feather flocking together. "It's too early for cake," she objected.

"Liz told me you said she could have cake."

"The truth bends in Lizard's hands," Birdie remarked. "All right, then, you and your bride eat your cake, and then you go home and have your honeymoon."

Joe glanced at the wall clock. It was nine-thirty. The party had been in full swing for hours, but he knew it would rage for hours more. He wasn't sure he ought to leave.

Now he was the one bending the truth. He wanted to stay at the party because he knew there was no honeymoon waiting for him and Pam once they left.

"It's past Lizard's bedtime," he noted. "I suppose we might consider getting her home."

"No, no, no." Birdie wagged a bony finger at him. "I take her home with me. You take your bride and have a honeymoon."

Joe sighed and looked apprehensively at Pamela. He had introduced her to Birdie right after the first dance, aware that Pamela and Birdie were going to have to get to know each other so they could coordinate Lizard's schedule. Pamela hadn't blinked at the older woman's odd attire—she could see where Lizard got her penchant for feathers—although she did have a little difficulty understanding Birdie's speech. Twenty years after she'd fled to Key West from Haiti, Birdie still spoke with an accent.

Evidently Pamela wasn't having much difficulty understanding her now. "You're going to take Lizard home with you?" she asked.

"That's right. You have a honeymoon tonight. You get Lizard back tomorrow."

Pamela nodded. "I think she's right. It's time for us to say good-night to all your friends."

It occurred to Joe that Pamela was exhausted. Her eyes were bleary, her hair limp.

"Okay," he said, wishing there could be a real honeymoon for him and Pamela. He was married; his wife belonged in his bed, didn't she?

No, of course not. This wasn't that kind of marriage, and he knew it. If he did anything that even remotely resembled what a husband did with a wife on their wedding night, she'd have the marriage annulled quicker than if he'd crammed cake into her mouth. He'd better keep a lid on his libido.

It took him and Pamela a good ten minutes to work

their way through the mob. At the front door, Pamela tossed her bouquet over her shoulder. Lizard elbowed at least three women out of her way so she could catch it.

A few guys showered Pamela and Joe with beer nuts as they swept out the door. Pamela's laughter was breezy. "Lord, it's hot out here," she said. "Does it ever cool down?"

"For three days in January." He took her hand again, casually, as if it didn't signify anything. It truly didn't, he told himself—other than the fact that he'd just gotten married and this woman was his wife.

His wife. What a weird concept.

"Well," she said, her laughter waning as they strolled to his parked car, "I owe you an apology."

"For what?"

"That champagne was delicious."

He feigned indignation at her implied insult. "You thought I'd serve lousy champagne?"

"As a matter of fact, yes."

"I'll have you know, Pam, that I'm a pretty classy guy."

"You are," she agreed, a serious undertone in her words. When he leaned past her to unlock the passenger door, she brushed her finger across the floppy petals of his orchid boutonniere. "It was a nice party, Jonas. Not like any I've ever been to before, but I had fun."

"I'm glad." He honestly was. If she was stuck with being his wife for the next however-many months, he wanted her to be, if not thrilled, at least passably happy. He wanted her to feel at home with his friends, in his place of business.

He helped her into the seat, then jogged around to the driver's side. "How about I detour to your apartment and we can pick up your car?"

"All right."

He revved the engine and eased away from the curb. A quick glance at her informed him that she'd grown subdued. He couldn't blame her. Just the two of them, alone in his car, driving through the darkness... It was a heavy dose of reality. God help them, they were married.

The silence made him uneasy. "You're a good dancer," he said.

"It's a miracle I can still walk. That bartender—Brick." Joe nodded, and she continued. "He kept stomping on my toes when we danced."

"He's a good guy."

"He doesn't talk much, does he?"

"One of his finest attributes."

"And Birdie... What is it with the feathers?"

"Why do you think everybody calls her Birdie?"

"Can she fly?"

"I wouldn't be surprised." He chuckled. "She and Lizard go down to the town beach almost every day. They like to collect gull feathers. When Lizard absolutely refused to carry flowers, it was Birdie's idea to make her a feather girl instead of a flower girl."

"It certainly was original. And in the spirit of compromise, it worked."

They had reached the parking lot of the apartment complex. Pamela smiled and let herself out of his car once he'd braked to a halt next to hers. His car seemed painfully empty without her in it.

He wasn't supposed to be thinking along the lines of a real marriage, of having Pamela fill his car and his life. He hardly knew her enough to consider her a friend, let alone a spouse. Why should he be so fixated on the slight shimmy of her hips as she settled behind the wheel of her own car? Why should he be inhaling deeply, trying to capture her lingering scent?

Too much champagne, he supposed. Too much dancing and laughing. The party had worked its magic on him, infused him with benevolence, made him want to embrace the world and everyone in it. Especially Pamela.

His wife.

He checked his rearview mirror to make sure her car was directly behind his. She knew the way to his house, but even so, he wanted her to arrive there with him.

He wondered what he was going to do with her once they were home. Kitty had brought Pamela's suitcases over earlier that day, and he'd put them in Pamela's room. When they got home, would she want to unpack and go straight to sleep? Or would she be practical and request that he show her where the utensils and spices were stored in the kitchen and where the laundry hamper was located?

He would rather talk with her awhile, maybe sit with her in the living room with a couple of cold drinks—lemonade would do, if she'd reached her booze limit. He wanted to get used to her presence in his house. He wanted to stop thinking of her hips, and her silver eyes, and the hollows of her cheeks. He wanted to stop remembering how soft her lips had felt beneath his when the judge had pronounced them husband and wife.

He'd left a couple of lights on inside the house so it would look warm and welcoming. He pulled all the way into the carport, and Pamela parked on the driveway behind him. They got out of the cars and met on the grass.

"Well, Mrs. Brenner, be it ever so humble..."

"There's no place like home," she concluded.

He was thrilled that she could think of his house as

home, even if only temporarily. He took her hand, then thought better of it and reached around her, hoisting her into his arms.

She let out a shriek, then a giggle. "Put me down, Jonas! I'm too heavy for you!"

"You're too light, is what you are," he refuted. "And I believe there's some sort of law that says I've got to carry you over the threshold."

"Well, I wouldn't want you breaking any laws on my account," she said, looping her arms around his neck, settling against his chest and smiling up at him.

Maybe it was the champagne. Maybe it was the bright half-moon or the spark of playfulness he hadn't glimpsed in her before. Or maybe it was Joe, high on champagne and moonlight and just as willing to play the game. Because the instant he'd swung open the front door, carried her inside and lowered her to her feet in *their* house, *their* home, the legal residence of Mr. and Mrs. Jonas Brenner, he knew he was going to kiss her. She was his wife, his mate, his partner in the dance of life.

And he was going to pretend it was real.

CHAPTER SIX

HE HAD LEFT ONE ARM around her when he set her down. He lifted his other hand to her cheek and angled her face to his. She gazed up into azure eyes that shimmered with trust. And then he touched his lips to hers.

Her mind told her this was a bad idea—but her heart was full of music and dancing and champagne. She was a married woman, and Jonas Brenner was her husband, and married people were allowed to kiss each other.

His kiss was light, tender, questioning. She answered with a sigh, and he covered her mouth with his once more, this time less tentatively. When she sighed again, he slid his tongue between her parted lips. Her eyelids grew heavy at the gentle assault of his tongue.

She sensed nothing demanding in the kiss. He was too clever to resort to force. Instead, he lured, he tempted, he made her want to give so he wouldn't have to take. He was, she conceded as her body warmed to his sensual advances, a sublime kisser.

She wedged her hands under his jacket and around his waist. His sides were lean and hard, ribs and muscle. Through the soft linen of his shirt she felt the contours of his back, sleek and supple, flexing beneath her touch.

He lifted his hand to her temple and into her hair, combing through it to the nape of her neck. As his tongue surged against hers, she heard him groan, and groan again when her fingers dug into his back. She was afraid that if she relaxed her hold on him, her legs would buckle, so she clung to him tightly, kissing him with a passion that matched his. A voice deep inside her soul whispered, *It's all right. He's your husband. It's all right.*

It wasn't all right, her conscience argued—but for the moment she didn't care. She cared only about the sweet seduction of his mouth, the restrained aggression of his lips and tongue, the possessiveness of his embrace as he pressed his body to hers.

He stroked the edge of her neckline, then slipped his fingers under the fabric to trace the ridge of her spine. His hand felt so good on her skin, too good. She wished he would move his hand forward to her throat, to her breasts. She wished he would touch her everywhere. She wished he would tear off his clothing, and hers, so the hard swell of him would no longer be seeking her, as it was now, through the barriers of his trousers and her dress.

She heard his breath catch as she brought her hands down to his hips and held him against her. A shudder of yearning rippled through her as he rocked against her, slowly, sinuously. She wanted him, wanted Jonas Brenner. Wanted the man with the devilish blue eyes and the earring.

She wanted her husband.

"Pam," he murmured, his breath caressing her lips. "Let's go to bed."

Bed. Wait a minute! This wasn't supposed to happen. She and Joe had entered into their marriage with the understanding that it wasn't about love or sex. It was about social workers and custody hearings, and it was about eluding a murderer until the said murderer was brought to justice. Having already risked her life, Pamela wasn't about to risk her heart.

"I..." She swallowed to clear the huskiness from her voice. "I don't think that's a very good idea."

He loosened his hold on her and leaned back so he could view her in the amber light of the entry hall. Letting out a long, weary breath, he shook his head and dropped his arms to his sides. "Sorry," he muttered, looking supremely disappointed. "I guess I broke a few rules, huh?"

No more than she had. She'd been as caught up in the kiss as he. Until he'd mentioned the word "bed," she had been quite content to yield to the mutual desire that had unexpectedly ignited between them.

She averted her gaze and fussed with her hair, which Joe had done an effective job of tangling into knots—just like her emotions. "I'm sorry, too, Jonas...."

"No. My fault." He held up his hands in mock surrender. He was smiling, but she saw no trace of his dimple, no glint of humor in his eyes. "Why don't you go upstairs and get settled in? I took all your stuff to your room."

"Thanks," she mumbled, not because he had lugged her suitcases up the stairs for her, but because he had taken all the guilt upon himself, even though she deserved at least fifty percent of it. If she had his courage, she would acknowledge her share. She would tell him he had nothing to apologize for. But she'd exhausted her supply of courage earlier that evening when she'd walked down the aisle to take Joe for her lawfully wedded husband. As craven as it was, she couldn't look at him, let alone share the blame for the passion that had briefly claimed them. She could scarcely admit to herself how much she'd ached for him when his arms and his mouth and his desire had held her captive.

It was a desire she was going to have to forget. Once the champagne wore off and she had a good night's sleep, she would come to her senses. So would Joe. They would make this marriage work the way they'd intended when they'd come to terms, and any errant longings would be squelched.

That was the way it had to be.

MICK MORROW drove smoothly and calmly out of the parking lot. After a few blocks, he steered to the curb, shifted into neutral and reached under the passenger seat.

It was there, just as Tony had promised: a thick yellow envelope.

Although Tony was supposed to be tailing Mick, he didn't want them to be seen together in public. So Mick had traveled to an agreed-upon suburban mall parking lot at an agreed-upon hour, parked his car in section 3-A and left it unlocked so Tony could leave the envelope under the seat. Mick had gone into a drugstore, browsed for ten minutes and bought a pack of gum. When he'd come back outside, there had been no sign of Tony.

The envelope was exactly where Tony had promised it would be, though. The guy had come through. Mick owed him.

He slid it back out of sight under the passenger seat and cruised home, resisting the temptation to open his special-delivery package until he was safely inside his apartment. The dreary drizzle of a Seattle summer evening couldn't get him down. In that envelope lay a route to Pamela Hayes. Let it rain—Mick was too pleased to care.

ords and her parents didn't know anything," Tony had told him over the phone yesterday. "But you mentioned she owned a condominium, so I thought, maybe she's sitting on a mortgage. Sure enough, I got hold of her credit report. Lots of interesting stuff, Mick. Stuff you might find useful."

Her credit report! Her charge accounts! Her bank accounts! The most intimate details of a woman's life, more significant than her height or weight or hair color, more personal than who she was sleeping with and what positions she'd rather die than try. "It could have possibilities," Mick had agreed, refusing to let Tony hear how thrilled he was.

"I can get these documents to you tomorrow, as long as we don't have to come face-to-face."

"Is anyone gonna be able to trace this to you?" Mick asked. His largess purchased only so much loyalty from Tony. If the guy got caught, Mick didn't doubt for a minute that he'd sing like the proverbial canary.

"I left no fingerprints. I know how to do this sort of thing."

"That's why I love you," Mick had said before working out the arrangements for the drop.

Inside his kitchen, he unlaced the tie that held the manila envelope shut, and pulled out the papers. Oh, yes indeed, this was interesting material, very useful. Her bank account numbers. Her credit card numbers. Previous apartments she'd lived in before she'd bought her condo. The condo price. Her income. The graduate school loan she'd taken years ago, paid back in full.

Mick resisted the urge to shout for joy.

One of her charge accounts was with a local bank. He dialed, asked for the credit office, and said, "Hello, I'm calling about my wife's credit card. Her name is Pamela

Hayes.'' He read off the account number, then continued, ''She's out of town, and I can't make head or tail of her bookkeeping—''

''Excuse me, sir, but according to our records, Ms. Hayes isn't married.''

He suffered a twinge of reflexive anger—it always flared when someone questioned him about anything. Smothering his temper, he faked a chuckle and said, ''Well, Pamela is a stubborn feminist. She kept her own name, her own accounts and everything else. She doesn't use my income to get her credit line higher. That's the way she likes it.''

''I see.'' The lady at the other end of the line hesitated. ''What did you say your name was?''

''Andrew Pitt.'' It had been one of his aliases back in the olden days, when he'd been running errands for a thug out of Newark.

''And your social security number, Mr. Pitt?''

He made up a number.

''Okay. Is Ms. Hayes planning to have a credit card issued in your name?''

''No. I'm just trying to sort through her receipts here. I think she may have run up some charges on this business trip she's taken, and I'd like a record of what she's billed so she doesn't bankrupt me. You know women,'' he added with another phony laugh.

The lady in the bank's credit department didn't share his amusement. ''In other words, you want to know her last few charges?''

''That's right.''

''We've received a motel charge of fifty-eight dollars and change in Boise, Idaho, and a gas station charge of nineteen dollars in Salt Lake City.''

''Great. Anything else?''

"No. That's it. Those charges came in two weeks ago. Apparently she hasn't used her card since."

Damn. "Okay, great," he grumbled, then remembered to thank the lady and say goodbye.

The bitch hadn't used her card in two weeks. She was smart; she must have figured out that by charging all her expenses she would leave a trail for him to follow. She could be anywhere right now. How was he going to track her down if she'd taken to using cash?

On the other hand, how much cash could she possibly have on her? According to her credit report, she had a cushy little nest egg sitting at the local bank, not to mention the treasury bills and the mutual fund she was into. Surely she hadn't liquidated her entire savings account. If she was smart enough to have eluded him, she was too smart to go driving around with tens of thousands of dollars in cash stuffed into her bra.

Maybe she'd switched to one of her other credit cards once she'd left Utah. Maybe she thought she could fool him by using one card one week and another card the next.

Nobody fooled Mick Morrow for long. Whistling to himself, he looked up the phone number of the company that had issued her other major credit card. If he didn't strike pay dirt there, he'd call back her bank and find out how much money she'd withdrawn before she'd left town. If he knew how much she had, he could calculate how far she would get before she ran out of legal tender and had to start paying her bills with plastic again.

Oh, he was going to track her down, all right. And once he did, she was going to be one very sorry woman.

PAMELA SAW NO POINT in lying in bed any longer. She hadn't gotten more than a couple of hours of sleep all night; lingering under the sheet for another half hour wasn't going to cure her of insomnia.

It was hard to sleep in a strange bed in a strange room, she told herself. It was hard to sleep after drinking too much champagne, and after not eating enough solid food, and...

Pamela saw no point in lying—either in bed or to herself. Her restlessness had nothing to do with the unfamiliarity of her surroundings or what she'd consumed at the wedding. There was only one reason she hadn't been able to sleep last night, and his name was Jonas Brenner.

She dragged herself out of the bed in the pretty yellow room and donned a pair of walking shorts and a camp shirt. They were among the garments Kitty had insisted that Pamela buy in the days before the wedding. She'd also stocked up on shorts and T-shirts—a Key West version of a trousseau. This wasn't a place where any of her professional suits and dresses were going to do her much good.

Once she was dressed, she brushed her hair and then inched open the door. The upstairs hall was silent. Joe must still be asleep. If she was lucky, she would be able to drink a cup of coffee and pull herself together before she had to confront him.

She tiptoed along the hall to the stairs and down. The aroma of coffee wafted from the kitchen, cheering her until she realized its significance: Joe was up, probably in the kitchen. She would have no caffeine in her when she came face-to-face with the man she'd married yesterday, the man who had spent his first night as her husband in a bed at the opposite end of the house.

Inhaling for fortitude, she followed the fragrance into the kitchen. Joe stood at the sink, his back to her as he

rinsed stray coffee grounds from the basket of the coffeemaker. He turned as she entered, and his blue eyes
froze her in place.

She hadn't thought he was so terribly handsome the
first time she'd met him, had she? She had thought he
was a bum—and he was, she told herself. He hadn't
shaved, his hair was tousled, and dressed in a pair of
fraying denim cutoffs and a T-shirt that read It's Better
In Bimini, he looked more than a little disreputable.

He also looked like someone who hadn't slept very
well. His eyes were bloodshot, underlined with shadow.
The smile he gave her could have passed for a grimace.

"Good morning," she said, trying not to wince at how
formal she sounded.

"'Morning." He scrubbed his hand through his hair,
then turned back to the sink and set the basket on the
drying rack.

When he said nothing more, she ventured timidly into
the room. It was bigger than the kitchen in her condo,
but not as nice. The cabinets were varnished pine, the
countertops Formica, the floor a checkerboard of scuffed
black-and-white tiles. The major appliances seemed
fairly old, but they'd been augmented with more up-to-
date equipment: a microwave oven, a food processor and
the blessed coffeemaker, its decanter full to the rim.

"I'm usually not up this early," Joe said without
looking at her. "What with the bar and all. If it's my
turn to stay till closing time, I don't get home till the
wee hours."

"I'm a morning person," Pamela told him.

He nodded, as if he'd expected her to be the antithesis
of himself. "Lizard's a morning person, too. She knows
she's not supposed to wake me up. She usually just grabs
a box of cereal and goes into the den to watch TV."

Pamela knew she ought to say something, but the house was too quiet, the atmosphere too formal. She eyed the cupboards, wondering which one held the coffee cups.

He answered her unasked question by pulling two mugs from a cabinet. Then he swung open another cabinet door to reveal a shelf stacked with assorted boxes of cereal. "We've got every sugary cereal known to man," he told her, smiling sheepishly.

Pamela smiled back, just as shyly. Looking at him seemed too dangerous, so she quickly focused direction on the selection of cereals. Indeed, they all appeared to be sickeningly sweet: chocolate puffs, honeyed wheat, sugared flakes, frosted corn and something that, according to the picture on the front of the box, was pink.

"It's supposed to taste like berries," Joe explained, noticing the angle of her gaze. "It's Lizard's favorite."

Grimacing, Pamela closed the cupboard door and opened the bread drawer. "I think I'll just make some toast."

He gestured toward the toaster, then pulled a plate for her from a shelf and got butter and jam out of the refrigerator. She felt him hovering behind her as she made her toast, as if he wasn't sure whether he ought to be making it for her. His nearness unnerved her. She wanted him either to give her a reassuring hug or to back off. Having him so close yet so distant only emphasized the tension between them.

"I get the daily paper out of Miami," he said, indicating the newspaper on the table. "They usually toss it onto the driveway. I don't know if you like to read the paper over breakfast...." He drifted off uncertainly, then smiled even more uncertainly.

His words brought home to Pamela how very little

they knew about each other. Not just the trivia about whether they liked to peruse the paper over breakfast, whether Joe liked to watch TV with his dinner, what day he usually did the laundry—but real issues, like whom he'd voted for in the last election or whether he had a bad temper, whether he liked sex hot and fast or slow and slinky or...

She felt her cheeks grow warm. She didn't care how he liked sex. For that matter, she didn't care whom he'd voted for.

Her toast popped up, and she carried it to the table and sat. He had the newspaper in front of him, but he didn't look at it. He only held his mug and watched her. She smiled bashfully, then fussed with her toast, meticulously buttering it so she'd have something to do. Her mind scrambled furiously for something, anything, to latch on to so she wouldn't have to wonder about how Joe liked sex.

"Bones," she said.

"Huh?"

"Kitty told me your mother digs bones." When Kitty had mentioned that, Pamela wasn't sure she'd heard her correctly. Now that she'd given voice to the notion, she was sure she hadn't.

Joe proved her wrong. "Yeah," he said, relaxing in his chair. "She's sifting soil at some old Mayan ruin in Yucatán."

"Is she an archeologist?"

"Nah. She's a dilettante."

"It's an unusual hobby."

He shrugged and lowered his gaze to his coffee.

Pamela studied him intently. Now that they were finally talking, she wasn't going to abandon the subject. "How did she wind up in Mexico?"

Joe seemed to understand how anxious Pamela was to keep the conversation alive. He raised his eyes back to her and smiled. "Her last boyfriend. They decided to sail across the Gulf of Mexico together. According to her, somewhere along the way they had a falling out, and the last few days were hell. He was ready to have her walk the plank, and she was ready to mutiny. Soon as they reached Cancún they parted ways. I figure she must have hooked up with somebody there who was on his way to the ruins, and the next thing she knew, she was digging up ancient artifacts."

"Isn't that odd?" Pamela asked carefully, hoping he wouldn't take offense.

He looked puzzled. "What do you mean, odd?"

"Well, I don't know...." As she chewed a bite of toast she pictured her own mother, as staid and stable a woman as ever existed. The only thing her mother ever dug was the soil in the flower beds in her own yard. To sail to another country with a boyfriend, break up halfway through the voyage and grab hold of another man was simply something her mother would never do.

"My mother is a character," Joe conceded. "Headstrong, bitchy and a whole lot of fun. You can't always rely on her, though."

"That's more or less what Kitty said."

"Kitty was speaking the truth."

Pamela ate a bit more of her toast. "How about your father?"

"He died ten years ago." Joe drained his mug, then stood and crossed to the coffeepot for a refill. "Thing about my mother, she was real loyal and steadfast as a wife. Then, when my father passed away, she spent a while mourning and then she cut loose. She'd had enough of the loyal, steadfast-wife routine."

"Yes, but then when you got Lizard, your mother wasn't there to help you."

"She tried," Joe defended her. "But you know, she'd already raised two kids of her own. And then she'd lost her daughter, and she just didn't want to settle down and deal with it." He shrugged again. "So I settled down and dealt with it instead."

"Your family has had more than its fair share of pain," Pamela murmured.

"Hey, what's a fair share? You get what you get."

"How did your sister die?"

"Ballooning."

Pamela almost choked on her coffee. "I beg your pardon?"

"She and my brother-in-law were ballooning. They got caught in a wind sheer and crashed."

"That's...pretty dramatic."

Joe smiled wistfully. "What you mean is, it's odd."

"Well...yes."

"They wanted to try ballooning. It's supposed to be fantastic. They didn't expect to die, and they didn't want to, but my sister was adventurous and nothing stopped her. She was absolutely fearless. That was what my brother-in-law loved about her." His smile grew bitter as he added, "And that's what my brother-in-law's family hated about her. He was a real stuffed shirt when she met him. She unstuffed him. He was crazy about her."

"Their daughter seems to have inherited their free spirits," Pamela noted.

Joe agreed with a grim nod. "Lizard'll die if she's got to go live with that bunch of stuffed shirts. They'll sit on her till her spirit dries up and dies."

"Was your father a free spirit, too?"

His smile returned. "My father," he boasted, "was a bar owner."

"Oh?"

"He left me the Shipwreck in his will."

"But ten years ago—" she eyed him speculatively "—wouldn't you have been too young to own a bar?"

"We got around that." He grinned. "This is Key West, Pam. People don't bother with the fine print around here."

She finished her coffee, pleased to have learned a bit about her husband, even if what she'd learned struck her as rather strange. Through the open window above the sink, she heard the chirping of a bird. Sunlight bathed the room in golden warmth. Joe continued to grin at her.

It was all too domestic, too cozy. If last night she'd been raging with passion, this morning she was awash in the tranquillity of home and hearth—which, in its own way, was just as dangerous.

Abruptly she stood and carried her empty plate and mug to the sink. "Speaking of small print," she said as she rinsed the dishes, "this morning I'd like to take care of some paperwork—getting my driver's license and car registration changed, making sure my name is amended to Pamela Brenner on all my records and that kind of thing."

"That's what you married me for," he commented.

She tried to interpret the hint of seriousness in his tone, then decided not to be so analytical. Joe was probably just sleepy. Not that she would dare to turn around and look at him. Just as he'd kept his back to her at the sink when she'd entered the kitchen, she remained at the sink with her back to him now. Life seemed marginally safer when she wasn't gazing into his glorious blue eyes.

"I was figuring I ought to go across the street and

pick up Lizard first. It's important for me to get to know Birdie a little better.''

"Sure."

"Do you think it's too early to call on them?" She glanced at the wall clock. Nearly nine o'clock.

"They'll be up. Probably performing some black magic ritual, even as we speak. Go on over."

Once again she struggled to interpret the wistfulness coloring his voice. Did he want to get rid of her? Did he feel as awkward with her as she did with him? Where had their temporary companionability gone? Were they going to be this uncomfortable with each other for the rest of their married life?

If so, how in God's name was Pamela going to endure it?

She shook the excess water from her hands, then dried them on a towel. "Well," she said, sounding wooden, "I'll need a key to your door."

"I have a spare upstairs. You won't need it to run across the street, though. I'll leave the door unlocked."

"Okay." She wanted to say something more: that she understood his discomfort and shared it. That if they both put their minds to it—or took their minds off it—they could keep the strain between them to a minimum. That if Joe maintained his derelict grooming, she would probably stop experiencing an unwelcome surge of lust every time she looked at him. That once Lizard was back home, they would have her to distract them from each other and to drain them of energy so completely that the thought of sleeping together would vanish.

Then again, Joe might have no interest in sleeping with Pamela. Last night might have been an anomaly. This morning, his edginess might simply be a result of his wanting to let her down easy, to back off from her without hurting her feelings.

And perhaps she was analyzing too much again.

She tried to smile, but it was a lame effort and Joe wasn't looking at her anyway. "See you later," she said, then raced out of the room with all the subtlety of an Olympic sprinter, hoping with all her heart that Joe wouldn't be around when she got back.

AS SOON AS HE HEARD the screen door clap shut, he rose from the table and hurried to the front door. Through the metal mesh he watched her saunter across the dewy lawn. *She's too thin,* he told himself. *No curves.*

But she did have curves, a slight flare to her hips, a nicely understated roundness to her bottom, an intriguing width at her shoulders. Her hair caught the morning sunlight and glittered with hints of silver and gold. Her arms were as graceful as a dancer's.

He wanted to be dancing with her right now. The way they'd danced last night to "Stand by Me." The way they'd danced in the front hall, the way their lips had danced, and their tongues, and their hips. He wanted his wife in his bed.

He felt a painful tug in his groin and cursed. Last night would have been perfect. They'd had the entire house to themselves. No five-year-old twerp to consider, no snotty little kid to startle them awake at the crack of dawn, no nosy young miss to ask how come Pamela hadn't spent the night in her own room. It would have been one of the most fantastic nights in Joe's life—and maybe Pam's, too.

Instead, he'd spent the night kicking his blankets, punching his pillow, engaging in all manner of bed-linen violence in a futile attempt to burn off what could be burned off only one way—and that required a woman in his bed. Pamela.

But Joe had exercised his scruples last night. What amazed him was that he actually had scruples to exercise. He never used to be bothered by right and wrong and all that. Sure, he had always tried to avoid bruising a woman's ego, and he was invariably a good boy when it came to protection, but the rest of it, the "shouldn'ts" and "mustn'ts"... When had he developed a sense of morality?

The day Lizard had become his responsibility, that was when.

How ironic that it was Lizard's fault he was suddenly hung up on setting a good example, behaving properly, toeing the line. If it weren't for the brat, he would have had no compunction about seducing Pam last night.

But if it weren't for the brat, Pamela wouldn't have become a part of his life.

He watched until she was no longer visible. Turning from the door, he tried to erase the image of her from his mind, her long, elegant strides, her fair hair, the curves of her not-too-curvaceous body.

Tried to, but failed. Pamela was his wife, and no matter how much he'd like not to be tempted by her, she was going to be a full-time, under-his-roof temptation for quite some time.

Blame it on Lizard, he thought, although he felt pretty damned guilty blaming the kid for his own wayward passion. It was Lizard's fault he'd had to get married. But it was his own fault for choosing Pamela Hayes as his wife.

CHAPTER SEVEN

PAMELA SHOULD HAVE expected Birdie's house to be strange. Any woman who attended a wedding dressed in feathers would be likely to live in a peculiar house.

Then again, Pamela conceded, it had been a peculiar wedding. And Lizard was a peculiar child, with a peculiar name. Of course she would have a peculiar babysitter.

Birdie answered the door wearing a flowing caftan printed with a tropical-bird pattern. Her wooden-bead earrings were long enough to brush her shoulders, and silver bangle bracelets were stacked several inches deep on each forearm. When she beckoned Pamela into her house, the metal loops clanked, sounding vaguely like dragging chains in a bad horror movie.

Enhancing the spooky mood were the candles that lit the angular hallway, lending the smell of hot paraffin to the air. Eerie paintings of brightly colored frogs adorned the walls, and the floor was covered with braided straw rugs. If a candle fell over, Pamela imagined the entire building would incinerate in less than a minute.

"We're making something," Birdie said vaguely, leading Pamela through the dim hall and into a kitchen too cramped and narrow to hold a table. The window above the sink looked out onto another room. Pamela figured that at one time the sink had stood against an outer wall. The room beyond might once have been a porch, since it featured a floor of painted concrete, and it seemed to be on a slightly lower level than the kitchen.

Through the smudged pane of glass she spotted Lizard kneeling on a chair, kneading a pink, doughy substance. If Pamela were an optimist, she'd assume it was modeling clay. But given its color—and everything else she'd learned about Joe's niece—she suspected that whatever the stuff was, Lizard was eventually going to eat it.

"Has she had breakfast yet?" Pamela asked Birdie, speaking in a whisper even though the child seemed totally oblivious to the two women spying on her through the window.

"She ate." Birdie eyed Pamela speculatively. "You and Joe, everything okay?"

"Everything's fine," Pamela lied, wondering whether as a boo doo chief Birdie could read her mind. "Thanks for keeping Lizard overnight."

"Lizard and I, we're pals. You want tea?"

"No, thanks." Pamela took a minute to survey the room where Lizard was playing with the pink dough. On the far end of the room was another door, leading to another room. "This is an unusual house," she remarked tactfully.

Birdie shrugged, her voluminous dress billowing in an aftershock. "Joe."

"Joe?"

"He put it together."

"He did?" Pamela glanced up at the beamed ceiling, the two rickety steps leading from the kitchen into another hallway, the plank floor and luridly painted cabinets. "It's awfully eclectic."

Birdie's eyes narrowed on Pamela. They were perfect for someone named Birdie—dark and sharp, leaving Pamela with the impression that she was being observed from above, even though Birdie was in fact shorter than she. If Birdie were truly a bird, she would be a hawk, or perhaps something colorfully exotic, like a mynah. Certainly not a cute little hummingbird or a domesticated blue parakeet.

"*Eclectic*," the older woman enunciated slowly. "I don't know what that means. I know *awful*."

"I didn't say your house was awful," Pamela clarified. And really, it wasn't. Just strange, with rooms tacked on here and there, floors on different levels and misplaced windows. There was something phantasmagoric about the place, as if it were a carnival fun house.

Birdie shrugged again. "It is awful. But me, I don't care."

"It's not awful," Pamela argued. As an architect, she viewed a building like this not as a disaster but as a challenge, a puzzle to be solved. "Did Joe really build it?"

"No. He put it together. He fixes it. Used to be, it was falling down. He propped and patched and painted. A good man, that husband of yours. You take good care of him."

"I'll certainly try." Refusing to dwell on the subject of her wifely duties, Pamela returned her attention to the house. "Mind if I look around?"

"Sure, you look around. Just don't step on the animals."

Pamela wasn't sure she wanted to know what sort of pets a woman like Birdie would keep. Spiders for her voodoo activities? Lambs for ritual slaughter? Snakes so Lizard would have some of her own species to cavort with?

Moving cautiously, Pamela left the kitchen for the

crooked hallway. The floor dipped in one part, apparently following the contours of the earth beneath it. The hall veered ninety degrees and ended in a small, trapezoid-shaped sitting room occupied by a small army of cats. On the other side of the sitting room, a door led to a bedroom with a cot against one wall and an abundance of toys on the floor. Lizard's room, Pamela guessed.

Turning, she found Birdie lurking behind her, a tiger-striped kitten cupped in her hand, her keen, dark eyes observing Pamela. Her face was ageless, but her hands showed the ravages of time, her fingers bony and her knuckles knobby. The kitten didn't seem to mind; it curled contentedly in her palm and closed its eyes as Birdie scratched behind its ears.

"I don't know if you were aware of it," Pamela said, watching Birdie as intently as Birdie watched her, "but I'm an architect."

"Lego," Birdie confirmed. "Lizard told me."

"Actually—" Pamela smiled "—I don't work with Lego. I build buildings. More precisely, I design them. But I do know a bit about construction. I'm just thinking..." She weighed the older woman's silence, wondering if what she was about to propose would offend her. "Your house has an awful lot of potential."

"*Potential* I don't understand. *Awful,* I know that word."

Pamela swallowed a laugh. "Potential means, well, something like raw ingredients. A house like this... If you opened a few walls, widened the hallways, brought more natural light into the rooms, it would really brighten the place up. And instead of all these tiny cubicles, you'd have wide-open spaces, with flow and cross ventilation and sunlight and..." She faltered, unable to interpret Birdie's opaque expression. "What I'm trying to say," she concluded, "is that it's a wonderful house, an architect's dream."

"You dream of a house like this?" Birdie snorted. Even the kitten in her hand seemed to snort.

"Well, not exactly, but..." The woman's toothy grin heartened Pamela. "It's just that I've always had a career, but now I'm married and living here in Key West, and I'm wondering what I'm going to do with my time while Jonas is at the bar and Lizard is with you. What I'm thinking is, I could renovate your house."

Birdie frowned. "Why?"

"To make it brighter and easier for you to live in," Pamela explained. "I could do that for you, if you'd like." *Please*, she implored silently. *Please let me do this. For me if not for you.* She needed something to keep her busy. If she didn't come up with an activity to absorb her time and energy, she would wind up spending that time and energy in dangerous ways. If she didn't work, thoughts of Joe would take over, fantasies of him, memories of his mouth on hers. Nature abhorred a vacuum, and if she didn't find something to fill that vacuum, Jonas and his wild little niece were going to occupy the empty space.

And once they did, Pamela would be in big trouble.

How much safer to pursue a project—and Birdie's house was ideal. Pamela could simplify the maze of rooms, make them more efficient and cheerful, and have something other than Joe to think about. That the work would benefit Pamela was clear, but it would benefit Birdie, too. The woman was getting on in years. Her hands were already arthritic; her hips couldn't be far behind. How was she going to navigate all the uneven hallways and steps in another decade?

"I'd do it for free," Pamela added. "How about if I

just draw up some sketches and you can look them over and tell me what you think.''

Birdie chuckled and shook her head. ''I like you, Pamela,'' she declared. ''Another crazy bird, that's you. No wonder Joe loves you.''

Pamela was too diplomatic to correct Birdie's misconception about their marriage. ''I don't think I'm such a crazy bird,'' she said amiably.

''Oh, yes.'' Birdie appraised her, then nodded. ''A loon, maybe.''

''Joe said I was a swan,'' Pamela murmured, although she had to admit he'd said that a long time ago. After her behavior last night, he probably thought she was a chicken.

''Another crazy bird, like me, like Lizard. Like Joe. You want to fix my house, be my guest. Joe is always fixing it, and now you're fixing it. You and he, you're two of a kind.''

''I'm not so sure about that,'' Pamela said quickly. She didn't want to think of herself and Joe as being two of anything.

Again Birdie's eyes took on an annoyingly wise look. ''Oh, yes. Two of a kind, you and Joe. Birds of a feather.''

Birdbrains is more like it, Pamela thought. ''We're really not that much alike—''

''If it makes you happy to fix my house, go ahead.'' Birdie tossed the kitten onto an old armchair with clawed, frayed upholstery and left the room, Pamela at her heels. ''For myself, I don't care. But if you're happy, you'll make Joe happy, and then Lizard will be happy. And that I care about. So make yourself happy and fix my house.'' They had reached the enclosed porch, where Lizard was hunched over the table, shaping her dough into gooey pink balls and then flattening them into pan-cakes with her fist. "Maybe Lizard can help you. She's good with Legos."

"She'll want to paint the whole house pink," Pamela warned.

"I don't want the outside pink," Birdie said.

"I may not have to touch the outside. I'll just tear down some inner walls...." She gazed around her, smil-ing at the prospect of digging in and making something out of the ramshackle house. "I won't do anything with-out your approval. I'll scribble some ideas on paper, and then—"

Birdie fluttered her hand, waving away an explanation she obviously didn't wish to hear. She'd already said she thought Pamela was crazy. "You do what you must do—as long as you make Joe happy. He's a good man, your husband."

Pamela's smile grew forced. She was supposed to be pretending her marriage was genuine, so she really shouldn't get all huffy and defensive when someone commented that she and Joe made a nice couple. If she could fool Birdie into thinking she and Joe were alike, maybe they would be able to convince the social workers and the family court judge.

But it was hard to pretend, hard to smile and nod. The problem with Birdie's comments was that they carried too much truth. No amount of hammering and tearing and replastering, no reconfiguration of rooms, no open-ing and brightening and ventilating, was going to alter the fact that Joe was Pamela's husband, that he was a good man, and, judging by her behavior last night, Pa-mela was a lousy wife, failing to make him happy. Jonas Brenner had taken her as his bride and saved her life. He deserved better.

Well, she would do what she could. She would change her name, change her driver's license and social security data and be as much of a mother figure to Lizard as possible. She would act like a proper, stable wife and lead the world to believe Lizard belonged with her Uncle Joe.

Pamela could do that much for him. She would try her best, within reason, to fool the world into believing she and Joe were two of a kind.

HE WANTED TO CLEAR OUT of the house before she got back with Lizard, but he couldn't. He had promised to leave the front door unlocked for her, and he couldn't very well take off while the house was unlocked. Not that he had much to steal, not that he didn't trust his neighbors, but Key West had been built by pirates and it was chronically overrun by mainlanders. People were wise to lock up behind themselves.

He held the spare key in his palm, flipping it over, tracing the notches and ridges with his thumb. There were commitments and there were *commitments*. For some reason, giving a woman the key to his home seemed like more of a commitment than marrying her.

That was a stupid thought. Pam was his wife, for crying out loud. Lizard's aunt by marriage. One half of the pretty little domestic scene he was going to present to the court. He had to give her a key to the house that, at least for the sake of appearances, was hers as much as his. He'd given her a ring, hadn't he?

And as soon as he gave her the damned key, he could split for the day.

He needed distance. Perspective. A path back to the self-control he'd felt before last night had whacked him upside the head—or below the belt. Hanging around the house with Pam all day wasn't going to cure him of lust. He needed to stay away from her until he could think of her once again as the too-slim, too-prim yuppie she'd been before he'd pulled that idiotic newlywed stunt and carried her over the threshold.

The Shipwreck didn't open for business until noon, but Brick and Kitty would probably be there this morning, cleaning up. God only knew how late the wedding celebration had raged on last night. Joe's friends weren't the sort to stand on ceremony. Just because the bride and groom had left didn't mean the party couldn't keep going in their honor.

Things probably hadn't wound down until the wee hours. If Joe hadn't gone and gotten himself hitched, he would have remained till the bitter end.

The hell with it. So he was hitched. He could still stay out late—he had to, and he would. Not just because his job demanded it, but because, if he wanted to preserve his sanity, it would be best to steer clear of Pam until she was safely tucked into her own bed, in her own room, with her door shut.

He heard voices through the screened front door, Pamela's and Lizard's. Pamela sounded stern; Lizard whined. "I *oh-weez* go to the beach. Every day. If you don't take me, I'll hate you forever."

"I've already told you, Lizard, I've got to run some errands first. If you behave yourself—"

"I am behaving myself!"

"Then don't behave yourself. Behave some other way. Behave like a nice, quiet girl."

"I hate you!"

Joe shuddered. Things were worse than he'd thought. Pamela was stuck not just with a man who had once regarded her as too bony and now only wanted to jump her bones, but also with a brat whose whine could shatter crystal a mile away. Joe could apply the brakes to his sex drive, but after coping with the Liz Monster for a morning, Pamela might decide to pack her bags and throw her lot in with the hit man in Seattle.

Hearing the screen door slam, he stood and left the kitchen for the hallway. "I'll take her to the beach," he offered, recalling that he'd promised Pamela he wouldn't saddle her with Lizard more than necessary. "You can do your errands. I'll take the kid."

"The kid," Pamela responded, glowering at Joe's pouting niece, "has been surly and sassy and doesn't deserve to be rewarded. If she wants to go to the beach, she can earn it by behaving nicely."

"You know what you are?" Lizard howled, crossing her arms over her chest and sticking her lower lip out as far as it could go. "You're a twit."

Joe relaxed. Lizard had picked up some nasty language hanging out at the Shipwreck. He'd taught her not to use bad words, but given how prickly she was at the moment, he had expected her to tag Pamela with some X-rated expression.

"Pam isn't a twit," he said. "She's my wife, Lizard, and I expect you to treat her with respect."

Lizard peered up with round, tear-filled eyes, evidently hoping to find an ally in him. "You know what she is? She's a rotten tomato."

"That's enough, Liz." He wasn't sure whether he should leap right in and discipline the kid or let her work things out with Pamela. If he interfered, they might never establish a truce on their own.

He glanced at Pamela, seeking guidance. But when his gaze met hers, he saw only stunning silver eyes, soft pink lips, a delicately sculpted chin, a slender throat begging to be kissed.

Man, he was bitten. Here he was, stuck in the middle of the first major quarrel that threatened to disrupt the peaceful domestic unit he'd worked so hard to achieve, and all he could think about was how this woman who was absolutely not his type was turning him on like a blender at the Shipwreck, crushing his resistance and pureeing his best intentions.

Pamela returned his gaze for a fraction of a second, then glared down at Lizard. "You don't win points with me for being obnoxious," she said in a starchy schoolmarm voice. "Right now, Lizard, you're being obnoxious."

"So what? You're noxious, too."

"We're going to run errands whether you like it or not."

"I don't like it! I don't like you! I think you're gross."

"The feeling's mutual." Pamela headed for the stairs, calling over her shoulder, "I'm going to get my purse. If you can convince your uncle I'm noxious before I return, more power to you." Her footsteps receded as she reached the top of the stairs. The house trembled slightly from the impact of her slamming her door.

Joe allowed himself a private smile at her long-distance show of anger. She'd kept her irritation in check downstairs, but Lizard had obviously pushed her too far. He kind of liked the idea of Pamela having a temper. He liked the idea that she had all sorts of volatile emotions churning inside her, ready to erupt at the slightest provocation.

Which wasn't to say that Lizard was a slight provocation. But he liked imagining Pam in the throes of some wildly passionate emotion, even if it was anger.

He shouldn't be imagining Pam in the throes of anything. Squatting down, he stared Lizard in the eye. "Listen up, toots. You aren't winning any points with me, either."

"I don't like her." Lizard sulked. "I was playing at Birdie's with this pink clay that Birdie said was magic, and we were going to make little dolls and bake them and then say chants over them and make curses and stuff? And she—" Lizard pointed accusingly up the stairs "—said I had to go learn to drive with her."

"She already knows how to drive," Joe corrected Lizard. "And you're about ten years too young. What she's got to do is get a Florida driver's license. She has to fill out some forms and pay some money at the motor-vehicle department."

"Well, she coulda left me at Birdie's."

"What did Birdie say about it?"

Lizard curled her lip. "She told me to go with her." She pointed toward the stairs again. "They were whispering. They were plotting behind my back and everything."

"What were they plotting?"

"Something with Legos." Lizard scuffed her toe against the rug. "I wanna go to the beach, Uncle Joe. Make her take me to the beach."

"I can't make her do anything." How true, he thought with a sigh. "Pamela's part of our family now, and if Birdie thought you ought to spend the day with her, Birdie must have known what she was doing. So my advice, Ms. Monster, is you go do errands with her, and if you don't drive her nutty, I bet she'll take you to the beach this afternoon."

"Why can't you take me to the beach?"

Because I can't stay around Pamela. "I've got to go to the Shipwreck."

"Bring me with you," Lizard pleaded, pressing her grimy little hands together prayerfully. "I'll help you. Please, Uncle Joe—"

Once again, he was faced with the option of doing the right thing. Like last night, he chose correctly, even though it broke his heart. "You've got to spend some time with Pamela. How else are you two going to learn to get along?"

"But I hate her!"

"She probably hates you, too. And given the way you've been acting toward her, I wouldn't blame her."

"I want her to hate me. Then maybe she'll go away and leave us alone."

"She's not going to go away," Joe declared, hoping Pamela wouldn't make a liar out of him. "So you'd best make peace with her."

Cocking her head, Lizard scrutinized him dubiously. "Why won't she go away? 'Cuz she's in love with you?"

If only, he thought, then scowled. He didn't want her love. He only wanted her help, right? Her help, her support and her sleek body wrapped around him at night. "Yeah," he muttered, unable to disguise the bitter disappointment shading his voice. "Pam and I are a real love match. So get used to it, Lizzie. This is the way it's going to be."

Deflated, Lizard slouched toward the kitchen. "Well, if I gotta go do errands with her, the least she could do is let me eat a cookie first."

"I don't think she'll kick up too much of a fuss about that." He watched his niece trudge away, then gazed up the stairs in time to see Pamela begin her descent. She carried her purse and wore sunglasses.

At the bottom of the stairs she faced him. Her lips formed a grim line; her skin smelled faintly of a sunscreen lotion. "You mentioned something about having a key I could use," she said hesitantly.

Unfolding his hand made him aware of how tight his fist had been clenched. The key was warm from his grip, and his palm bore its outline. "Here," he said, dropping it into her hand so he wouldn't have to touch her.

"Thank you."

"I'm sorry about Lizard."

"She's going through a lot. I guess she's entitled to have a snit."

"Sometimes I think she was born with PMS."

Pamela gave him a faint smile. "All females are born with PMS, Jonas." She stashed the key in the pocket of her shorts, drawing his attention to her long legs. They were too pale, but a few more days of Florida sunshine would rectify that. Her calves, while slender, had muscle to them, and her knees shaped perfect ovals. Her thighs—

"I've got to go to the bar," he said abruptly.

She looked at her watch. "It's ten in the morning."

"People in these parts tend to start drinking early." *Especially when they're in a state of intense sexual frustration,* he added silently. "I'll be home late. The Shipwreck closes around 2:00 a.m., depending on how many customers are in a take-his-keys-and-call-a-cab state."

Pamela nodded.

"So I won't be home till very late. No need to wait up."

She nodded again. Evidently she understood what he was really saying: that he didn't want to have to see her when he rolled home. "Well," she said, then mulled over her thoughts for a minute. "Have fun."

"You have fun, too."

"I'm sure the Department of Motor Vehicles will be a barrel of laughs," she said dryly. "The next time you see me, all my documents will say I'm Pamela Brenner."

His wife. His partner. His legal mate.

The woman living at the other end of the house.

He strode out without bothering to shout a farewell to Lizard. Let the two females with their PMS forge a truce. Let them find a way to coexist. Joe had already found his way to coexist with Pamela: stay as far away from her as he could.

AS IT TURNED OUT, arriving at the Shipwreck early had been a wise move. Lois was the only one there, and she was having a time of it dragging the heavy tables from the main room back to their usual places. She'd already swept and mopped the floor, but the rafters were still draped with white ribbons, and empty plastic champagne cups kept turning up in odd places—on a windowsill, under the jukebox, lined up like ducks in a shooting gallery along the ceramic edge of a urinal in the men's room.

"So," Lois said, holding a trash bag open for him to toss in his collection of used cups. "How's holy matrimony treating you?"

"I'm not sure it's holy," he grumbled, refusing to meet her dark-eyed gaze. "Pam and I were married by a judge, not a minister." He climbed onto one of the tables and started uncoiling the white streamers from the rafters.

"Okay, so how's legal matrimony treating you?" Lois

chattered up at him. Fortunately she didn't give him a chance to answer, but instead launched into a monologue about how lovely the wedding had been. "I wept through the entire ceremony, Joe—and for hours afterward. It was so beautiful. The judge's words, the ring, the music... By the way, who the hell is this Pamela person, anyway? Where did you meet her? I mean, really, Joe, how long did you even know her before you went and got yourself leg-shackled? Not that it wasn't one of the most beautiful leg-shacklings I ever saw, and the cake was incredible if I say so myself. But honestly, Joe, what the hell was it? Love at first sight?"

Lois's words reminded him how very few people knew the truth about his marriage. Kitty knew, and his lawyer, and the happy couple themselves. "Yeah," he fibbed, trying not to sound too gruff. "It was love at first sight."

"I don't know about love at first sight. It's supposed to be very romantic, but it doesn't seem all that practical."

"It can be damned practical," he argued. If any word described his marriage to Pam, it was practical. He carefully unsnagged a thread that had gotten caught on a splinter in the wood, then let the long white ribbon drop.

Lois scooped it up and shoved it into the trash bag. "Well, I would never have guessed her to be your type, Joe."

Neither would I, he thought uneasily.

"I mean, you always used to go for big bazooms. This Pam person, whoever the hell she is—if I may speak frankly, Joe, she has more class than your usual squeezes."

"Maybe that's why I married her," he snapped, wishing Lois would shut up. He leapt down from the table and took the trash bag from her. "I'll go stick this in the Dumpster." He would do anything—even volunteer for a garbage run—to get away from Lois and her unintentionally annoying banter.

Outside in the alley, he unwound. What the heck—he couldn't be having a worse time with Lois than Pamela was having with Lizard. The notion of Pam standing in one of those interminable lines at the motor-vehicle department, with Lizard screeching and moaning and making an all-around nuisance of herself, brought a smile to his lips. It wasn't that he wished Pamela ill. It was just that if he was going to be miserable, he wanted his wife to be miserable, too.

It turned out that the remainder of his day was more or less unremittingly miserable. The early crowd started dribbling in shortly after noon. They tended to be mostly dissolute would-be writers, many of them sporting Hemingway beards and running at the mouth about the Great American Novels they were going to write if only they had a free half hour. Yet instead of rambling self-indulgently about their great oeuvres and their chronic writer's blocks as they usually did, they all spent the afternoon slapping Joe on the back, congratulating him and dishing out advice on how to keep the little lady in line, or on her back, or whatever. Joe had to grin good-naturedly and pretend he appreciated all their suggestions.

"Never bring her flowers when you've done something that would upset her," one of them admonished him. "Like, if you fool around on the side, don't bring her flowers. It's like hanging a neon sign around your neck saying Guilty."

"You're the boss," another chimed in. "Don't ever let her forget that."

"If things get stale, go the vibrator route," yet another recommended. "Works every time—as long as you've got fresh batteries on hand."

Joe barely had time to recover from the afternoon regulars when the evening crowd arrived. They were worse because they were his friends. The fishermen and navy guys couldn't stop riding him about his impetuous marriage. The ladies seemed to think Joe was twice as irresistible now that he was officially out of reach. Men shook their heads and offered their condolences; women whispered that if he had any problems with his wife, he could unburden himself to them. A few romantically inclined women played "Stand by Me" on the jukebox so many times Joe almost stopped liking the song.

No, he still liked the song. It was just that whenever he heard it, he wanted Pamela in his arms, dancing with him, smiling, looking slightly dazed, slightly amazed and utterly beautiful in her simple white dress. The song made him remember how easily he and Pamela had moved together on the dance floor, how well their bodies had matched, how natural it had felt to have her in his arms. It made him remember how much he'd wanted to take her home, carry her into his house and make her his wife.

He stayed until closing time, ignoring Brick when he grunted that Joe should go home to the missus. Joe stayed after Kitty sashayed out the back door, swearing she was bushed. He stayed until the last bleary-eyed beer drinker shuffled out the door.

The bar's silence was eerie. In the shadows, in the whisper of the air-conditioning, he could almost hear the echoing strains of "Stand by Me." He contemplated removing that disk from the jukebox, but decided to leave it in for now. By tomorrow night, the novelty of his marital status would have worn off; people would leave him—and the song—alone.

He gave the bar one final wipe, then locked the cash register. Glancing up, he noticed that the steering wheel clock on the wall read ten past two.

She had to be safely in bed by now. He would be able to go home and get to his own room without running the risk of seeing her and yielding to temptation. And he'd sleep late tomorrow, and maybe, if luck stayed with him, she would go out early and he wouldn't have to see her in the morning, either.

He drove down Duval Street, which was still lively with traffic and noisy pedestrians, and south into his own slumbering neighborhood. The front porch light of his house glowed. Pamela must have left it on for him.

Damn her for doing something so thoughtful. The plan was that he'd dive into bed without thinking about her, without being touched by anything she did or was or meant to him.

Okay. So she was considerate. As long as he didn't see her, he could stand a bit of consideration on her part.

He climbed up the porch steps and let himself into the house. The hall light was on, too, but the upstairs was dark and silent. Everybody was asleep.

He tiptoed down the hall to make sure the back door was locked—and spotted her on the screened porch, sprawled out on the cushions of the wrought-iron sofa in the corner. She was sound asleep, a book open across her chest.

She must have tried to wait up for him. Like a good wife, a *real* wife, she'd sat up and read, waiting for her man to come home from the late shift at work.

Damn her all over again. If she was going to do stuff like this, leaving lights on for him, struggling to stay awake so she could greet him when he finally got home…if she was going to act like a wife, he was going to have one hell of a time trying not to act like a husband.

Sighing, he went out to the porch, located a bookmark on the table, and tucked it into her book. Then he gathered her into his arms. She seemed heavier tonight than she had last night, because she was asleep. But he'd gladly take the extra weight. If she woke up, if she opened her eyes and smiled and whispered his name, he would turn left at the top of the stairs, not right, and refuse to release her until he'd reached his own room, his own bed.

Thinking about it made him hard. Feeling her silky hair brush against his arm, her cheek nestle against his shoulder and her knees bend around his other arm as he carried her up the stairs made him more than hard. It made him feel protective and bewildered and—damn her to high heaven—affectionate.

He blew out a long, weary breath. Affectionate he could handle. Protective wasn't like him—at least when it came to anyone other than Lizard—but it was part of the deal he'd agreed to when Pamela told him about her predicament back in Seattle. And affectionate and protective were enough to make him feel bewildered.

But he felt something more, too, something restless, something troublesome, something as hot and steamy as Key West in July. It made him walk faster, as fast as he could without waking her, and practically hurl her onto her bed. Without even stopping to pull off her sandals, he hightailed it out of her room, sweating and aching and wondering how he was going to survive this stupid marriage without losing his mind.

CHAPTER EIGHT

"WHEN YOU SAY 'BINGO,'" Mick asked, "exactly what are you saying?"

"I'm saying, I got a line on her driver's license."

Mick pressed the mute button on the remote control and leaned back in the overstuffed chair. The silent drama being played out on the television screen across the room from him—some gonzo was throttling some lady—was a scene Mick would ordinarily have found engrossing. But Tony's news was even more engrossing, even if he didn't trust the chump from here till tomorrow. Sometimes he wondered whether having Tony on his payroll was worth it.

Other than keeping the Seattle Police Department out of Mick's hair while he tried to put the bitch out of commission, Tony hadn't delivered. Or more precisely, he hadn't delivered enough. Mick had been able to trace her credit-card charges as far east as St. Louis, but from that point on she'd disappeared into the black hole of cash purchases, leaving no records, no trail. Where the hell had she gone? North to New York? South to Atlanta? Back to the West Coast? He knew she wasn't likely to have flown out of the country; none of her bills was to an airline. And besides, if she'd wanted to go continent-hopping, she would have booked a flight out of Seattle, not St. Louis.

It was safe to assume she was still in the U.S., and

sooner or later she was going to run out of cash. But where would she be when she had to go back to living on plastic? When was she going to stick one of those gold cards of hers into an automatic teller machine for a cash advance and send Mick another clue as to her whereabouts?

"Her driver's license," Mick said impassively. He wasn't going to let himself get excited about anything Tony had to tell him. Not until it panned out.

"More than that, Mick. Her name."

"I know her name."

"Not anymore, you don't. She changed it."

Mick squelched the optimism that threatened him. Until he had everything—which meant until he had her—he refused to get his hopes up. "What did she change it to?"

"This wasn't easy to find out," Tony hedged.

Squeezing me for more money, Mick thought angrily. "I don't give a rat's ass how hard it was to find out," he snapped. "Tell me her name."

"Brenner."

"Brenner what?"

"Pamela Brenner. And she's traded in her Washington State license for a Florida one."

Mick's pulse sped up. She was in Florida, apparently planning to stay long enough to have changed her license. Evidently she was really afraid of Mick if she'd changed her name, too.

Well, he'd never taken her for a fool. She had enough brains to recognize that Mick was somebody she *ought* to be afraid of.

"Florida's a big state," he remarked. "Give me an address."

"I couldn't get the address. My contact in Florida got

the heebie-jeebies and hung up before I could wring anything more out of him. According to Florida's central computer system, someone whose license number matched Hayes's Washington State license changed her papers to Florida, but my source wouldn't say for sure that Pamela Brenner is the same person as Pamela Hayes.''

"Don't pull my chain, Tony. If I've got to travel all the way to Florida, I need to know where to go. Miami, Tampa, Orlando... You've got to get me her address.''

"You aren't allowed to leave the state while you're out on bail, Mick.''

"That's not your problem. Your problem is, I need to know if this Pamela Brenner is the same broad as my good friend Miss Hayes. And I need to know where she lives. And frankly, her plate numbers would be more useful to me than her driver's license, which she no doubt will be carrying in her wallet where I can't see it. Like I'm supposed to pick the pocket of every skinny blond bitch in Florida to see if she's got the right license? Get me tags, pal. Get me an address. Florida's a big state.''

"I'll do what I can," Tony promised.

"Just get me what I need, and we'll all live happily ever after.''

"Yeah," Tony promised again. "That sounds about right to me." He hung up without saying goodbye.

Mick lowered the receiver and grinned. He might have been heavy-handed with Tony, but the guy was a wimp, and he responded well to being scolded. Mick didn't even have to spell out a threat. He just had to give a little nudge, and Tony would go back to risking his neck to get Mick what he was after. After all, Mick had as much on Tony as Tony had on him.

Florida. Pamela Brenner, neé Hayes, lived in Florida. Once again Mick could taste success.

Still smiling, he lifted the remote control and turned the sound back on. The lady on the screen was lying dead, the man looming above her, looking mighty satisfied with what he'd accomplished.

Jury selection for Mick's new trial wasn't supposed to begin for months. If necessary, his lawyer could drag things out even longer. But it probably wouldn't be necessary. Mick would soon be feeling the same smug satisfaction as the guy on the TV show, taking pride in a job well done—and walking free when the state's star witness was unable to testify against him.

Oh, yes, he thought, gazing at the female corpse on the screen. Things were definitely looking up.

IF ANYONE HAD TOLD PAMELA she was destined to be married to a man she never saw, she would never have believed it. Then again, if anyone had told her she was going to observe a murder, put herself in jeopardy by testifying against the murderer in court, and flee to a steamy, sticky island off the southern tip of Florida, where she would take an utter stranger as her husband and accept his wild little niece as part of the package, she wouldn't have believed that, either.

None of this had been a part of her life plan.

She wanted to see her husband. She wanted to talk to Jonas, tell him how her day had gone, boast about how she'd persuaded Lizard to behave with the assistance of a dish of peppermint-stick ice cream and a pad of graph paper that had so pleased the little girl she'd forgotten all about her demands to be taken to the beach. Pamela had purchased pencils, a ruler, a protractor and the graph paper so she could begin jotting ideas for the overhaul of Birdie's house. Lizard had insisted that she knew Birdie's house—and Birdie—better than Pamela did, and therefore she should have some graph paper to jot ideas on, too.

If peace could be bought for the cost of a pad, Pamela wasn't above spending the money. More than peace, Pamela had bought victory over the Liz Monster. It would have been cheap at twice the price.

Pamela wanted to tell Joe. She wanted to brag that, for a single, professional woman who'd never had any dealings with five-year-old brats, she had acquitted herself with Lizard rather nicely. Joe had told her not to wait up for him, but she'd wanted to see him, so she'd pulled a paperback novel from the shelf in the den and settled on the porch to read until he got home from the Shipwreck.

And then, apparently, she'd fallen asleep.

She hadn't seen Joe, but he'd seen her. When she woke up the next morning, she found herself in her own bed. Who but Joe could have carried her up the stairs?

She knew he was strong enough. She knew how easily his powerful arms could lift her and cradle her against his chest. He'd carried her across the threshold, hadn't he? And embraced her, and kissed her...

She supposed she should be grateful that he'd left her fully clothed when he'd brought her to her room last night. It would have been simple enough for him to undress her when she was too soundly asleep to protest. For that matter, it would have been simple enough for him to have kissed her awake like a scruffy Prince Charming arousing Sleeping Beauty from her century-long slumber. Pamela wasn't sure she would have stopped him.

But obviously he hadn't wanted to kiss her, or undress

her, or join her in bed. Now that the enchantment of their wedding had worn off, he had come to his senses and decided to keep his hands, and his lips, to himself.

Pulling herself out of bed, she removed her wrinkled clothing, tossed it into her laundry basket and donned her bathrobe. She passed the bathroom to peek at his bedroom door, which was firmly shut. No doubt he was still sleeping.

Feeling out of sorts, she showered, returned to her bedroom and dressed in the Key West uniform: fresh shorts and a T-shirt. Then she went downstairs.

Lizard was seated cross-legged on the floor of the den, no more than a couple of inches from the television, an open box of sugar-laden cereal in her lap. She wore a tank shirt and sweat pants cut off at the knees, with a feather tied into the drawstring at the waist. Her attention glued to the cartoon, she didn't acknowledge Pamela's quiet "Good morning."

Pamela could have urged Lizard to put a few more feet between herself and the screen, or to turn it off altogether. But Lizard wasn't her child, and training her not to pig out on junky cereal while watching junky cartoons wasn't Pamela's job. At the moment, she wasn't really in the mood to be sociable, either.

Abandoning the den, she went outside to get the newspaper. A light drizzle was soaking the earth, and the newspaper was soggy despite its plastic wrapper. Her spirit felt soggy, too.

Really, she assured herself as she returned to the kitchen and spread the sections of the paper out to dry, she didn't care about seeing Joe. He was just her husband, and Lizard was just her niece by marriage. Nothing important. Hardly a family. Pamela would fix herself

a pot of coffee and read the waterlogged paper, and she
wouldn't mind a bit if she was all alone.

AS IT TURNED OUT, she didn't see Joe once during the
entire day. After breakfast, she and Lizard went across
the street to Birdie's house to measure the rooms and
make a diagram of the building's foundation on their
graph-paper pads. When they went back home for lunch,
Joe was gone. In the afternoon Pamela traipsed through
the mud of Lizard's garden, listening to Lizard pontificate on the balance of nature and the fact that Birdie
knew how to make dandelion wine, which proved that
dandelions were just as valuable as grapes, and that if
weeds weren't good, God wouldn't have made them.
Pamela refrained from pointing out that God had also
made thugs like Mick Morrow, so maybe not all his
creations were good. Lizard was too young to become a
cynic.

For dinner Pamela served salmon. Lizard argued that
it was in fact orange and not pink, but Pamela held firm
and the kid ate it. Afterward, Lizard endured two
baths—she flunked Pamela's inspection after the first
bath—and Pamela read her a chapter from a book chron-
icling great battles in world history. "I like the parts
about weapons," Lizard told her. "Read about the catapults, okay? They're neat. I wanna build one."

Pamela read the chapter on catapults, then tucked Lizard in. "I'll tell Uncle Joe you said good-night," she
said, although heaven only knew when she would have
the opportunity. Maybe it was just a coincidence, maybe
today had been an anomaly, but Pamela couldn't shake
the suspicion that Joe didn't want to talk to her, didn't
even want to be in the same room with her.

"Give him a kiss from me," Lizard requested.

Pamela gritted her teeth. "Okay."

"And tell him I don't really think you're ugly. Just kinda skinny, is all."

"I'll tell him."

"And you should grow your hair longer, so you can have braids, like mine."

"Okay. Bedtime, now, Lizard."

"And tell Uncle Joe we're gonna borrow his tools to build Birdie's house."

"I'll tell him." *If I happen to bump into him anytime in the near future,* Pamela grumbled under her breath. "Have you ever gone a whole day without seeing him, Lizard?"

Lizard peered up from her pillow. Her small round face was surrounded by a mass of hair, and then by a menagerie of stuffed creatures that included an alligator, a possum and what appeared to be a rat. "No, but that's on account of we didn't have you. Sometimes he'd bring me to the Shipwreck with him. But now you're here, and I bet he never brings me there again." This prospect clearly did not sit well with her. She scrunched her face into a scowl. "He keeps telling me a bar is no place for a kid. I like it, but he doesn't like me hanging out there. He says now that I'm older I gotta clean up my act. If you ask me, two baths is clean enough."

"Well, I'm glad you're not going to the bar. I agree with him—that's not an appropriate place for a child to be."

"But I like it there. And Kitty's teaching me how to mix drinks, and she always makes me pink stuff. Strawberry daiquiris or pink ladies, only she leaves the booze out."

"Thank heavens for that," Pamela muttered. "You're better off drinking milk."

"Milk is yucky. I like daiquiris better."

"You definitely need to clean up your act, young lady." Pamela ruffled Lizard's hair, then smiled and turned off the light.

"Don't forget to kiss Uncle Joe for me!" Lizard called after her.

She closed Lizard's bedroom door and descended the stairs. The house was unnervingly quiet, as still and silent as her condominium back home when she wasn't listening to one of her Mozart CDs. It didn't seem right that she should have changed her residence, her name, her marital status, her entire existence—and still feel so alone.

She wandered into the den, perused the television listings in the newspaper and decided there was nothing she felt like watching. Joe had a modest stereo system, and she studied his collection of disks and tapes. Not a single classical recording among them. Mostly rock—oldies as well as an assortment of the latest grunge bands.

She wondered if he owned a copy of "Stand by Me."

The closest he would get to standing by her would be a song on a disk, she thought grimly. Joe was doing exactly what she had once hoped he would do. He had married her and now was giving her as much independence as she'd had as a single woman.

She didn't want a relationship with him, she reminded herself. She didn't want to become overly involved in his family. All she wanted was a disguise, protection from Mick Morrow. Not a lover, just an adult to talk to at the end of the day. Someone to confide in, to boast to, to describe Lizard's zany concepts for Birdie's house: "I think we should build a tree house in the living room, with a rope ladder. And then if the company got boring you could hide up there and shoot arrows down at them.

And you know what? We should put a *chimbley* in the middle of the kitchen, just in case Birdie's food catches on fire.''

Perhaps, given her voodoo activities, Birdie's food did spontaneously combust. Perhaps, given the woman's apparent obsession with all things avian, she could use a tree house.

If only Joe were home.

Sighing, Pamela picked up the book that had put her to sleep last night. She was about to stretch out on the sofa when the telephone rang.

The shrill sound was so unexpected she flinched. Her heart thumped wildly; her breath caught in her throat. It took her a full minute to remember that no one who was in any position to do her harm knew where she was. The call would be for Joe, not for her.

Either that, or the caller was Joe himself. Calling to say hello, maybe. Calling to say he would try to get home earlier tonight, or wake up earlier tomorrow so they could exchange a few words like a married couple.

Refusing to give in to pleasure at the thought of getting a phone call from her absentee husband, she hurried into the kitchen and lifted the receiver. "Hello?"

"Mary DiNardi here," said Joe's attorney. "Is this Pam?"

Pamela tried to stifle her disappointment. "Yes," she said, recalling the brisk, dark-haired lawyer she'd met a few days before the wedding. She had gotten the impression that Mary didn't like her much—or at least didn't like the notion of her marrying Joe. Mary had treated her with a slightly cool formality totally at odds with her easy humor and congeniality with Joe.

Well, Mary didn't have to like Pamela, and Pamela didn't have to like Mary, but they were united in keeping

Joe and Lizard together. The least they could do was tolerate each other.

"Hello, Mary. Joe isn't in right now. He's—"

"At the bar. I know. I figured if I called him there, he might get the message garbled or whatever. Anyway, since you're the lady of the house..." She cleared her throat, as if speaking was a strain. "I've received a correspondence from the Prescotts' lawyer saying they've filed custody papers with the court. The court has appointed a guardian for Liz."

"A guardian?"

"A legal representative, basically. The judge assigns her to make sure Lizard's best interests are represented during the custody hearing. The judge named a local social worker, and she's coming to visit you tomorrow morning, to have a look at Lizard's home life."

Pamela had expected such a visit. Joe had married her for no other reason than that he knew the home he provided for his niece was going to be evaluated, and he wanted that home to have a mommy figure as well as a daddy figure. Yet hearing that the visit was actually going to occur—*tomorrow*—sent a chill down Pamela's spine.

"Isn't it a little soon for the court to be taking this step?"

"Honey, it was a little late that Joe got around to taking a wife. I hope you can pull off this charade."

"As his lawyer, how do you think we should handle this?"

"Don't make the house spotless. You want it to look clean but comfortable. Tell Lizard not to wear any feathers. And tell Joe not to wear an earring that dangles. And for God's sake, pretend you love each other."

Pamela bit back a retort. She didn't need Joe's lawyer

lecturing her on how she and Joe were supposed to act. They had forged their alliance with a clear understanding. Of course they would pretend they loved each other.

Damn it, there was no "of course" about it. She and Joe hadn't even been in the same room at the same time for the past two days—at least not while she was conscious. How was she going to act as if she loved him?

She'd just have to do it, that was all. That was the deal she'd made with Joe.

"Do you know what time we should expect the social worker to show up?" she asked, filtering all emotion from her voice. "Joe tends to sleep late."

"Tell Joe he'd better tend to wake up early tomorrow. They didn't give me a time. They like to drop in unexpectedly, so they can catch you in your normal routine. It's the way they do things. You're lucky you got this much warning."

"I see."

"Knock 'em dead tomorrow, Pam. Joe deserves to keep that little girl."

Pamela recollected that little girl's whining, her muleheadedness, her aggressiveness...and decided that Joe definitely deserved her. "I'll do my best," she promised Mary before saying goodbye.

Once again, silence swelled to fill the house. It wasn't a lonely silence, though; it was a tense, prodding silence, a void Pamela intended to fill with work.

She gazed about her at the kitchen. She knew where the food, dishes and pots were kept, but she had no idea where Joe stored his cleaning supplies. After all, he had assured her she wouldn't have to take care of the house. That had been part of their deal. She hated housekeeping, and in Seattle she paid a service to do those chores for her. Then again, in Seattle she lived a calm, childless existence, her condominium tidy and rarely in need of major cleaning.

The same could not be said for Joe's house. The kitchen, while not filthy, was far from neat. Weeks-old third-class mail shaped a sloppy heap on the counter; newspapers lay piled on the floor in the corner for recycling; the sink was decorated with crumbs and soggy celery leaves; the calendar hanging from a hook on the broom-closet door displayed the April page.

She crossed the room, flipped the calendar to July and opened the closet door. Not surprisingly, she found everything she needed inside: a broom, a mop, a bucket and a shelf filled with scouring supplies. Just the sight of all that cleaning gear made her groan.

She really, truly, did not want to spend her evening putting Joe's house in order. His custody battle with his in-laws wasn't her problem.

Yes it was. She was his wife, for better or worse, until they got a divorce. She had married him for Lizard's sake, and for Lizard's sake she was going to have to pretend she was a devout homemaker, the little woman, Joe's better half. Pamela wasn't going to renege on her obligations.

She permitted herself a few pungent curses, then pulled a can of cleanser and a few rags from the shelf and got to work.

THREE HOURS LATER, the house was indeed clean but comfortable. Tabletops and shelves were polished. The dust balls under the sofa had been harvested. The chairs had been pushed in around the dining room table, and Lizard's toys had been transferred from the living room to the den and arranged to convey that this was a user-friendly house. The few houseplants had been watered, the framed crayon artwork had been hung straight, and the utilities bills Joe had left pinned under the base of the food processor had been tucked discreetly into a drawer.

If Pamela had had the time, she would have looked at the bills. She had no idea what it cost Joe to keep his house running. She would have liked to contribute to the household expenses, but she'd already fought that particular battle with Joe and lost, so she had spent this evening contributing in another way, a stereotypically wife-ish way. Surveying the living room, admiring the plumped pillows on the sofa and inhaling the tangy fragrance of lemon-scented furniture polish, she acknowledged that her efforts had given her a greater sense of accomplishment than merely writing a cheque would have done.

She glanced at her watch and scowled. Ten past eleven. Her labor had exhausted her; after a quick shower, she would head straight to bed. She would have to be up early tomorrow morning to get Lizard fed and dressed—sans feathers—before the social worker arrived. Pamela would have to hold things together until Joe surfaced. Heaven knew when he would be getting home tonight.

She wasn't in the habit of making late-night calls, but she realized she ought to try to reach him at the bar and let him know about the court-appointed guardian's planned visit. She should have phoned him earlier, but she suspected he wouldn't be easy to connect with while he was at the Shipwreck. If he were, Mary would have called him instead of Pamela.

Still, she ought to try. Swallowing a yawn, Pamela trudged to the kitchen and dialed the bar's number. After five rings, Kitty answered the phone. "Shipwreck," she shouted above the raucous din that filled the barroom.

"Kitty? It's Pamela."

"Pam? Hi! How's it going? Wait, hang on a second...." Pamela heard a scratchy sound as Kitty held her hand over the mouthpiece and screamed something about being out of Heineken. Then she came back on the phone. "So, how are you? Why don't you come on over and say hello?"

"I'm watching Lizard," Pamela reminded her. "She's fast asleep."

"Oh—oh, yeah. Well, we've gotta get together. I've got to tell you about this guy I met, he looks just like Ernest Hemingway...." She went on and on, occasionally interrupting herself to holler something to someone in the bar. Through the cacophony of voices Pamela heard the high-pitched croon of Neil Young warbling "Helpless."

"Listen, Kitty," Pamela said quietly, trying to break Kitty's stream-of-consciousness chatter without raising her voice. She didn't want to wake Lizard by yelling into the phone. "I need to talk to Joe."

"So, how are things with you lovebirds? Didn't I tell you the man's a prince?"

"Sure." If Joe was a prince, Pamela must be a scullery maid, if not one of the serfs. "I really do need to—"

"But I keep telling him, what he ought to do, once everything dies down, is take you on a real honeymoon. I mean, yeah, I know, the whole thing is kinda bogus—"

"Please, Kitty! You're in public!"

"My lips are sealed. Don't worry your little West Coast head, Pam. Everybody just knows it's a love match."

"Fine. Can you put my love match on the phone right now?"

"Matter of fact, I can't. There was a scuffle here. This guy was massively stewed, and he took a swipe at someone and lost his balance. He hurt himself, is all. Fell into a chair and needed a few stitches on his chin. Joe took him down to the hospital. The last thing he wants is to have this bozo suing him."

"Oh, God. Is there a danger of that happening?"

"Nah. This sort of stuff happens all the time. Joe'll just fill out an accident report and have the cops administer a sobriety test to the guy. Once it's established the guy's way over the limit, Joe won't have to worry about much."

He'll only have to worry about having the court and his in-laws find out that he earns his living by carting drunks to the hospital to get stitches, Pamela thought grimly. "Will he be back soon?"

"Can't say. Hang on a second…" Kitty again muffled the mouthpiece with her hand and shouted, "Lois, get your butt over here! These margaritas have been sitting here for years!" Back to Pamela, she said, "So, you want me to give him a message?"

Pamela sighed. "Ask him to get home early if he can."

"Don't hold your breath, honey. Tonight's been a rough one. I wouldn't expect any nookie if I were you."

Pamela wasn't expecting any nookie in any case. She considered telling Kitty the reason she wanted Joe home early, but decided not to. Kitty was clearly in a garrulous, dangerously indiscreet mood. If Pamela mentioned the social worker, everyone in the Shipwreck would know about it before Joe got back from the hospital.

"Just tell him I called," she requested, then said goodnight and set down the phone.

She pulled open the drawer where she'd hidden Joe's bills, rummaged inside it, came up with a sheet of paper and a pencil, and began to write.

Dear Jonas,
A court-appointed guardian is coming tomorrow morning to check up on Liz. Please wake up as early as you can, and don't wear a conspicuous earring. I'll do my best to take care of everything else.
Pamela.

She taped the note to the newel post at the bottom of the stairway, where Joe would be sure to see it. After double-checking to make sure the porch light was on for him, she climbed the stairs.

Her back ached. Her hands were chapped from the cleansers, and the flesh under her fingernails felt gritty. Sweat glued her hair to the nape of her neck. She grabbed her robe, then trudged down the hall to the bathroom for a shower.

Fifteen minutes later, her hair still damp from her shampoo, she sank into bed and closed her eyes. She thought about the impending visit from the social worker, about Joe's in-laws, about trying to convince the court that she was a good mother-figure to Lizard when she herself wasn't terribly convinced of that. She thought about Joe, staggering home at some ungodly hour, wearing a drunkard's bloodstains on his shirt and finding her note with its unwelcome news.

She had always thought of marriage as a shimmering vision on the horizon, beautiful yet distant, something to aim toward, to dream about, to reach for, something that would be waiting for her once she was ready for it. She had imagined marrying a man who shared her tastes, her rhythms, her low-key demeanor and her preference for intellectual pursuits and aesthetic pleasures.

She had not imagined that it would entail an exasperating five-year-old child, a mop and an out-of-touch husband. She had not imagined that it would result in sleeping alone.

She had not imagined that being married would compel her to take care of everyone, putting their needs and concerns ahead of her own. Yet deep in her heart, she knew that that was exactly what marriage was all about.

So much for pretending that this was a real marriage. Except for the empty pillow beside her, she felt incredibly married—and not terribly thrilled about it. Marriage, she realized as she rolled over and hugged her blanket to herself, was damned tiring. She fell asleep wondering whether she'd gotten more than she'd bargained for, or less.

CHAPTER NINE

AT SEVEN O'CLOCK the next morning, Pamela emerged from her bedroom, her head pounding and her nerves twitching like the quills of a porcupine sensing danger. She moved quietly down the hall, pausing at the open door to Lizard's bedroom and surveying the bedlam within. The floor was strewn with toys, clothing, a pillow, peanut shells and, not surprisingly, an impressive assortment of feathers. Picture books were stacked haphazardly on the bureau, several drawers of which hung open. The bed's mattress wasn't lined up with the box springs. The roller shade hung at a drunken angle.

Lizard herself wasn't there. Not that Pamela blamed her; she wouldn't want to spend a second longer than necessary in that room, either. With a shudder of disgust, she continued down the hall to Joe's room. Halting outside his closed door, she listened for sounds of life within.

She heard nothing.

Wonderful. He was sleeping late, and she couldn't count on him to assist her with Liz's court-appointed guardian. The first true test of the contrived Brenner marriage, and Joe wasn't going to do his part. He was going to sleep the morning away.

A strange mixture of emotions seized Pamela: disappointment, exasperation, sympathy for a man who might lose his niece simply because he worked odd hours—

and a sudden, treasonous pang of doubt. Perhaps a man who couldn't wake up early on what was conceivably the most important day of his niece's life didn't deserve that niece.

As soon as the thought took shape in Pamela's mind, it self-destructed. Joe deserved Lizard because he'd raised the child for three long, difficult years, because he'd rearranged his entire life around her, because he'd sold his houseboat for her. Because he kept her drawings on permanent exhibit in his living room. Because he'd taught an obstinate little girl that before she left the table she had to ask to be excused. Because he loved Lizard as much as any parent had ever loved a child.

Because he was either stupid enough or noble enough to have given his hand, his name and his protection to Pamela, knowing the threat she was living under.

For that noble stupidity—or stupid nobility—Pamela would deal with the social worker. With or without her husband by her side, she would convince the court official that Lizard belonged in Key West with her uncle.

Sighing, Pamela U-turned and stalked back down the hall to the stairway. At the bottom of the stairs she saw that the note she'd left for Joe last night was gone. Evidently he'd read it and didn't care, or he'd slept through his alarm or had an unjustifiable degree of faith in her ability to handle the social worker without his assistance.

She wished she had that much faith in herself.

She located Lizard in the den, seated on the floor in front of the television, gaping at a cartoon program and shoving fistfuls of dry cereal into her mouth. A feather protruded from the back pocket of her shorts.

"No feathers today," Pamela announced briskly.

"Huh?"

"No feathers. And," she added, recalling news stories

from a few years back that had revealed a relationship between sugar consumption and hyperactivity in children, "you're going to have a healthy breakfast this morning."

Whatever peace she and Lizard might have negotiated yesterday was dashed by Pamela's announcement. "I'm not eating anything healthy!" the kid shrieked. "I'm already healthy! And I'm strong, too. I bet I'm stronger'n you. I bet I could beat you up."

That was a bet Pamela wasn't foolish enough to take. She decided to rely on her superior intellect and what few scraps of control she still had left.

She strode purposefully into the den, plucked the feather from Lizard's pocket and spoke before Lizard could protest. "Have you ever eaten pink grapefruit?"

Hearing the word pink gave Lizard pause. She eyed Pamela dubiously, obviously searching for a trap. "Grapefruit's yellow," she finally said. "And it's yucky."

"Pink grapefruit is sweet. I think Uncle Joe has some in the refrigerator."

"I won't like it," Lizard said ominously, although she sounded tentative.

"It's pink," Pamela crooned. "Pink, pink, pink. Come on, let's have some pink, pink grapefruit."

Lizard's expression changed from skeptical to incredulous. "You're gonna eat some, too?"

"If you're willing to share it. Once you taste it, though, you may wind up wanting the whole thing for yourself. Come on." Not waiting to see if Lizard was following her, she strolled into the kitchen, swung open the refrigerator door and pulled a pink grapefruit from the bottom shelf.

Lizard might be stronger than Pamela, but she was

only five years old and incurably curious. Sure enough, she trailed Pamela into the kitchen and hovered at her elbow, observing as Pamela cut the fruit in half. "That's not pink," she scoffed, sounding less than surprised at Pamela's lame attempt to trick her. "It's orange, like that icky fish you made me eat." She reached around Pamela for her cereal box.

Pamela swiftly lifted the box and set it on a high shelf in one of the cabinets. She didn't care whether Lizard ate a healthy breakfast of any color. She could eat refined sugar straight from the bowl as far as Pamela was concerned. But if the social worker arrived while Lizard was stuffing her face with junk, she might decide Joe's house wasn't wholesome, and Lizard would wind up with the Prescotts.

"Pink grapefruit is very sweet," Pamela said, stretching the truth as much as she dared. "Try it, and I'll make you some whole-wheat toast. With strawberry jam."

"Strawberry jam's red, not pink," Lizard muttered, scowling at the fruit.

"Just try it."

"I don't want it. It's yucky."

"Try it." Pamela carried the plate to the table. "It's pink. Try it." Refusing Lizard the chance to argue further, she turned her back on the child and slid two slices of whole-wheat bread into the toaster.

Behind her she heard a slurping noise—and then a gagging noise. "It's disgusting!" Lizard whined.

"It's delicious."

"It's poison! I hate you!" Lizard dragged her chair across the room, used it to climb onto the counter and pulled her beloved box of cereal from its high shelf.

If Pamela weren't so anxious about the social worker's visit, she would have yielded. But she was in no mood for Lizard's shenanigans. "You can't have cereal today," she said, wrapping her arms around Lizard's knees to keep her from falling off the counter. "And you shouldn't climb up there. It's dangerous."

"I climb all the time," Lizard retorted, popping open the flaps of the cereal box.

"Lizard, I'm warning you—put that cereal away and let me get you down."

"I'm getting down," Lizard acquiesced, kicking free of Pamela's loose hold on her legs. But she didn't get down, and she didn't put the cereal away. Instead, she dug into the box and pulled out a handful of sugary pink puffs.

Pamela reached for the box. Lizard gave a war whoop and hurled it into the air. The box overturned, spilling granular pink nuggets across the floor. Lizard leapt from the counter, knocking the chair on its side with her foot and letting out a howl of pain. "My toes! Ow! I think they're broke!"

Pamela didn't agree with Lizard's diagnosis—especially after Lizard managed to run across the room when Pamela tried to catch her. "I told you climbing up there was dangerous," she scolded, righting the box of cereal and glowering at Lizard.

"Climbing wasn't dangerous. Coming down was dangerous. I hate you! You wanna poison me and kill me, too! And the house is on fire, too!"

As soon as Lizard mentioned the word fire, Pamela smelled something burning. Spinning around, she saw a plume of smoke rise out of the toaster. Cursing under her breath, she yanked the plug from the socket and peered into the slots, almost expecting to see flames. All she saw, however, were black crusts and more smoke.

"You're trying to kill me," Lizard declared, then

squatted on the floor, gathered the cereal near her feet into a small mound, and scooped it into her mouth. "When Uncle Joe wakes up I'm gonna tell him you're a murderer."

"You do that," Pamela snapped, jiggling a knife into the toaster slots until the two charred slices of bread emerged. "I'll defend myself by saying it was justifiable homicide. I bet he'll believe me, too."

"I hate you, I hate you, I hate you!" Lizard hollered.

The doorbell rang.

"Oh, God." Pamela stared in dismay at the cereal-covered floor and inhaled the stench of incinerated crumbs. In a firm voice, she said, "Clean up this mess right now, young lady."

"I'm not a young lady! I'm a boo doo chief."

"Not at the moment, you're not. Sweep up the mess. There's a broom and a dustpan in that cupboard." She pointed to the broom closet.

"It's *your* mess," Lizard retorted. "You grabbed the box. You made me spill it. You clean it up."

"Clean it," Pamela spat out.

"I don't got to. The doorbell's ringing. I bet it's Birdie. She lets me eat anything I want!" With that, Lizard flounced out of the kitchen, Pamela at her heels.

Her heart was racing, her eyes stinging with tears of anger and frustration. Hadn't there been a time, not so terribly long ago, when she'd been in complete control of her life? Hadn't there been a time when her daily existence was calm and orderly?

Lizard's words echoed in her skull: *It's your mess.* That said it all, the ultimate truth. This was Pamela's mess.

Lizard was already swinging open the inner door when Pamela reached the front hall. She smoothed her camp shirt into the waistband of the neat denim skirt she'd chosen to wear, and arranged her face into a polite smile for her visitor.

The social worker appeared as calm and orderly as Pamela's life used to be. On the far side of middle age, the woman was slim and well groomed in a cotton sheath, a stylish linen blazer and stack-heeled sandals. In her left hand she gripped a thick leather briefcase; in her right she held a business card.

Pamela ran her fingers through her disheveled hair, discreetly unraveling a piece of cereal from the strands behind her ear. "Hi," she said to the woman, whom Lizard was regarding with blatant distrust. "I'm Pamela Brenner." Thank heavens the name glided naturally off her tongue.

"I'm Mona Whitley from the Department of Social Services," the woman introduced herself. "I'm here at the behest of Judge Roger Ephraim, who's going to be presiding at the custody hearing—"

"Yes, I know," Pamela said hastily, shooting a quick look at Lizard. She didn't want the social worker discussing the custody fight in front of the child.

Mona Whitley smiled and nodded, apparently understanding Pamela's desire to protect Lizard. "May I come in?"

"Of course." Pamela nudged Lizard out of the way and held open the screen door. "I was just making some coffee. As a matter of fact, we've just barely gotten out of bed—"

"I've been up for hours," Lizard declared. "And I'm starving."

Great, Pamela thought—Mona Whitley was going to think Pamela and Joe weren't feeding her. "Anyway,"

Pamela went on breezily, accepting Ms. Whitley's card, "the kitchen is a little bit messy at the moment—"

"A little bit?" Lizard hooted. "It's a lot messy. Remember Hurricane Andrew?"

"Indeed I do," Ms. Whitley said, her eyes narrowing on Lizard. "You must be Elizabeth."

"I'm Lizard," Lizard said petulantly. "Nobody calls me Elizabeth. I'm Lizard, and I'm a boo doo chief, and I can eat whatever I want." With that, she swiveled on her bare foot and stomped back to the kitchen.

Pamela's spirits plummeted. "Elizabeth is always a little cranky in the morning," she fibbed, gesturing toward Lizard's retreating form. "Perhaps I could get you a cup of coffee. If you'd like to have a seat in the living room..." *Which I spent last night dusting and polishing so it would pass muster with you,* she wanted to add. At the moment, the living room was in better shape than she herself was.

"You don't have to entertain me," Ms. Whitley said. Her smile revealed too many teeth. "What I'd really like is for you to let me just fade into the background while you go about your usual routines."

"I see. Well. As I said, we just had a spill in the kitchen, and I'm in the middle of getting breakfast for Liz—" She silenced herself before adding -*zard.* "And I'm afraid my husband is—"

"Right here," Joe's voice came from the stairway. "Good morning. Glad you could stop by."

If hearing Joe awake and coherent surprised her, seeing him absolutely astonished her. She turned and glanced toward the stairs in time to see him descend the last few steps. Clean-shaven, his hair parted and damp, he wore a fresh shirt and untorn, unfrayed jeans. His ear

was decorated with a gold dot so modest she almost
didn't notice it.

Reaching the bottom step, he extended his right hand
toward Mona Whitley. His smile was as cool and confident as hers. "I'm Jonas Brenner," he said.

Maybe it was because Pamela hadn't seen him for the
past couple of days. Maybe it was because she felt over-
whelmed by the social worker's visit and her own over-
wrought mental state. Maybe it was just that, with his
riveting blue eyes, his thick, tawny hair, his tall, lean
physique and that smile, announcing that he had nothing
to fear, nothing to hide, nothing to worry about, Joe was
like the morning sun, bright and steady and dependable.

Or maybe the emotion she experienced at his arrival
was simply a result of being his wife. Because as she
gazed at him, she felt exactly what a wife was supposed
to feel when she saw her husband: Comfort. Relief. Joy.

HE'D MEANT TO MAKE IT downstairs earlier, but it was
hard to get your ass in gear when you'd been tending
bar till 2:00 a.m. Sure, he could have gotten home earlier—Brick would have taken the closing shift—but Joe
was so damned busy avoiding his wife that he'd turned
down Brick's offer and waited until the last patron had
departed before locking up and rolling home.

He'd been exhausted, and he'd had a few spots of
blood on his shirt from that jerk who'd cut his chin. But
carting an inebriated yahoo to the hospital had seemed
easy compared to the prospect of facing Pamela and
keeping his desire for her in check.

When he'd found her note for him, though, he'd regretted his cowardice. He'd regretted it even more as
he'd taken a quick walk through the house and seen how
neatly everything was arranged. She must have worked

her tail off to straighten the place up. And he'd promised she wouldn't have to take care of the house.

The least he could do was make sure she wouldn't have to solo in the morning, too. When his alarm clock had buzzed, he'd wrestled against the urge to bury his head under the pillow, and he'd gotten himself together enough not to send the social worker off in a huff.

He shook her hand as she introduced herself, and then he casually slipped his arm around Pamela's shoulders. He had thought his only challenge would be pretending he was a true husband to Pam. But the real challenge was going to be acting like her husband without responding to the sexy angularity of her shoulders, the soft fragrance of her hair and the glittery silver in her eyes. "Is the coffee ready yet, honey?" he asked, sounding so natural he very nearly frightened himself.

"The kitchen's a disaster," Pamela murmured through clenched teeth.

He chuckled. "The kitchen's always a disaster. If Ms. Whitley wants to deduct points for sloppiness, we're in big trouble." May as well own up to it, not try to hide what couldn't be hidden.

He released Pamela and sauntered down the hall to the kitchen, refusing to let his apprehension show. He found the Liz Monster sitting on the floor, scooping up spilled cereal and tossing it into her mouth—although her aim wouldn't win her any tryouts with the Orlando Magic.

Keep it light, Joe coached himself. *Don't let the social worker see you sweat.* "Oink, oink," he addressed Lizard. "You're a pig this morning, aren't you."

Lizard leapt to her feet and threw herself into his arms. "Uncle Joe! You got up!"

"Of course I got up." No sense letting the court lady know his usual hours.

"Pamela tried to make me eat burned toast," Lizard wailed. "And this yucky stuff, some kind of grapefruit that she said was pink but she was lying, and—"

"Well, that *is* pink grapefruit," he argued gently, hoisting Lizard higher in his arms and glancing over his shoulder at the fruit on the counter. "I know it's got kind of a peculiar flavor, but I bet Pamela thought you were so mature you could handle it. Now, do me a favor, Lizzie, and get that broom, and we'll get this place all spiffed up." He shot an affable grin toward Ms. Whitley, who was watching from the doorway. Little did the lady know, but his kitchen had rarely been as spiffed up as it was right now, even with all the cereal on the floor.

He would have to thank Pamela for the unusual cleanliness of the place. He could have flowers delivered, or take her out to dinner—but then she might think he was making a pass at her, putting pressure on her. And he wasn't truly sure that assessment would be wrong.

She materialized next to Ms. Whitley, looking worried. That she should be so eager to make a good impression on the social worker touched him. She had her own problems; she didn't have to carry the full weight of his as well.

"You know what?" he asked as Lizard handed him the broom. "I bet Ms. Whitley would like to see your herb garden. Why don't you take her out in the yard and show her around while Pam and I get the floor swept?"

Lizard would have agreed to anything that got her out of having to help clean up. "Okay," she said happily. With a skip in her step, she led the way out onto the screened porch and from there into the backyard.

Pamela watched, her lips pressed together, her eyes a

bit too bright. "She listens to you a lot more than she listens to me," she muttered.

"She's known me a lot longer," he pointed out, handing her the dustpan and then setting to work sweeping up the cereal.

"Besides which, you let her have her way. She made this mess—she should have cleaned it herself."

"And if we didn't have that spy in our midst—" he angled his head toward Ms. Whitley's business card, still in Pamela's hand "—I would have crazy-glued the broom to the little beast's hands before I'd let her off the hook. I just didn't think this was the time or place for a showdown."

Pamela nodded. She looked suddenly weary. "I guess I'm not very good at parenting."

"You're fine." He propped the broom against the table and planted his hands on Pamela's shoulders. "You're better than fine, Pam. Okay?"

She peered up into his eyes. He recalled the anguish he'd seen in her face the first time she'd come to his house, when her tears had seeped inside his soul and softened him up. He really hoped she wasn't going to get weepy on him again. If she did, he'd have to hug her, and if he hugged her, he'd kiss her.

"I tried to dress nicely for Ms. Whitley—"

"You look great."

"And I tried to neaten up the house—"

"This house hasn't been so neat since the last owner moved his stuff out. Really, Pam—you're terrific. Okay?"

Instead of tears, he saw something else in her eyes— a glint of anger. "If I'm so terrific, why are you treating me as if I had leprosy?"

He smothered a groan. "If you had leprosy," he argued, giving her upper arms a reassuring squeeze, "would I be touching you?"

"This is the first time I've seen you in days, Jonas."

"I work lousy hours," he rationalized. "You know that."

"I also know when someone is avoiding me. Where were you yesterday morning? Why did you sneak out of the house the minute my back was turned?"

It occurred to Joe that her words could be taken as good, old-fashioned shrewishness, the stereotypical nagging-wife stuff. He didn't have to account for himself or his whereabouts, did he? Even if this were a real marriage—especially if it were a real one—he wouldn't necessarily tell his wife where he was going, or when, or why.

Yet the way Pamela put it made it sound as if he was stepping out on her or something. She had to understand that the only reason he was avoiding her, sneaking out of the house and all, was because if he hung around he would start treating her the way a wife should be treated, and that would destroy their arrangement.

He took up the broom and started sweeping. "I don't suppose you'd believe me if I said it was for your own good."

The anger spread from her eyes to encompass her entire body. Her spine stiffened, and she brandished the dustpan as if she wanted to whack him with it. "My own good? What am I, another little child you've taken custody of? *My own good?*"

He shot a quick look toward the window above the sink, which overlooked the backyard. "Can we talk about this some other time?" he asked quietly.

"No, we cannot." She knelt down where he'd amassed a pile of cereal and held the dustpan so he could sweep the cereal into it. "I thought we were equal partners in this, Joe. Equal means you don't make decisions for me. If it were for my own good never to see you, I wouldn't have married you."

There was a compliment embedded in her rage: she wanted to see him sometimes.

The trouble was, *all* she wanted was to see him. When he saw her, he wanted a whole lot more.

He heard a gale of laughter, Lizard's and Ms. Whitley's, through the screen in the window. If he could hear them, they could probably hear him and Pamela. This was no doubt the worst time in the world for them to be quarreling. Tactics demanded that he concede for now.

"All right," he said. "I'll try harder to wake up early."

"Don't do me any favors," Pamela retorted.

Oh, swell. She really was a wife, wasn't she? Here he'd swallowed his pride and given in, and Pamela refused to accept his surrender. The woman was asking for a fight.

Joe would love nothing more than to give her one. If she wanted to argue both sides, he would gladly argue right back. He was nimble; he could take anything she said and throw it back in her face. She wanted to be equals with him? He didn't pull his punches with his equals.

But that damned social worker was here. "Make up your mind," he grumbled. "You want me to wake up early? Say so. You want me to sleep late? No problem. Just make up your mind."

"I want you to treat me like your partner, not a pariah."

Whatever the hell did she mean by that? "Fine," he said, just to be done with it.

"Because it's ridiculous that I should have to leave you notes, for heaven's sake. If I need to talk to you, I should be able to."

"I said fine," he repeated in a quiet growl.

"This is important, Jonas. I don't want to be brushed off."

He was tempted to take the broom and brush her into the damned dustpan. But Lizard and Ms. Whitley came waltzing back into the kitchen, denying him the chance. "Well," the social worker said grandly, "Elizabeth certainly knows a lot about weeds."

"She's a smart kid," Joe grunted, relieved to have someone other than Pamela to think about.

"I also told her we're gonna ock-attack Birdie's house as a project."

"You are?" This was news to Joe—and garbled news at that. He sent Pamela a questioning glance. Her answer was a smug look, as if to say his ignorance about this so-called project was just one more thing he didn't know about because he'd been treating his wife with less than husbandly respect.

Lizard nodded vigorously. "With a tree house in the living room, right, Pamela?"

"We still have to run that concept past Birdie," Pamela said, smiling at Lizard with a warmth Joe wished she felt toward him, even if at the moment he wanted to throttle her.

"Birdie is your neighbor?" Ms. Whitley asked.

"Also Liz's baby-sitter," said Pamela, then gazed around the room. "I think we're done here. Liz, would you like something to eat?"

"Yeah. Pink cereal."

Pamela pursed her lips but didn't refuse Lizard her choice. Even though he would rather not do anything for

Pamela, Joe courteously filled a cup of coffee for her, asked Ms. Whitley one last time if she wanted some, and when she declined, filled a cup for himself. Then he excused himself and walked outside to get the newspaper.

The morning was hot, the grass soaked with dew and the air dense with the fragrance of greenery and sun-kissed flowers. His footsteps crunched on the gravel as he ambled halfway to the street and picked up the paper. He stood in the driveway for a long minute, the paper tucked under his arm and his mug balanced in his hand. The sky was cloudless, the palm trees motionless. A single cricket played a lazy tune somewhere to his left.

As riled as he'd been indoors, out here he felt surprisingly buoyant. He wasn't the sentimental sort who got all mushy at the sight of a butterfly, but the butterfly he saw flitting above his azaleas made him smile. And the lawn was so green, the heat enhancing its tangy scent. Inside the kitchen he'd been in turmoil. Out here, the turmoil was gone.

When was the last time he'd actually stood in his front yard and appreciated a summer morning? Did the tranquillity seem greater than usual because of what had preceded it? Or did Joe simply feel it more deeply because, for some reason, he was feeling everything more deeply lately?

So much was on the line: Lizard. Pamela. A marriage. A court battle. His sex life, or lack thereof. His future. Behind him his house held challenges, responsibilities, the life he'd somehow stumbled into.

Yet without that life, without those challenges and responsibilities, he might not have felt the golden heat of the sun on his cheeks so keenly. He might not have recognized the distinct perfumes of the rhododendrons and lime trees, the wisteria and the magnolias. Without the spilled cereal and the heated tempers, he might never have realized what a gorgeous morning he'd awakened to.

Maybe it was the contrast between inside and out, his suppressed male urges, the fear that he was about to lose a little girl who meant the world to him, but suddenly everything seemed precious, worth fighting for. Suddenly Joe Brenner felt as if everything mattered.

With a bemused smile, he turned and went back into the house, more than ready to face off with the social worker, his niece and his wife.

CHAPTER TEN

HER OWN GOOD?

The nerve of him, patronizing her that way! Acting as if he knew what was best for her! Pamela Hayes was a mature adult. She was intelligent, well educated, the mistress of her own fate.

Well, not exactly. For the time being, she had to lie low and keep her cool—and for the time being, she had to be Pam Brenner, the happy housewife. She had to make this marriage work.

She would begin by playing her surrogate-mother role as best she could. She doubted Mona Whitley would be thrilled by Pamela's attempts at maternal behavior thus far: dragging Lizard through the bureaucratic tedium of the motor-vehicle department, measuring the rooms in Birdie's dilapidated house, bickering over the color of salmon.

Today would be different. Regardless of how annoyed she was with Joe, Pamela was going to be the best damned mother-figure she could be. She hated failing at anything, and she wasn't going to fail at this.

She filled her cup with fresh coffee, took a sip and set off in search of Lizard and Ms. Whitley. She found them on the screened back porch. Lizard had lugged a carton to the table and was systematically emptying its contents: glossy white paper and jars of finger paint.

What a perfectly domestic activity. Lizard might be

rude and crude, but she knew how to impress a social worker. She and Pamela could finger paint together, just like a mother and daughter would, and Joe could sulk outside, for all Pamela cared.

Smiling, she carried her coffee to the porch and declared herself ready to tackle an art project. "I asked that lady if she wanted to make a picture," Lizard announced, pointing to Ms. Whitley. "She said she didn't want to get her hands dirty."

"Well, I certainly don't mind getting my hands dirty," Pamela lied, accepting a sheet of paper from Lizard's supply. She stared at the clean white rectangle for a minute, trying to remember how one went about finger painting, something she hadn't done since her nursery school days.

Lizard seemed to realize that Pamela was stumped. Rolling her eyes at Pamela's ineptitude, she poured two pools of paint, one red and one blue, onto Pamela's paper. "Smear it," she instructed her.

Pamela smeared it—on the paper, on her palms, on her wedding band. On her blouse. On her chin when she scratched an itch. The paint was thick and slick and viscous. It was disgusting. But somewhere in the midst of all her smearing, she lost track of Ms. Whitley observing from the couch. She forgot about her spat with Joe, the spilled cereal, the fact that back in Seattle a hit man was undoubtedly still stalking her. She forgot all the tenets of architectural design. There were no parameters here, no client's specifications, no environmental impact studies. This creation was devoted to oozing color, shapelessness, anarchy.

To her utter amazement, Pamela loved it.

Within minutes, she became so engrossed with the swirls and spirals and loops she was creating that she forgot Ms. Whitley's presence. She blended the red and blue into a rich violet shade and traced flowerlike shapes. She added yellow streaks, green squiggles, more red, more blue. When she decided her picture was done, she took a deep breath, smiled proudly and straightened up. Ms. Whitley was gone.

Pamela gazed around her, blinking back to full consciousness. Lizard was currently smearing paint across her third sheet of paper; her first two masterpieces were spread on the floor to dry. "I'm going to wash up and change my clothes," Pamela said, eyeing the daubs of paint on her shirt and sighing.

As she entered the kitchen, she heard the low murmur of voices, Joe's and Ms. Whitley's, emerging from the living room. *Isn't Joe lucky I dusted and vacuumed in there,* Pamela thought, a twinge of her earlier anger returning. Cleaning last night, finger painting this morning—she ought to be in the running for Mother of the Year honors.

She rinsed her hands in the sink, then walked down the hall to the living room doorway, where she had a clear view of Joe and the social worker seated side by side on the sofa, drinking coffee and chatting. Joe spotted Pamela and rose. "Hey," he said quietly.

"Hey" didn't qualify as an apology. But now, with Ms. Whitley sitting beside him, wasn't a very good time for apologies. "I'm going upstairs to put on a clean shirt," Pamela said.

"Good idea." Joe's gaze skimmed the front of her shirt. She knew he was staring at the splotches of paint, but she couldn't help feeling as if he were ogling her bosom.

As if that part of her anatomy deserved to be ogled. Joe ought to save his ogling for the Shipwreck, where he could feast his eyes on the generous endowments of Kitty and the other women who frequented the joint, half naked in their tank tops and short shorts.

Pamela decided she rather enjoyed thinking the worst of him. It made her less likely to remember those few precious moments of closeness they'd shared on their wedding day. From the start she'd been determined not to let this marriage serve as anything more than a survival strategy. Labeling Joe a breast man, whether or not the label was true, helped Pamela to keep her feelings for him in perspective.

With a nod toward Ms. Whitley, she turned from the doorway and headed for the stairs. To her dismay, Joe excused himself and hurried after her, reaching the foot of the stairway a step ahead of her and blocking her path.

His gaze wasn't on her chest anymore. He stared directly into her eyes, searching. "Are we okay?" he asked, his voice muted, husky.

She bit her lip. No, they weren't okay—but it didn't matter, as long as they could pretend to be okay for the social worker. "Jonas..."

"That paint looks kind of cute on your blouse," he said, although his gaze never left her face.

"My blouse is ruined," she said coldly. She wasn't in the mood to be teased.

"You ought to dress a little less formally when you're finger painting."

"I dressed for Ms. Whitley," she hissed, darting a quick glance toward the living room. "I really don't think we ought to be having this conversation right now."

"Well, we aren't going to have it later," he said reasonably. "I'll be at the Shipwreck."

She checked her watch. "Gee, it's after ten. Maybe

you ought to be on your way right now. It's not as if anyone expects you to be home at this hour."

Instead of matching her sarcasm, he laughed. The skin around his eyes crinkled; his teeth flashed white. "I'll be on my way real soon," he promised. "As soon as Ms. Whitley is done raking me over the coals."

Pamela put aside her hostility long enough to consider the woman in the living room. "Is that what she's doing?" she whispered.

"She's trying to get a handle on our marriage," Joe whispered back. "She's been giving me a hard time about our whirlwind courtship."

"Courtship?" Pamela snorted softly, then cast another quick look toward the living room to make sure Ms. Whitley couldn't hear them. The woman was hunched over a notebook, scribbling. Reassured that she wasn't eavesdropping on their conversation, Pamela turned back to Joe. "I don't recall our having any sort of courtship."

"Honey, if I courted you, this marriage would be a whole other thing. My style of courtship doesn't lead to separate bedrooms."

Pamela felt her cheeks grow warm. She didn't want to be teased—and she didn't want to be wondering about Joe's style of courtship. "I'd rather not discuss this," she muttered through pursed lips.

"I know you wouldn't. That's why I'll be leaving for the bar in a few minutes. Meanwhile..." He trailed his index finger lazily along her jawline, behind her ear and around to the nape of her neck, leaving a tingling trail of heat on her skin. "I think we ought to put on a little show for the lady, so she'll believe my song and dance about how it was love at first sight between us."

"Is that what you told her?" Pamela asked, her voice unfortunately faint.

He slid his other hand along her side to her waist. "What else could I have said?"

Certainly not the truth. Actually, the truth seemed kind of cloudy to Pamela at the moment. Every time Joe stroked his fingertips across the nape of her neck, every time she peered up into his eyes, she became less sure about truth.

It wasn't love at first sight; that much she knew. But their marriage wasn't merely a survival tactic, either. At least, it wasn't merely a survival tactic when Joe was this close to her, his lips an inch from hers, his gaze boring into hers and his hand molding to the curve of her hip.

He brushed his mouth against hers, then straightened up and smiled hesitantly. "Faking it is easy, isn't it?" he murmured, drawing his hands away and clearing his throat. His eyes were luminous, his breath uneven. He didn't seem to be faking anything. "I'll be on my way as soon as I'm done with Whitley."

Pamela understood then why he was avoiding her: it wasn't just for her sake, but for his. The instant his mouth touched hers, she felt his yearning. She felt the air temperature in the hallway rise, the beat of her heart accelerate. This must be Joe's style of courtship—and it definitely didn't lead to separate bedrooms.

"I'm going to go change my clothes," she mumbled, gripping the railing for support as she started up the stairs.

"Yeah, slip into something more comfortable," Joe joked, although she heard no laughter in his words. She didn't dare turn around. She didn't want to see him. And she didn't want him to see her all flushed and flustered.

Reluctantly she acknowledged that he was right. For

her sake—and his—it was better if he stayed away from her.

"BEING MARRIED has changed you," Kitty opined.

Joe avoided eye contact with her, focusing instead on the blender, watching the rum, bananas and crushed ice turn into a thick beige froth.

He knew being married had changed him—far more than he'd ever expected. It was different from the change he'd undergone after his sister's death, when Lizard had invaded his life. That change had entailed moving to a real house, developing a certain sense of responsibility and devoting his free time to the kid instead of to boating and flirting.

Pamela had changed him in a completely different way. He had always thought the up side of marriage was that you could have sex whenever you wanted, and the down side was that you couldn't have sex with anyone but your wife—at least, if you took the relationship seriously. Instead, he was finding that the only lady he wanted to have sex with was his wife—and sex was out of the question.

Part of his and Pamela's agreement, he recalled, was that they could take lovers if they were discreet about it. But he didn't need Mona Whitley's court-appointed intrusion into his life to remind him that screwing around with women who weren't Pamela would pose a grave risk. Even if a stacked, leggy woman sauntered up to the bar right now, handed him a key and purred, "Meet me at midnight, I'll bring the condoms," he wouldn't follow through.

He poured the banana daiquiri into a chilled glass and gave Kitty a bland look. "Sure, marriage has changed

me," he drawled. "Ever since Pam and I tied the knot,
I've been speaking with a British accent."

"Cheerio, old chap," Kitty scoffed. "You're still
talking like the same guy you always were. You're just
acting different."

Joe studied her through the haze of blue cigarette
smoke that clouded the air. Her hair looked less brassy
in the Shipwreck's muted light, but her tank top was too
snug; her breasts bulged from the scooped neck like two
yeasty mounds of dough. He used to admire her luscious
curves, but now…it was too much of a good thing.

Yeah, marriage had changed him, all right. If he could
find himself looking at Kitty and thinking wistfully
about Pamela's modest proportions, the change was profound.

"Okay, I'll bite. How has marriage changed me?"

"I don't know. I'm trying to put my finger on it."
Kitty scooped a few cocktail napkins from the pile on
the bar and set them on her tray. "It's like you under-
went an attitude adjustment. You seem more serious or
something."

It wasn't that he was serious, he almost argued, but
rather that he was tired. And hornier than any newlywed
ought to be.

"I mean," Kitty persisted, "I want to know if everything is going okay with you and Pamela. Because, I
mean, I feel kind of responsible, on account of I set you
guys up and all."

"You didn't exactly set us up," Joe said, thinking he
was doing Kitty a favor by letting her off the hook. She
had set them up, but if the marriage was a mistake, he
didn't want her to feel guilty about it.

Actually, the marriage wasn't a mistake. In terms of
proving to the court that Joe could provide a good home

life for Lizard, the marriage was a stroke of brilliance. The only mistake was that he'd gone and married some-one he found himself lusting after.

"I mean, I knew Pamela before you did," Kitty re-minded him. "And she's kind of serious. Is she making you serious?"

"I've always been serious." Right. And the sun al-ways rose in the west. "Isn't there a customer waiting for that banana daiquiri?"

"Let her wait. Brick? Help me out here. Doesn't Joe seem more serious to you than usual?"

Brick joined them at the bar, carrying a cutting board heaped with the lime wedges he'd been slicing. He eyed Joe up and down and grunted.

Kitty pounced on this as corroboration. "See? He thinks you're serious, too."

"I am serious. I'm seriously going to fire you, Kitty, if you don't serve that banana daiquiri soon."

"Come on, Joe, what is it? Pamela isn't a good wife?"

"She's an excellent wife."

"She's not getting along with Lizzie Borden?"

"She and Lizard are getting along phenomenally. It's weird how well they get along. This morning they did finger painting together. They run errands together. Lately they've been collaborating on a scheme to reno-vate Birdie's house together."

"No! You're kidding! You hear that, Brick? Lizard and Joe's wife are going to renovate Birdie's house."

"Uh-huh," Brick grunted.

"Thing of it is," Kitty continued, then noticed Joe's lethal frown and lifted the daiquiri onto her tray, "Pa-mela's smart, you know? She must have had a good reason to marry you. Something beyond wanting to finger paint with Lizard.''

Joe knew Pamela's reason. He wondered if Kitty did. "You think she had a good reason, do you?" he asked casually. "Like what?''

Kitty shrugged. "Like, you're a great guy."

He was tempted to reveal Pamela's true reason, which had nothing to do with Joe's greatness. But, as Kitty had pointed out, she'd known Pamela longer than he had. If Pamela had wanted Kitty to know about her Seattle assassin, she would have told Kitty herself.

He nudged Kitty's tray, giving her the choice of either lifting it or letting it crash to the floor at her feet. Rolling her eyes at his impatience, Kitty balanced the tray on one hand and moseyed through the dense evening crowd.

Free of Kitty's badgering, Joe contemplated Pamela's reason for marrying him. Ever since they'd tied the knot, she hadn't said a word about the hit man. She'd been in a big hurry to change her name and her legal papers, but that was it. She didn't behave as if she were paranoid, barring the windows and carrying a firearm at all times. As far as he knew, she wasn't constantly on the phone to Seattle, tracking the moves of her nemesis. She didn't act like someone with a price on her head.

What if there wasn't a hit man? What if she'd made the whole thing up?

The idea jolted him. He gripped the bar, nodding vaguely as Lois hollered for a malt liquor and a Seven-and-Seven. God, he thought—it was possible. Pamela could have invented that cock-and-bull story as an excuse to marry him. She was smart, and anyone as smart as she seemed to be wouldn't testify publicly against a professional murderer, right?

But why would Pamela have made up such a yarn?

Why, if her life wasn't hanging in the balance, would she have married Joe?

Surely not because he was a great guy. Kitty's concept of what made a guy great would likely bear little resemblance to Pamela's. Joe happened to agree with Kitty that he himself was a great guy, but he doubted Pamela would agree.

She couldn't have married him for his money. He was no millionaire—and if she were a gold digger, she wouldn't hook up with a guy raising a kid. Someone like Pamela had enough class to reel in a stockbroker or a bank executive if finding a sugar daddy had been her goal.

"Come on, Joe, wake up. I need a Seven-and-Seven," Lois declared, rapping the bar with her knuckles to get his attention.

"Oh. Yeah." He glanced around and saw Brick about to slice lemons. "Hey, Brick, cover for me for a minute. I've got to make a phone call."

"Uh-huh."

Ignoring Lois's frown of bewilderment, Joe hurried to the end of the bar and around it, down the hall and into his office. He nearly stumbled against Lizard's box of toys in his haste to slam the door shut. Even with it closed, he heard the noise of the bar, the cacophony of voices, laughter and jukebox music infiltrating his private haven.

Tuning out the din, he slumped into the chair behind the desk, propped his head in his hands and glowered at the telephone. If he called Pamela, what would he say? "Hi, honey—I crave your body but I don't trust you." "Hi, Pam—just checking to see if your life is truly in danger." "Hi, wife—I want to know the *real* reason you married me."

His uneasiness surprised him. Why should he give a damn about her real reason for anything? She'd done him a favor by marrying him, and she was continuing to do him favors by making his house presentable and taking care of his niece. So what if she'd lied about why she married him? He'd gotten what he was looking for.

Even so... Back in the beginning he'd had a few qualms about marrying someone with a price on her head. He'd swallowed those qualms, and, rational or not, it ticked him off royally to think those concerns might have been baseless. Not just ticked him off—it made him wonder what Pamela was after. No sane human being would take on Lizard without expecting something in return.

He fingered the phone, trying to decide whether to call her and demand proof that her life was in jeopardy. It didn't seem like something he ought to do over the phone, but if he faced off with her in person, it could turn into a nasty scene. A man couldn't accuse his wife of scamming him and expect her to laugh and kiss him on the cheek for being so perceptive.

One thing Joe couldn't afford was a nasty scene, not when he had Ms. Whitley breathing down his neck. He'd rather be conned by Pamela than let the social worker catch a whiff of trouble between the oh-so-happy Brenners.

He ran his fingers over the phone buttons again, then hauled the phone directory from the bottom drawer of his desk and looked up the area code for Seattle. He dialed directory assistance and requested the number of the Seattle Police Department. When the operator asked which precinct, he faltered for a moment, then said, "The main office, whatever. Cop Central."

He jotted down the number she recited and thanked

her. A deep breath, a brief, silent pep talk about how he wouldn't panic if it turned out that the woman he'd married—the woman he lusted after—had invented a cockamamy story about a hit man for some ulterior purpose, and then he punched the buttons and listened to his call connect.

"Seattle Police Department," came a woman's voice. "This phone call is being recorded."

Joe took one more deep, steadying breath. "Hi," he said in a ridiculously casual voice. "I'm hoping you can answer a question for me. It's about a woman named Pamela Hayes, who testified in a murder case in Seattle a few months ago."

The woman on the other end of the phone didn't respond right away. "A murder case?"

"She witnessed a professional murder, and she testified against the hit man. I don't know his name, but—"

"Who is this?"

Now it was Joe's turn to hesitate. "Do I have to give you my name?"

"If you want your call taken seriously, yes."

He sighed and assessed the situation. These were law enforcement folks he was talking to. They were supposed to be on Pamela's side. Joe could give them his name without doing harm to her. "I'm Joe Brenner. I'm…a friend of Pamela's. A very good friend. And I'm worried because she thinks she's in danger from this murderer she testified against."

"I'm going to have to transfer your call to Homicide," said the woman at the other end. "Perhaps they can help you."

He heard a few clicks as his call was transferred, and then a man came on the line. "Detective Wilcox here," he identified himself. "What can I help you with?"

Joe started all over again. "I'm concerned about a friend of mine, Pamela Hayes. I mean—*she's* concerned, and I'm concerned for her." He was rambling, and he gave his head a sharp shake to clear it. "She testified against a hit man at a trial a few months ago, and she's worried that the hit man might come after her."

"Pamela Hayes?"

"Yeah. She's a *very* good friend of mine, and I want to make sure she's safe."

"Ah, yes. I know that case," Detective Wilcox said. "I understand she got so spooked after the conviction fell through, she left town for a while. The DA says her only contact with Seattle is that she occasionally calls her lawyer. No one else knows where she is. Then again, even if I did know where she was, I wouldn't tell you."

"That's all right," Joe said magnanimously. *He* knew where she was, and he wasn't going to tell Wilcox, which he figured made them even. "I was only wondering—is she still in any danger?"

Detective Wilcox chuckled. "*Still* in danger? I don't think she was *ever* in any real danger."

"But she *did* testify against a hit man?" Joe reminded him, although his voice curled up at the end, turning the statement into a question.

"Yes, indeed she did. She's a gutsy lady."

"So what makes you so sure she isn't in danger?"

"Look," Detective Wilcox said gently, "if I had my druthers, the perpetrator wouldn't have been released on bail once his conviction was overturned. The guy's guilty as sin, but these courts, you know—one snafu, one minor technicality, and the process has to start all over again. That's the American legal system for you."

"I see." Joe should have been appalled that Pamela's story was checking out—if she'd testified against a hit man, then she very well might be in danger, regardless of what this detective was telling Joe. But he was too relieved by the knowledge that she hadn't lied to him. "So…is she in any danger?"

"We have the perpetrator under constant surveillance. We've got a cop permanently assigned to him. He hasn't been anywhere near Ms. Hayes since he got out on bail. He hasn't come within a mile of her. If he had, our man would have stepped in."

"She said that when she was in Seattle the creep was following her."

"It's understandable that she's nervous. Let's face it, she witnessed a murder. It could make anybody a little crazy, right? But, no, he wasn't following her. He's under watch, twenty-four hours a day. If she thought she saw him following her, it was just her imagination playing tricks on her. She's perfectly safe. Our officer is making sure of that."

"I'm glad to hear it," Joe said. Thanking the detective, he ended the call.

So, she was telling the truth—or, at least, the truth as it appeared from her perspective. The cops in Seattle thought she was paranoid—just as she'd said. And maybe, if the murderer was under full-time surveillance, she *was* being a little paranoid. Maybe, as Wilcox had said, she was a little crazy.

Joe could handle that. Just that morning she'd proved to be as close to the absolute, ultimate, picture-perfect mommy as an alleged thirty-year-old architect who didn't know anything about children could be. If she happened to be a little crazy on the side, so be it.

This marriage wasn't made in heaven; it was made on a handshake. And within a reasonably short time, it would be over. By then, Joe fervently hoped, he would have regained his old taste in women. He would stop fantasizing about a pale, flat-chested, angular-shouldered, possibly demented woman, and he would stop being so damned serious. Once he had permanent custody of Lizard, he could forget Pamela Hayes had ever entered his life.

He shoved away from his desk, strode across the office and opened the door. Someone had programmed the jukebox to play "Stand by Me." Suppressing a groan, Joe squared his shoulders and returned to his post behind the bar.

CHAPTER ELEVEN

PAMELA SUPPOSED EVERY marriage took time to find its routines and rhythms. That she and Joe had managed to settle into their own patterns of functioning after less than two weeks of wedded bliss ought to have satisfied her.

Except that the patterns Joe had settled into chafed at Pamela's nerves, leaving her troubled and glum.

He no longer seemed to be going to great lengths to avoid her. On rare mornings, he would actually venture into the kitchen before 10:00 a.m. and mumble a good-morning to his wife and niece before he buried himself in the pages of the newspaper.

He would spend the morning with Lizard if Pamela wanted to run errands. She had learned from experience that grocery shopping was sheer torture if Lizard accompanied her. Lizard had a habit of running up and down the aisles, grabbing junk food and tossing it into the shopping cart before Pamela could stop her. When Pamela made her put the junk food back on the shelves, Lizard whined in a pitch that could shatter fine crystal. And when Pamela got home and emptied the bags, she always discovered among her purchases some sugary pink item Lizard had smuggled past her.

In the afternoons, when Joe left for the Shipwreck, Pamela would engage in various activities with Lizard. Sometimes they would toil in Lizard's weed-infested herb garden. Sometimes they would go to Birdie's house to begin their first renovation project: breaking down the windowed interior wall of the kitchen and turning the room beyond it into a spacious dining area. One afternoon they went to see the latest Disney animated feature at the theater in town.

It rained every day. The air was thick, sticky, soupy with humidity. Every now and then the sun would peek tentatively through the clouds, and Pamela would feel an answering ray of hope inside her. But then another army of clouds would march across the sky, obliterating the sunlight, and her mood would plummet once more.

The atmosphere inside the house was as overcast as the atmosphere outside. Even though Pamela's and Joe's paths intersected several times a day, he never touched her. His smiles were reserved, his eyes lacking the warmth she'd seen in them the last time he'd kissed her—when he'd been putting on an act for Mona Whitley's benefit. Key West might be in the tropics, but the Brenner household was currently operating under an arctic freeze.

Pamela told herself Joe was keeping the emotional thermostat set on zero to avoid complications. She told herself they would both be better off if he never again flirted with her, gazed at her with longing or indicated in any way that he desired her. She'd been clear about not wanting a passionate relationship with him, and he was accommodating her wishes. She ought to count her blessings.

What blessings? None—unless boredom was a blessing, and isolation, and resentment.

She recalled how, during her single days, she had imagined that the ideal marriage would be not all that different from her present situation: a partnership in which her husband made no demands on her, didn't expect her to discuss sports knowledgeably and let her hold the remote control when the television was on. She'd dreamed of a husband who respected her independence and didn't try to change her. She supposed Joe fit the bill.

But marriage wasn't supposed to leave her feeling so alone, was it?

Thank God for Lizard. The little girl kept Pamela company—and kept her sane. To her amazement, she was growing rather fond of the Liz Monster, even though every activity they did together seemed to end up in a mess: puttering in the garden, sawing through the wall in Birdie's kitchen, baking brownies, cleaning Lizard's bedroom and laundering the mildewed clothing and stuffed animals they excavated from the darkest recesses of Lizard's closet.

After more than a week of rain that transformed the yard into a swamp and Pamela's usually limp hair into a frizz to rival the bride of Frankenstein's, Joe lifted his nose out of the newspaper one morning to announce that the weather page was forecasting clearing skies and high temperatures.

"Let's go to the beach," said Lizard. She was eating Cocoa Puffs with her hands, but at Pamela's disapproving look she emptied her fist into the curve of her spoon and smiled sweetly. "I'll eat nicely if you take me to the beach," she wheedled.

Pamela almost blurted out that Lizard could stuff Cocoa Puffs up her nose for all she cared—if the weather was pleasant, they would definitely go to the beach. Day after day of rain had left her emotionally waterlogged. She was as eager as Lizard to get out of the house and into the sunshine.

She wondered what a Brenner family outing would be like: husband, wife and child, picnicking in the shade of a palm tree, digging in the sand, romping in the surf. Briny breezes, laughter, the crash and fizz of the waves striking the shore. The fragrances of salt and seaweed, coconut oil and aloe from the sunscreen lotions of beachcombers around them. Buckets and shovels, sand castles with elaborate turrets and moats, Joe in a swimsuit. Joe's bare chest. His broad shoulders. His strong, sleek back. His muscular thighs and calves. His lean abdomen. His windswept, sun-streaked hair. His eyes as blue as the sky.

"Pam will have to take you, toots." Joe addressed Lizard directly, not sparing Pamela a glance. "My distributor's coming to the Shipwreck this morning. I've got to be there to go over my orders with him."

"Of course I'll take you," Pamela said, clearing the unexpected hoarseness from her throat. She didn't want to picture Joe undressed. Surely it was just as well that he couldn't come with them. If she saw him in a swimsuit, she would probably wind up hating him for having a magnificent body—whereas, if he saw *her* in a swimsuit, all pale and skinny and gawky, he would probably be cured of any wayward interest in her.

The hell with him. She and Lizard were going to have a grand time at the beach, just the two of them, no guys allowed. Jonas Brenner could spend the rest of his life holed up at the Shipwreck with his distributor, for all Pamela cared.

Once Lizard was done playing with her Cocoa Puffs, Pamela began organizing for their outing. She packed sandwiches, carrot sticks and boxes of apple-cranberry juice, which Lizard conceded was pink enough to be worthwhile. She located two huge beach towels in the upstairs linen closet and stuffed them into a canvas tote, along with an old blanket, a paperback novel from the den and the lunch she'd prepared. She slathered Lizard with a thick layer of sunscreen, even though Lizard swore she didn't need it. "I'm already tanned," she complained.

"That's not a tan. That's dirt," Pamela argued, rubbing the lotion into the squirming girl's arms and legs. "Where I come from, you never go to the beach unless you're wearing sun block." Where she came from, it rained ninety-eight percent of the time, but Lizard didn't have to know that.

"It smells yucky," Lizard declared. "Like macaroons. Birdie once gave me macaroons and I threw up all over the place."

"Why doesn't that surprise me?" Pamela muttered, wiping her greasy palms on a paper towel. "I want you to wear a sun hat, too. And no feathers."

"I always wear feathers at the beach."

"Do you want to go to the beach or do you want to give me a hard time?"

Lizard weighed her choices and backed down. "Okay, no feathers. But if I find feathers there, I'm gonna keep them."

"As long as they aren't attached to any live animals," Pamela said before stepping into her bedroom and closing the door.

She'd brought one swimsuit with her from Seattle. When Kitty had taken her shopping for her "trousseau," Pamela had considered buying a new swimsuit. But beachwear in Key West, like nearly everything else on the island, breached the boundaries of good taste. Pamela wasn't a prude; she could handle a bikini, even though she believed no woman over the age of twenty-five ought to wear one in public. But the bikinis for sale at the boutiques Kitty had taken her to made G-strings and pasties look puritanical in comparison. "That's called a thong," Kitty had told her when she gaped at one swimsuit bottom, unable to tell the front from the back.

"What it's called is repugnant," Pamela had argued, wrinkling her nose and hanging the garment back on the rack.

So there she was, a married woman in a modest maillot that was faded from wear and swimming laps in the heavily chlorinated pool at the health club she belonged to in Seattle. She would no doubt be the dowdiest woman on the beach. Lizard would probably announce, at the top of her lungs, that Pamela was ugly.

So be it, she thought wryly, slipping a baggy T-shirt on over her suit and settling a broad-brimmed straw hat onto her head. If Mona Whitley had any spies at the beach, they would see Pamela and report that she was the most demure, primly attired woman there.

Lizard was waiting impatiently on the porch, clutching a bag of plastic beach toys, when Pamela came downstairs. She detoured to the kitchen to get the tote. Joe was gone.

She suffered a pang of irritation at his having left without saying goodbye to her. *She* wanted to be the one to leave without saying goodbye to *him*.

Something was bugging him, something more than unfulfilled lust. She tried to recall when Joe had transformed from being merely conflicted to outright icy. Sure, they'd kissed a few times, and they'd both responded more passionately to those kisses than was wise, but so what? They were adults; they could deal with their shared discomfort. But Joe had gone from treating Pamela as if she had leprosy to treating her as if she were irrelevant.

And she couldn't begin to guess why.

"Are you comin' or what?" Lizard hollered through the screen door.

Sighing, Pamela hoisted the tote off the counter and carried it out to the porch. She locked up, took Lizard's hand and stepped down off the porch with her. "Isn't this sunshine lovely?" she remarked, savoring not just the clear sky but the absence of the thick humidity that had clung to the earth for so many sodden days.

"You know how to get to the beach?"

"I'm not sure. It's a few blocks from here, right?"

"Yeah. We can walk if you want."

"I'd love to walk."

Pamela and Lizard strolled side by side down the driveway to the street. Lizard thought for a minute, then turned left. That seemed correct to Pamela, who had driven past the municipal beach a couple of times.

"I'm gonna build the greatest sand castle in the whole entire universe," Lizard boasted. "Birdie told me about this place, it's called Versatile or something?"

"Versatile?" Pamela repeated.

"It's this big palace in France."

"Versailles," Pamela corrected her.

"Yeah, that's it. Anyway, that's what I'm gonna build in the sand. And I'm gonna decorate it with seashells and dead kelp."

"Just like the original Versailles," Pamela noted, even though she knew Lizard wouldn't get the joke.

The further they journeyed from the house, the more Pamela's spirits lifted. Partly it was the weather, the pleasant shock of walking from sunlight to shade to sunlight again. For so long the sky had been too dark for the trees lining the street to cast shadows. Today, after so many days of rain, the flora smelled fresh and green and alive. Cars cruised past with their convertible tops down and their radios blasting. People coasted by on bicycles. The world was drying out and coming back to life.

But part of Pamela's cheerfulness might also have been a result of getting away from Joe, from the strain of living in his house yet being totally shut out by him.

"Can I ask you a question, Lizard?"

"You can ask me anything," Lizard assured her. "I'm very smart."

Pamela mulled over whether she ought to drag Lizard into her problems with Joe. But she wasn't expecting Lizard to solve those problems, or to take sides. All Pamela wanted was to figure out what the problems were.

"Is something bothering your uncle?" she asked.

Lizard nodded somberly, her round little face taking on a mature cast. "Yup."

"Do you have any idea what it could be?"

"Joyce and Lawton."

"Who?"

"Joyce and Lawton. They're this other aunt and uncle of mine."

"Ah." It hadn't occurred to Pamela that Joe's withdrawal might simply be a result of his stress over the looming custody battle.

"They're these people, they were related to my daddy."

Pamela nodded. "Jonas has mentioned them to me."

"They're supposed to come and visit me soon. I don't think Uncle Joe wants them to come."

"You may be right, Lizard. I think that's part of what's bothering him."

"It's up to us to keep him happy. I figure I'll bring him some gull feathers from the beach. There's always tons of gull feathers lying around. That might make him happy. And maybe we could make some more brownies."

"Your Uncle Joe didn't get to eat too many of that first batch," Pamela reminded her. "You gobbled up most of them."

"And they weren't even pink. I bet if we made pink brownies... Hey! We could call them pinkies!" Lizard wiggled her pinkies in the air and chanted in a singsong, "Let's bake pinkies!"

Pamela rode out Lizard's silliness with a tolerant smile. After a while the child wound down, and Pamela once again pursued the subject of Joe's state of mind. "Anything else you think might be bothering your uncle?"

Lizard meditated for a few minutes. "You know what? He doesn't get to do anything fun. He has to hang around with his *disliberator* instead of coming to the beach with us. I think he needs more fun in his life."

"I agree." Not that Pamela was volunteering to be the source of his fun. But there were other kinds of fun than that. Family togetherness, for instance. Trips to the beach. Lizard was right: Joe ought to spend less time sitting in meetings with his distributor.

"You know what?" Lizard continued. "We ought to let him help us with Birdie's house. He's always fixing stuff over there. She had this leaky ceiling once, and he fixed it. And her toilet backed up one time, it was real gross. It flooded all over the bathroom floor and everything! You shoulda seen it. There was soggy toilet paper gushing out of the toilet, and poop, and—"

"Spare me the details."

"Yeah, well, it was really gross." Lizard let out a delighted laugh. "Anyway, Uncle Joe fixed it. I bet he'd like to help us fix her kitchen."

"Do you think so? Do you think he'd enjoy plastering the new wall with us?"

"Yeah. He likes getting messy. He has to. He's my uncle."

Pamela smiled. Apparently Lizard didn't know what was wrong between Joe and Pamela—or even that anything was wrong at all. But her suggestion made a certain sense. Joe had declined their invitation to go to the beach today, but if they kept asking, kept trying to include him in their activities, perhaps in time they could break down the barriers he'd erected between himself and Pamela. She remembered the way he'd been at their wedding, smiling and tender, dancing with her again and again as Ben E. King crooned from the jukebox. *Stand by me...*

If she was going to be married, that was the man she wanted to be married to. The dimpled, grinning man, the man who would stand by her. Maybe, if she and Lizard could somehow entice him to roll up his sleeves and join them in their daily mess-making, Pamela and Lizard could make him happy.

THE BEACH WASN'T too crowded, although Pamela suspected that by afternoon it would be packed. She staked out an area in the shade of a palm tree, spreading the blanket and using her sandals, the towels and the tote to hold the corners down. Lizard grabbed her bucket and shovel and raced down to the water's edge, eager to build her replica of the "Versatile Palace."

Pamela arranged herself comfortably on the blanket and sighed contentedly. The air was laced with the scent of salt and the gleeful squeals of children splashing at the water's edge. The sun glazed the sand, imbuing it with a gentle shimmer.

Lying in the shelter of the palm tree, absorbing the therapeutic warmth and the soothing sounds of youthful laughter and the surf, Pamela could almost forget that anything was amiss in her life. An uncommunicative husband? A murder trial? A temporarily sidetracked career? Who cared? She had the beach, the sea, a good novel and the company of a little girl who could obviously entertain herself without constant adult supervision. On a morning like this, it was possible to believe everything was going to work out okay.

The heat tranquilized Pamela. Above her, the caws and mews of the sea gulls sounded like a lullaby. The words of her book blurred; she closed her eyes and felt the tension drain out of her. Giddy shrieks amid the thudding surf nibbled at the frayed edges of her consciousness.

A long moment passed, and she opened her eyes and searched the shoreline. A shot of pink sprang from the foaming waves, then vanished, then sprang up again, arms wheeling, hair dripping.

Pamela frowned. Hadn't Lizard been wearing a lime-green swimsuit?

There it was, lying on the sand. The pink creature bounded out of the waves, darted along the water's edge and plunged in with another cheerful shout.

Pamela sprang to her feet and sprinted to the water's edge in time to see Lizard soar out of the water again, stark naked.

She snatched the swimsuit off the sand and charged into the water, ignoring the shock of its coldness. "Lizard! Elizabeth! Get over here now!" she roared, fear and fury battling inside her. The chilly water lapped at her knees as she forged deeper and grabbed hold of Lizard's slippery arm. "Put this on!" she commanded, then cast a quick look around to see how many people might have seen the nude little girl.

Lizard stared up at Pamela and blinked with phony innocence. "How come?"

"Because I said so!" Pamela retorted.

"So what? Birdie says—"

"I don't care what Birdie says!" Pamela reached down and grabbed Lizard's foot, determined to shove it through the leg hole in her swimsuit. Lizard tumbled backward with a shivery splash that sprayed water all over Pamela.

Lizard obviously found Pamela's outraged sputtering hilarious. She leapt back up, giggling and dancing out of Pamela's reach.

"Get over here!" Pamela chased her through the water and out onto the beach, scrambling across the sand after the naked child, who continued to flap her arms and shriek with laughter. If onlookers hadn't noticed Lizard before, they certainly noticed her now.

Pamela's long legs compensated for her lack of speed. After a minute she caught up to Lizard, snagged her around her wet belly, hauled her off the sand and lugged her back to the blanket, where she wrapped her in a towel. "Don't you ever, ever do that again!" she chided.

"How come?"

"Because." Pamela dried her in brisk, frantic strokes, then yanked the swimsuit onto her. *Because I said so* wasn't going to work a second time. "Because you're not supposed to be undressed in public," she explained.

"Birds don't wear clothes," Lizard pointed out.

"Birds wear feathers." Anticipating Lizard's argument, she continued, "And no, you can't wear feathers. Birds are different from people."

"But Birdie said if you strip to your essence you can be as free as the birds. You can fly in your spirit...or something like that."

Scowling, Pamela smoothed the straps across Lizard's shoulders. "Do you know what essence means?"

Lizard shrugged, the motion jarring one of the straps out of place. Pamela nudged it back. "I think it means kinda like your skin or something."

"Listen to me." Pamela kept her hands on Lizard's shoulders, holding the girl in place. "It's a sad fact of life, Lizard, but you can't go running around naked in public. There are a lot of sick people in this world."

"What do you mean, sick? Like, they have chicken pox?"

"No. It's more like they're sick in the head." Pamela took a slow breath and sorted her thoughts. In her wildest dreams, she would never have imagined she would have to have this discussion with a little girl—someone else's little girl, at that. It was the sort of task a childless professional woman shouldn't have to face. Pamela had never studied the subject; she hadn't read instructional articles or pamphlets on it.

Someone else should have told Lizard these things. Birdie, or Joe, or Joe's mother, or someone. No child should reach the age of five without knowing about perverts. Nevertheless, it seemed as if the other adults in Lizard's life had failed to warn her. Pamela was just going to have to muddle through on her own. "Some sick-in-the-head people might want to touch your private parts," she said carefully. "You know what your private parts are, don't you?"

"What I keep under my bed?"

"No. The private parts of your body. The parts that are supposed to be covered by your bathing suit."

"You mean, like my butt?"

Pamela sighed. Why bother with discretion? "Yes, Lizard. Like your butt."

"Why would anyone want to touch my butt?"

"Because they're sick."

"Do they think touching my butt'll make them better?"

Pamela sighed again. "It doesn't really matter what they think, because they're sick in the head. In any case, Lizard, I want you to promise me you won't go running around nude anymore."

"Even in the bath?"

"In public, Lizard. That's what we're talking about. No nudity in public."

Lizard looked peeved. Her eyes narrowed and frown lines pleated her brow. "What if Uncle Joe says I can?" she tested.

"If he says you can..." *I'll kill him,* Pamela concluded silently. He didn't have the right to say anything on this subject. He'd relinquished his rights when he'd decided to meet with his distributor at the Shipwreck instead of coming to the beach with his family. "If he says you can, you can," she said. "But I'm sure he'll say you can't."

Lizard stuck out her lower lip in a plump little pout. "I bet he says I can. I'm gonna go build a castle. And you can't help." She stomped off in a snit.

Pamela permitted herself one final sigh that ended in a shudder. She would rather have Lizard angry at her than running around in her birthday suit. Her gaze glued to Lizard, she felt some of her tension fade, but not all.

One part of her remained tight with rage—rage that Joe hadn't taught Lizard how to protect herself.

Damn it. This had nothing to do with Mona Whitley and the courts. It had nothing to do with persuading the authorities that Lizard belonged in Key West. This wasn't a game, a staged performance. This was real life. When Pamela thought about all the weirdos in the world, and all the terrible things that could have happened to Lizard, she wanted to weep.

She wasn't going to weep. What she was going to do was give that husband of hers a piece of her mind about his responsibilities as a family man.

IT HAD ALL SEEMED so simple when Mary DiNardi first raised the idea. You get married, you make a pretty family picture for the judge, you keep Lizard. No emotions, no involvement, just a straightforward deal, as neat and fair as the contracts he drew up with his distributor.

He'd even picked a woman who didn't turn him on— except that she did. He'd picked a woman who had as good a reason to stick with him as he had to stick with her—unless she was simply a crazy lady. Was it any wonder that he wanted to keep as far from her as possible?

"Go home," Kitty scolded him. "You look like hell."

How she could see what he looked like in the murky light of the bar was beyond him. "You used to think I was cute," he shot back.

"You used to look like you got a few hours of sleep every night. Go home."

He glanced toward the steering-wheel clock on the wall. Nearly midnight—the busiest time at the Shipwreck. "The bar's too crowded."

"Nothing the rest of us can't handle. Go home, Joe—and do us all a favor this time: don't stay up all night making whoopee with Pamela. Get some sleep."

Making whoopee. Real funny. "I'll leave in an hour."

"You'll leave right now or Brick'll escort you out. Right, Brick?"

Brick grunted. Joe eyed his fellow bartender with resignation. Besides making the best tequila sunrises on the island, Brick was built like a linebacker on the Dolphins, which enabled him to double as a bouncer when things got too rowdy. Joe didn't doubt that Brick could "escort" him from the premises—either by tossing him over one brawny shoulder or by dragging him out by his feet.

"All right," he relented. "I'm outta here."

Driving home, he admitted to himself that he really was exhausted. His fatigue wasn't just a result of the nocturnal restlessness caused by knowing a woman—an available woman with snow-blond hair and the sexiest shoulders this side of the Continental Divide—was lying alone in a bed at the opposite end of the hall from him. It was also an outgrowth of living with doubt.

He'd trusted Pamela once. He wanted to trust her again. But he wasn't sure how, short of investigating her mental health records. And what would he do if he found out she was really messed up? If he gave her the boot after less than a month of marriage, the courts sure wouldn't consider Lizard's home life stable.

He'd gotten himself into jams before. Jams with women, on occasion. Given all the women he knew, he'd have had to be God himself not to have messed up at least a few times. But he'd never gotten mixed up with marriage. And he'd never had so much at stake.

A light was glowing in the living room window when he pulled into the driveway. Pamela usually left the hallway light on for him, as well as the light above the front door. It wasn't like her to forget to turn off the other lights.

Fatigue weighed him down as he climbed out of his car, trudged up the front walk and let himself into the house. His neck was stiff, his back aching. Tonight he was going to put his distrust and desire on hold and get some serious, uninterrupted shut-eye. Whatever lay ahead, he needed his strength to confront it.

What lay ahead, it turned out, was Pamela. He had barely closed the door behind himself when she charged at him from the living room. She was wide-awake, so full of energy he recoiled a step as she advanced toward him. "We've got to talk, Jonas. This is really important. And so help me, if you try to avoid me—"

"Hey, hey." He held up his hands to stop her. He'd just come home. He wasn't expecting to see her; he wasn't used to seeing her. He was tired, he was sore... and she was a vision of beauty.

She must have been out in the sun all day. Her cheeks and the tip of her nose were pink, her arms and legs—exposed by her shorts and a tank top—more of a golden hue. Her hair seemed a few shades lighter than it had been that morning, her lashes and eyebrows bleached to platinum above her silver-bright eyes.

"This is important, Jonas," she said.

"Fine. It's important." He sidled past her, heading for the kitchen. If it was all that important, he might need a beer to get him through it.

"It's about Lizard."

Thank God it wasn't about him and Pamela. He paused and turned. "What about her?"

"Did you know she likes to run naked on the beach?"

Actually, he hadn't known that. But what the hell?

She was a kid. A remarkably uninhibited one. "Naked, huh."

"From her head to her toes."

"Well." He continued down the hall to the kitchen, Pamela hot on his trail. Without turning, he pulled a couple of beers from the fridge, extended one to her and then set it on the table when she didn't take it. He twisted the cap off the other bottle and took a swig.

She crowded him against the counter, her hands fisted and her eyes ablaze. "Damn it, Joe! Don't you realize what a terrible thing this is?"

"Terrible thing?" He'd suspected Pamela of having a prudish streak—after all, she'd passed up the opportunity to make love with him. But jeez, a little kid running around bare-ass on the beach was no big deal. "Come on, Pam. She's five years old."

"Old enough to keep her body covered."

"For God's sake. So she ran around naked. It's no big deal. You know how kids are."

"I know how adults are."

He knew some of them were prigs. Pamela, for instance. "What happened? Did some bluenose come over and tell you to cover her up?"

"Bluenose? Do you think I'm talking about morality? You think that's what this is about?" Pamela's knuckles turned a bloodless white. The tendons in her neck stood out. Slowly it dawned on him that she was really in a state about this.

He lowered his bottle and regarded her cautiously. "I'll admit Lizard can be wild, but come on. She isn't even in school yet. Kids are always losing their bathing suits at the beach. They love skinny-dipping."

"This isn't about Lizard's wildness, or skinny-dipping, or losing her bathing suit. This is about the real world, Joe. It's about creeps who get their jollies with little girls.''

"Oh, God." His heart lurched in his chest. Had some creep touched Lizard? Had someone approached her? He'd strangle the guy with his bare hands, so help him. He'd tear off his head—and other parts of his body, too. He'd—

"Maybe you don't see the danger. Maybe you think I'm being hysterical—"

"Who touched her?" His voice emerged low, raw, the rage barely suppressed. "Did someone touch her?"

"No. But you let her run around naked, and you're asking for trouble." Pamela began to pace the kitchen, not so much burning off steam as charging herself up. "I'm not talking about fun and games, Joe. I'm not talking about skinny-dipping. We were on a public beach, and Lizard removed her bathing suit because Birdie told her it would free her essence. Well, let me tell you something, Joe—I'm not going to let that precious little girl free her essence on a public beach. The world is full of creeps. And Lizard thinks she's perfectly safe exposing herself when who the hell knows what kind of perverted beast might be on that beach with her, watching her and getting ideas. I don't know what you allow, what you think is just children being children, what you consider acceptable Key West behavior. And frankly, I don't give a damn what you allow and what you consider acceptable. As long as I'm here, as long as I'm Lizard's aunt by marriage, that child is not going to go naked on the beach. I absolutely refuse to let her expose herself to that kind of danger—and if you disagree with me, well, tough luck, buster.''

Her eyes flashed at him, shiny with tears. Joe realized that this wasn't about Lizard's lack of decorum, or the hang-loose atmosphere of the island, or Pamela's arguable paranoia. She cared about Lizard, cared about his niece so much she was willing to wait up for Joe, to rant and rave and wave her fists in the air. For Lizard's sake. Because she cared.

He still wasn't sure he believed she was in any danger. But for the moment, it didn't matter. All that mattered was that Pamela loved his niece as much as he did, loved her enough to go to the mat with him about her, fight for her, worry about her.

How could he not believe in a woman who cared so much about Lizard? How could he not want her?

One long stride carried him across the room to her. He snagged her in midcircuit around the room, wrapped his arms around her and pressed his lips to hers in a hard, fierce, angry, loving kiss.

CHAPTER TWELVE

KEY WEST. Mick supposed it made sense that she would get herself as far from Seattle as her car would carry her. Although she could have crossed the border into Canada. More's the pity she hadn't. If she had, it would have been a hell of a lot easier for Tony to track her down, what with certain acquaintances of his who happened to be affiliated with the border patrol.

Okay, so whatever. Key West might be far away, but it wasn't inaccessible. All Mick had to do was fly to Miami, rent a car, scoot down Route 1 on the causeway that connected all those dinky little islands, find the lady currently going under the name of Pamela Brenner and pop her. Easy as pie.

Mick inventoried the contents of his suitcase one more time. Underwear, toiletries, fake mustache, sunglasses, baseball cap. Traveler's checks. Auto club directory of lodgings in Southern Florida. Unassembled plastic gun, the pieces neatly stashed inside the suitcase lining.

He would buy the bullets once he got to Florida.

He couldn't believe how simple it had been, once some homicide detective had mentioned in passing to Tony that he'd heard from a friend of Pamela's. "She's still running scared, according to her friend," the detective had told Tony, all innocence, all goo-goo helpfulness.

Tony, bless his little heart, hadn't given anything

away. "A friend of hers, huh? Did you happen to catch her name?"

"It was a he. Let's see, we got it on the tape: Joe Brenner."

Bull's-eye. Pamela Hayes had changed her name to Brenner, hadn't she? It was easy enough for Tony to trace Joe Brenner's phone number to a bar on Key West. From there, a quick flip through the phone directory had produced Joe Brenner's home address: Leon Street, same address that appeared on Pamela Hayes Brenner's new Florida license.

Thank you, God.

Mick had considered contacting someone on the East Coast to do the dirty deed for him. Technically, he wasn't allowed to leave the state while he was free on bail. But technicalities could be smoothed over with a little cash, and Mick wanted the Hayes woman for himself. No one had ever had the guts to stand up to him before. She was a prize, and he wanted her scalp on his belt.

He zipped his bag shut, grabbed his car keys and left the apartment. A cool drizzle bathed the road and created halos around the streetlights. A sign, he thought, smiling to himself. A sign that the angels were with him on this mission.

Oh, he was going to get her, all right. He was going to plug her with so many holes she could do service as a colander. And he was going to enjoy it. Nobody testified against him in court and walked away.

The clock on his dashboard read eight o'clock. He'd arranged to have a ticket waiting for him at the airport. The red-eye's departure time was nine-fifty. When he woke up tomorrow, he'd be in the Sunshine State.

He hummed a tune in time to the clicking of his windshield wipers. This was going to feel good, he thought. Pamela Hayes deserved to die, and not just because she'd fingered him. Women didn't belong on construction sites. It was a man's business: designing, building, raising capital and keeping the union in line. What the hell had they brought in a female architect for? Female architects ought to be designing dollhouses.

Yeah, she deserved to die. The world would be a better place minus one uppity professional woman.

He drove onto the highway, southbound. The asphalt was slick with rain, forcing him to slow down. He batted down his rising frustration. So what if he got to the airport five minutes later? The less time he hung around the terminal, the less chance some security bozo might spot him and do a thorough check on his background—or his suitcase.

Up ahead he saw a swarm of red lights. Brake lights. Traffic jam.

"Damn!" He banged his fist against the steering wheel, then struggled to rein in his temper. Traffic happened. He was just going to have to be patient.

This wasn't merely traffic, he realized after his car caught up to the mass of motionless vehicles clogging the highway. No one was moving, period. A few drivers climbed out of their vehicles to see what was going on. Mick climbed out, too.

Around a bend in the road he saw a jackknifed eighteen-wheeler, the trailer of which had skidded sideways to block all three southbound lanes. Somewhere behind him, Mick heard the approaching wail of a siren.

He spat out a few foul words. It could take hours for the truck to be removed from the highway. Mick didn't have hours.

He yanked open his car door, slumped onto the seat

and slammed the door shut. In his rearview mirror he saw two state troopers cruising along the shoulder, their blue lights flashing. Behind them was another vehicle, with a flashing yellow light. A tow truck.

Oh, right. One little tow truck was going to clean up this mess.

Drumming his fingers against the dashboard, he watched the troopers and the wrecker cruise past. He counted to five, then eased his car onto the shoulder. Shifting into reverse, he backed up to the exit ramp, all the while praying that no more cops would be coming along for a few minutes.

A couple of cars honked at him as he coasted backward past them. A van pulled onto the shoulder, following his example. Good thing, Mick thought. He would be less conspicuous if he wasn't the only driver breaking the law to escape the gridlock up ahead.

Slowly, cautiously, he made his way down the ramp to the street. At the bottom, he navigated a three-point turn and headed west, leaving the traffic-snarled highway behind. "Yes!" he hissed triumphantly.

Okay. One disaster averted. Now he had to find an alternate route to the airport—and he had to make tracks. That damn eighteen-wheeler had cost him twenty precious minutes.

He veered around the block, meandering through damp, dark streets, weaving his way toward Route 99. He tried not to look at the dashboard clock, but its digits glared at him, taunting him.

Damn it. If he didn't catch this flight, he'd have to wait a day—assuming he could even get a seat on the next flight. The longer he waited, the greater the chance that Pamela Hayes would move on, change her name again, do something to screw him up the way she'd screwed him up in court. He just wanted to take care of her so he could get on with his life.

He pressed harder on the gas pedal. He was a better driver than that idiot trucker. He wasn't going to skid. Seattle residents knew how to drive in wet weather; it was the only kind of weather they had.

The light ahead turned from green to yellow. Mick didn't have time for red lights. He floored the pedal and zoomed through the intersection. And heard a siren as a traffic cop turned the corner, switched on his lights and chased him down.

"JONAS?" HER VOICE emerged as a whisper, uncertain. Just a minute ago she'd been steaming with rage. She'd actually wanted to punch him, shake him, force him to acknowledge her.

She hadn't been prepared for him to acknowledge her like this, though. Even worse, she hadn't expected to respond to his kiss, to feel the steaming rage turn to steamier desire as he twined his fingers through her hair and slid his lips from her mouth to the bridge of her nose, to her forehead.

"I'm sorry," he murmured.

For what? Making light of Lizard's nudist proclivities? Treating Pamela so cavalierly? Or kissing her?

She hated him for his ability to arouse her with his touch, with the lean grace of his body as he closed in on her. She struggled valiantly to resist her treacherous reaction to him. "What's going on, Jonas?" she asked. "Why are you doing this?"

"You're my wife." He said it as if it were news to him, a profound revelation.

"You could have fooled me."

He slid one hand from her hair to her shoulder and

down her arm, to capture her left hand in his. With his thumb he traced the thick gold band that marked her as his wife. "Why did you marry me, Pamela?" he asked.

She frowned, momentarily bewildered by both his question and her own uncertainty as to her answer. For a strange, unnerving moment she believed she'd married Jonas Brenner because his eyes were so blue. Because his smile was so deliciously wicked. Because deep in some hitherto unknown part of her soul she'd been longing for a bum in torn jeans and an earring to become a part of her life.

"I told you," she said, lowering her gaze so she wouldn't have to see his handsome face, his intense stare. "There's a hit man after me."

"Tell me about him."

Her frown intensified. She took a step back and found herself pressed against the counter. She'd thought—maybe even hoped, in that same hitherto unknown part of her soul—that Joe was going to seduce her. Obviously he was more in the mood for a chat. But if they were going to talk instead of make love, they ought to be talking about Lizard, not Mick Morrow.

"Tell me about this hit man who's after you." Joe remained close to her, his thumb gliding across her knuckles. His chest remained an inch from hers; his feet remained parted, framing hers.

She didn't want to talk about the murder she'd witnessed. Whenever she talked about it—whenever she even thought about it—dread welled up inside her, making her feel weak and wretched.

"Pam." He released her hand and let out a long breath. "No one is stalking you," he said, sounding oddly disappointed.

"Someone most certainly is," she retorted. "His name is Mick Morrow, and he's a cold-blooded killer."

"Mick Morrow." Joe scratched his chin thoughtfully. His fingernails made a rasping sound against the day-old stubble of beard. "It doesn't sound like a hit man's name."

"What name would you prefer? Black Jack Morrow? Homicide Morrow? AK-47 Morrow?"

"He uses an AK-47?" This took Joe aback. "A semi-automatic?"

"No. He uses an ugly little pistol. At least, that was what he used to kill Larry Ebersole."

Joe regarded her with what appeared to be strained patience. "Who's Larry Ebersole?"

Pamela sighed. It was going to be a long night. Edging past Joe, she reached for the unopened bottle of beer and gave the cap a sharp twist. "If you really want to go into all this, let's sit down."

Joe nodded, but instead of pulling out a chair at the kitchen table, he took Pamela's hand and his beer and led her to the old sofa along the back wall of the screened porch. Light from the kitchen spilled through the door, and the air was stirred by the songs of the night—crickets, bullfrogs and the whisper of the wind as it sifted through the fronds of the royal palms surrounding the house.

Pamela eyed the wrought-iron table on the other side of the porch. She remembered the luncheon Joe had hosted there to press his case for marriage. Lizard had called her ugly that afternoon, and Pamela had felt emotionally battered and afraid.

She no longer felt battered. She probably should have felt afraid—the word from Seattle was that Morrow was still out on bail—but somehow, being married to Joe had given her courage. If she could take on Lizard and win, if she could endure this farcical marriage, if she could survive the dense, muggy heat of Key West, then surely she could handle Mick Morrow's being at liberty in Seattle.

Joe sat a couple of feet away from her on the couch, angling his body so he could view her. The diffuse light from the kitchen transformed his face into a study of amber-lighted planes and shadows.

Despite her reservations about him in the past, she knew he was a man she could trust. An honorable, caring man, and she owed him nothing less than the truth.

"I was the architect on a project," she began, then took a sip of her beer and turned to stare out at the dark backyard. "A suburban minimall. Larry Ebersole was the contractor."

Joe nodded.

"Larry had lowballed the project, snagged the contract, and found a million ways to jack up the price once ground-breaking began. That's how contractors work—they write up as cheap an estimate as they dare, and once the project is under way, they tell the owner, 'Oh, you wanted double-glazed windows? The estimate was only for single-glazed. Double-glazed is going to cost you more.' Or, 'You want French doors? Read the small print. The estimate stipulates sliders, not French doors.' And they inflate the price to cover all the specs they pretend they didn't know about when they'd gone to contract."

"Pretty sleazy."

"That's the way they work. Anyway, the owner of this project wasn't having any of it. He insisted he'd contracted for double-glazed windows from the start, and if Larry Ebersole didn't bring the job in at the agreed-upon price, the owner intended to sue the pants off him. So Larry was in a financial bind.''

''What did you have to do with this?''

''Nothing—except that as the architect on the project, I would visit the site every now and then to see how things were moving along. A few times when I was there, I saw Larry talking to this fellow, Mick Morrow. Larry told me Morrow was a money man who could extend him the credit he needed to get the job done on budget. That was all I knew. The financing of the project was none of my business. My firm had gotten its design fee directly from the owner.''

She drank some more beer and glanced at Joe, wondering how such details could possibly interest him. He appeared fascinated, though, so she lowered her bottle and continued.

''One evening, I was supposed to meet some friends at the symphony. I decided to detour to the construction site, just to see how things were progressing. When I approached the trailer I heard voices through the window. Mick Morrow was yelling at Larry Ebersole for failing to make timely payments, or some such thing. I have the feeling Morrow had bankrolled him for a lot more than just this one project.

''In any case, Larry bolted from the trailer, and Morrow followed him. He kind of...tackled Larry.'' Her voice trailed off, her hands grew clammy in her lap and shivers traveled the length of her nervous system. Describing the scene forced her to relive it. She could even feel the cool evening air at the construction site as she hid in the dank shadows of the construction tractors. ''When Larry was on the ground, Morrow pulled out this little gun and shot him in the back of the head.''

She had to force out the words. Her throat was squeezed shut, choking her.

Joe slid along the sofa cushions until he could put his arm around her. "Not a pretty picture," he said.

"No." The single syllable slid out on a whimper.

Joe ran his hand up and down her arm, consoling her. "I take it this thug didn't realize he had an audience."

She confirmed his guess with a shake of her head. "I stayed in the shadows. I probably should have stepped forward, though. Maybe Larry would be alive today if I had."

"Or maybe you *wouldn't* be alive today. If the guy could kill one person, he could kill two. You think he's still trying to kill you now. I'm sure it would have been easier for him to off you then and there."

She nodded, trying to shrug off the chills that continued to rack her. Joe tightened his arm around her. "I suppose I knew instinctively that I ought to stay in the shadows. I didn't move until Morrow had driven away. Then I went over to Larry. He...he was..."

Joe spared her from having to say it. "I get the idea." His hand continued to caress her, his palm warm and strong on her bare skin. It was the gesture of a friend, a husband. "You didn't have to testify against him, did you?"

"Of course I did. Testifying against him was the proper thing to do. The moral thing. He was convicted of first-degree murder, thanks to my testimony."

"Which has endeared you to him forever."

"I wouldn't be in trouble today if the conviction hadn't been set aside." The chills lost their grip on her, thanks to the warmth of Joe's body.

"How did that happen? What went wrong?"

"One of the jurors had gone to primary school with

Larry's widow. Why that fact didn't emerge during jury selection is a mystery, but the judge had to throw out the verdict and schedule a new trial. And meanwhile, Morrow somehow got himself released on bail. He's free to roam the streets and hunt me down."

"Do you have nightmares?" he asked.

She shot him a surprised look. Nobody—not even her parents—had ever thought to ask her that. "Yes," she admitted. "Sometimes. I see Larry Ebersole lying on the ground, with that little hole at the base of his skull. There wasn't much blood. It was just…this horrible little hole." She closed her eyes, trying to erase the image.

Joe eased her against him, guiding her head to rest on his shoulder. "So…once they put this ass back on trial, you intend to testify against him again?"

"I have to. If I don't, he goes free."

"I can't believe they released him on bail."

"I think he has friends in high places."

"How do you know he's still in Seattle?"

"I call my attorney on a regular basis—and once the phone bill comes, I'll reimburse you for those calls."

"Forget that," he said sharply. His tone was gentler when he asked, "Who keeps your folks up on things?"

"The DA's office. He's on my side, at least. He needs me alive to make his case." She relaxed in the protective curve of his arm, soothed by the patterns his fingers traced against the skin of her upper arm. She hadn't felt this close to him since their wedding. "Why did you ask me all this tonight, Jonas?"

He sighed, set his bottle down beside hers on the floor and closed both arms around her. "I don't know," he said, then shook his head. "Yeah, I do know. I didn't believe you."

She flinched. Wriggling out of his arms, she twisted to confront him. "What do you mean?"

"Pam." Without her to hold, he didn't seem to know what to do with his hands. He folded them, then separated them and tapped his fingertips against his knees. "You showed up on the island one day, out of the blue, and when Kitty told you I was looking for a wife, you actually agreed to meet me. Look at us, Pam—we're a total mismatch, right? You're a fancy-dancy architect and I'm a no-frills barkeep." He spread his hands palms up. "We swapped stories, got hitched, and—let's face it—you've had proof that my story is true. Lizard exists, the social worker's been here, you've talked to my lawyer. You know I was telling the truth about why I wanted to marry you. You've seen my evidence."

"And you haven't seen mine," she said quietly, her voice edged with indignation.

"That's right. I haven't." All this time—had he thought she was lying? Misrepresenting herself? Marrying him under false pretenses? Trying to trick him for some reason?

Perhaps she didn't have the right to resent him for not trusting her—but for heaven's sake, he trusted her with his niece. He trusted her with his home. "Maybe if you were around more often, you would have found plenty of reasons to believe me. You would have seen me telephoning my lawyer—"

"Pamela." He gathered her hands in his. "I haven't been around very much because I want you. And I kept asking myself, 'Who is this woman?' I had no answers, Pam—and it scared me, because even though I didn't know who the hell you were or what you were up to, I still wanted you."

"Well." She wished she could stay angry, but his candor wouldn't allow it. "Do you have answers now?"

"I guess I have enough." His hands were so much larger than hers, his fingers long and blunt, his palms thick and smooth. "Tonight, when you lit into me..." He grinned and shook his head. "It didn't matter anymore what your story was or how much evidence I'd seen. All that mattered was that you cared enough about Lizard to fight for her. You were ready to go the distance for her, just because you cared. And damn it, Pam, that made me want you even more. More than I thought I'd ever want a woman."

He kissed her again, slowly this time, not to shut her up, but to open her. His lips caressed hers, brushed and brushed again, teasing, enticing, melting the last vestiges of her resistance. Joe didn't want her because she was pretty. He didn't want her because he was horny. He wanted her because she'd cared enough about his niece—and about what was right—to fight him.

And that, she realized, was exactly what she wanted him to want her for.

He drew her onto his lap and circled her waist with his arms. His mouth opened against hers, and she welcomed the sweet invasion of his tongue. He slid his hand across her back, exploring the ridge of her spine, the width of her shoulders. "Pam," he whispered, "Pam..."

She felt his tension in his legs, in the motion of his hips as he shifted under her, in the swift beat of his heart as she skimmed her hands across his chest. Through his T-shirt she discerned the smooth lines of his torso, the sleek, firm muscles, the convulsive clenching of his abdomen when she approached the waistband of his jeans. And then he shifted again, lifting and turning her until she was lying on the cushions, under him.

His kisses grew hungrier, greedier. His body, stretched on top of hers, grew harder. He pulled her shirt free of her shorts and yanked it up over her head; she shoved his shirt up until it was bunched around his arms and then removed it. This wasn't just about Joe wanting her, she acknowledged. This was about *her* wanting *him,* wanting his trust, his friendship, his passion.

His chest was magnificent, the muscles cleanly defined, enhanced by an arrow of dark-blond hair aimed at his navel. She ran her hands over his skin, savoring its warmth, savoring even more the way his breath caught and then emerged in a low moan when she rubbed her fingertips across his nipples. He propped himself up so he wouldn't crush her, and she took advantage of the space between them to caress his shoulders, the arch of his ribs, the indentations below his stomach. When she once again reached the waist of his jeans, he nudged her hands aside and tugged open the snap of his fly, and then the zipper.

She peered up at him. Her eyes had grown accustomed to the dimness, and she could make out the silken tumble of his hair across his brow, the profound yearning in his gaze—yearning, and desire, and...trust. She saw it, recognized it, and knew that even if they were a total mismatch, even if this marriage was a sham, an understanding existed between her and Jonas Brenner, an empathy as precious and binding as love.

She skimmed her hands up his back and into his hair, and pulled him down to her. His lips crushed hers, placated hers, teased and coaxed and then abandoned hers to trail down her chin to her throat, to the satin shoulder strap of her bra. He wedged his hands beneath her to pluck open the clasp, then pulled the undergarment off and let it fall to the floor with their shirts. He continued grazing downward, pausing to suckle one breast and then the other. She dug her fingers deep into his hair, holding him to her, wanting his kisses never to end.

He nestled one leg between hers, and she rose instinctively, undulating against his thigh. She heard him groan, heard herself sigh as ripples of longing coursed down from her breasts to her hips. He rose to strip off her shorts and his jeans, and then settled back into her embrace, warm and naked and aroused.

Her hands roamed along his back, learning its supple contours. Her fingers skimmed the firm curve of his bottom, the lightly haired skin of his thighs. He sat back on his haunches, allowing her to touch him, and she did, stroking the steel-hard length of him and smiling as he closed his eyes and gasped and surged against her palms. *Control,* she thought, curling her fingers tighter. She loved being in control, exciting him until he seemed ready to burst.

But she had little time to enjoy her mastery over him. With a final shudder, he pulled her hands from him and pinned them to the cushions. Then he kissed her again, traced a line with his tongue along her midriff, across her belly and down to the points of her hipbones, to the tops of her thighs, to the soft curls of hair between her legs. His breath danced over her, his lips, his tongue, and her body lurched, hot, desperate, melting for him, for Jonas, her husband, her lover.

He slid back up her body, pulling her legs around him, and planted a fierce, fiery kiss on her lips as he plunged into her. She returned his kiss with the same ferocity, her hands tight around his shoulders, her body moving in rhythm with his. His thrusts urged her onward, closer and closer to the edge. She felt her control slipping, snapping, shattering. With a soft cry, she let go, soaring, falling, lost in the ecstasy Joe had given her.

After a long moment he sank onto her, spent and weary. His breath was harsh, his skin slick with sweat. She closed her arms loosely around him, savoring the pleasant heaviness of his body and her own exhaustion.

Another long moment and he eased onto his side, wrapping her in his arms and looping one leg around hers. She hadn't realized how narrow the sofa was, how much she needed him to keep her from tumbling onto the floor.

Her head rested snugly against his shoulder; her lips were less than an inch from his collarbone. Her arms were folded between their bodies; her hips stayed against his, even as he softened and slid from her.

Slowly, agonizingly, her consciousness returned. She heard the screech of the crickets, felt a humid, tropically scented breeze wrap around her body, remembered who she was, who Joe was and what they'd agreed to when they'd gotten married a month ago.

This wasn't love, she told herself. She didn't love him, she couldn't love him. It was a total mismatch.

His voice reached her from above, muffled by her hair: "Any chance you'll consider moving down the hall to my bedroom?"

"No." Her answer popped out before she could give much thought to his request, and she decided to stick with it. She needed to rely on her self-protective reflexes, and they were warning her that if she moved into Joe's bedroom, into his bed, she would make love with him every night, whenever she could. No man had ever made her feel what he'd made her feel just now—even if it was only physical, even if he wasn't her type, even if she didn't like his earring, even if…

"You didn't have to think long about it, did you?" he muttered, although she detected an undercurrent of wry amusement in his tone.

She *couldn't* let herself think long about it. If she thought at all, she would think about how good it felt to lie in Joe's enveloping arms, his glorious body sheltering hers. She would think about how she'd never in her life been given to casual sex, and this sex certainly hadn't been casual. Its very seriousness made it dangerous to her.

She would think about how Joe's lovemaking had eradicated her rationality, obliterated her composure, stampeded her self-control. Good God, she hadn't even stopped to ask him to use protection. She'd been too transported to care.

It simply couldn't happen again. Once his crisis and hers were resolved, she was going to be leaving him. That was the deal they'd agreed to.

"Joe." She sighed, wishing it didn't feel so downright comfortable to snuggle this way with him. "You know we haven't got a real marriage."

"I recall signing a legal piece of paper. Don't you?" Again she discerned the mixture of amusement and solemnity in his voice. "But what the hell. I'm not talking about marriage. I'm talking about sex."

And I can't talk about sex without thinking about love, she almost retorted. She forced herself to wriggle out of his embrace. Sitting up, she felt a chill that had nothing to do with the air temperature and everything to do with not having Joe's arms around her anymore.

He rolled onto his back and gazed up at her. His eyes were lucid, cutting through the midnight gloom like twin blue lasers. They seemed to slice right through her, penetrating all her defensive layers and burning into her soul.

"Jonas," she said sternly, trying but failing to disguise her exasperation, "you can't just barge into my life after ignoring me and Lizard for days and days and expect me to welcome you with open arms."

"But you did welcome me with open arms," he pointed out with infuriating logic. He undercut his words by gathering her hand in his and touching his mouth to her palm in a tender kiss. "Not that I'm complaining. This was great."

"It doesn't matter how great it was," she argued, withdrawing her hand. "And it doesn't matter that we signed a legal document. We're practically strangers."

He contemplated her charge and shrugged. "That could change," he said cryptically.

Only if he changed it, she thought. Only if he decided to participate in Lizard and Pamela's world. Only if he joined them on outings to the beach and helped them with Birdie's house and talked to them instead of hiding behind the newspaper at the breakfast table.

But if the change occurred, if he worked his way into their life, how would Pamela keep herself from making love with him again? How would she keep him from eroding her control? How would she keep herself from falling in love with him?

A total mismatch, she reminded herself, swinging her legs off the sofa and gathering up her clothes. Maybe she and Joe were a total mismatch, but right now, the worst mismatch she could think of was her head and her heart—her head warning her to keep her distance from Jonas Brenner and her heart aching to love the man she'd married.

CHAPTER THIRTEEN

LONG AFTER SHE'D LEFT the porch he was still sprawled out on the couch, enveloped in the wee-hours darkness. His body was spent but his mind was on red alert, transmitting all sorts of scrambled signals. Fortunately, he was a night owl. Decoding those signals might have been impossible for most people at that time of night, but not for Joe.

The signals, once he translated them, were telling him how wrong Pamela was for him. From the instant he'd seen her, he'd understood that she was too straitlaced, too prim and proper, too *everything* that had always turned him off in a woman—which was what had made her a perfect wife for his particular needs. And yet...in spite of it all, wrong just didn't seem to be the operative term at the moment.

"Right" didn't fit the bill, either. She was too skinny for his taste. She had hardly any upholstery on her. He'd been too conscious of the angles of her knees, the sculpture of her shoulders, the delicate protrusions of her ankle bones. Her breasts had flattened into nearly nothing when she'd been lying on her back, just two slight swells peaked with round, red, alluring nipples that begged to be kissed....

Start again, he admonished himself.

Too skinny and too pale, even after her day at the beach. Her complexion reminded him of milk. Or maybe cream. Then, too, her face had flushed a delicate pink when she'd been aroused, and her lips had turned crimson from his kisses. Those gloriously enticing nipples of hers had been the color of ripe berries and just as sweet, and her skin—that pale, pale skin—had felt like silk against his hands, and she'd felt even more like silk, a hot, tight sheath of silk, when he'd plunged into her....

Damn. He was hard again. And she was planning to spend the night in her own room, in her own bed. Probably with the door locked and a chair wedged under the knob, just in case.

Get back to right and wrong.

Okay. She'd been absolutely right to decline his invitation to spend the night with him. The agreement they'd cobbled together didn't include sex. And even if it had, Joe didn't have any rights when it came to making love with her, not after he'd treated her so coldly. If he'd wanted her to get friendly, he should have gone to the beach with her and Lizard today, should have made more of an effort to overcome his skepticism about her hit-man story, should have been a number one, first-class hubby to her. Signing that piece of paper hadn't given him special privileges. He'd signed it only because he had to have a woman like Pamela in his home, the way you had to have a refrigerator or dependable plumbing.

Requiring her services as if she were a household fixture guaranteed him nothing in the way of bedroom activity. What had happened on the porch just minutes ago had been a fluke. It wouldn't happen again.

What a tragic prospect. To hell with that stupid notion that Pamela wasn't his type. She'd definitely been his type when he'd kissed her, and touched her, and taken her body with his. Thinking about her now, running up a list of all her shortcomings and finding himself getting more and more aroused with each addition to the list indicated that she was as much his type as any woman had ever been.

You know we haven't got a real marriage, she'd said. A real marriage, he conceded as he pulled himself languorously off the sofa and tugged on his jeans, would obligate him to make a commitment. It would mean accepting as fact everything she'd told him about Mickey Mouse, or whatever the hit man's name was, and including himself in her life in all sorts of ways. It would require him to show up every day, no excuses.

He could do it. For another chance to experience the most incredible sex he'd ever had, sure, he could turn this thing into a real marriage—as long as Pamela gave him a chance.

And if the sex had been even half as good for her as it had been for him, the odds were pretty decent that she would.

"I'M GOING TO HELP YOU at Birdie's today," he announced over breakfast the next morning.

"Oh?" Pamela flicked a brief glance at him, then drank some coffee, hiding behind the mug. For the first time in the month they'd been married, she had monopolized the newspaper. Joe had come downstairs to find her immersed in the paper, devouring news of foreign insurrections and international politics along with a slice of whole-wheat toast and an orange sliced into wedges.

Lizard was on the screened porch, constructing her version of the Taj Mahal out of modeling clay—or maybe it was supposed to be a hippopotamus. Joe couldn't tell, and he was too tactful to ask. As it was, he didn't even want to acknowledge the fact that his niece was creating a clay sculpture of any sort just a few feet from where, last night, he and Pamela had created the beast with two backs.

Nor did he want to think about the fact that one of the beast's heads was right that minute facing him across the breakfast table—or would be facing him if she ever lifted her nose out of the damned paper.

She seemed to be laboring hard to avoid eye contact with him. Her effort not to look at him allowed him an unabashed view of her. He could stare at her for as long as she refused to acknowledge his staring. As he sipped his coffee, he took in the straight white-blond fringe of her hair, her elusive eyes, the tension in her pursed lips, the taut line of her throat.

Had he actually considered her too skinny? Too pale? Not his type?

"The way I figure it," he continued, after her silence became unendurable, "is that if you're really tearing down Birdie's walls, you could probably use a little help."

"We're doing all right without you," Pamela said tersely.

"Since when is 'all right' good enough?"

She flashed a silver-eyed look his way. She seemed to be framing her reply. "Is that a rhetorical question, Joe, or do you really want to help us?"

"I really want to help you."

He wished her gaze wasn't so guarded, so dubious. Then again, who was he to resent her for distrusting him? Hadn't he been busy distrusting her for the past few weeks?

She fingered the newspaper nervously. The pages made a faint rustling sound. "It's messy work," she warned.

He chuckled, but the laughter carried an edge. "Oh,

well, in that case, forget I offered. A gentleman like me would never want to get messy.''

"Jonas…" She sighed, and he saw a hot blush rise in her cheeks, as it had last night when she'd come while he was deep inside her. "Forgive me for being suspicious, but why, all of a sudden, do you want to do this?''

"You know damned well why," he answered calmly, then took a healthy swig of his coffee. He was actually feeling far less confident than he sounded. Not that she could ban him from Birdie's house, but if she decided to crank up the drawbridge at his first attempt to march across the moat, getting her into his bed was going to be more difficult than he'd imagined.

"All right," she relented, then frowned in deep concentration as she perused an article about a budget crunch in the state's welfare system. Her abrupt surrender, mixed with a tantalizing measure of evasiveness, appealed to him as much as her pink cheeks and her bony shoulders and the small swells of her breasts beneath the fabric of her loose-fitting yellow T-shirt.

He'd messed up last night with Pamela, and he had no regrets. He certainly wouldn't mind getting messy with her today.

SHE HAD TO ADMIT he was an enormous help.

They stood side by side in the erstwhile enclosed porch, removing huge chunks of the wall that had once separated it from the kitchen. They had sent Birdie and Lizard, along with most of Birdie's cats, across the street to Joe's house to occupy themselves with Lizard's herb garden. The absence of Birdie and Lizard had proved as useful to Pamela as the presence of Joe.

The air was warm and cloudy with plaster dust. Joe had supplied Pamela with an old duck-billed cap of his, and he wore one himself. He'd also provided bandannas for them to tie around their noses and mouths to keep from inhaling the dust.

Wearing the bandannas prevented all but the most necessary talk. When a slab of plasterboard came loose, Joe lugged it out to the backyard, freeing Pamela for the more painstaking work of scraping excess plaster from the counter and removing shreds of drywall from the vertical studs. Much as she hated to admit it, they made a good team.

Just like last night.

A treacherous thought. She tried not to pay attention to Joe's strength, his lithe movements, the powerful flexing of his back as he hoisted the heavy debris and hauled it outside. She tried not to notice the beautiful blue of his eyes, visible in the space between his improvised face mask and the visor of his cap. She averted her eyes.

"Why did you sha-she-booty?" he asked.

She lowered her chisel and scowled at him. "Huh?"

He set down the slab of drywall he'd been holding and enunciated more carefully through his bandanna. "Why did you decide to do this?"

She turned from him to stare at the tattered remains of the wall. She could have told him she'd done it to make Birdie's house more livable, or because it was the closest she could come to practicing her profession while she was living in Key West. She could have told him she'd done it because she wanted to work hard, sweat hard, keep Lizard busy and keep her mind off her own problems. All of that would have been true.

"It was something to do," she mumbled, then read his perplexed look and repeated her answer, mouthing the syllables clearly through the soft cotton fabric.

"I was thinking, maybe it was kind of—what's the word—sublimation?"

She was not going to discuss the matter with him. "If I had anything to sublimate, it was fear."

"Are you afraid of me?"

She shot him a quick look. He appeared to be inspecting a vertical stud, but she wasn't fooled. "I'm afraid of Mick Morrow. Or are you planning to kill me, too?"

He laughed. It didn't sound like laughter through the bandanna, but she could tell by the humor in his eyes and the motion of his shoulders that he was enjoying a good chuckle. "Hey, sweetheart, dead ladies don't do a damned thing for me. I want you very much alive."

She felt her cheeks grow hot beneath the broad triangle of cloth. A laugh escaped her, partly from embarrassment and partly from relief at being able to talk to Joe again and relax in his company. Even if he wasn't the man of her dreams—although last night he'd done an estimable job of redefining those dreams—she hadn't liked being frozen out by him.

"What we're going to do," she explained, changing the subject, "is break down the door frame and leave this open." She paced to the end of the counter and gestured with her hands to indicate the opening. "We'll put a half wall behind the sink to hide the plumbing. It's going to look wonderful."

"I think it will," he agreed, scanning the area with his gaze. "You've got a knack for this sort of thing, don't you?"

"It's what I do best."

"I'm not so sure of that," he teased, then grew still. His eyebrows dipped in concentration. "What's that knocking?"

"What knocking?"

He touched his index finger to his bandanna to silence her. She heard it, then—a rhythmic rapping sound.

"One of the cats, maybe?"

"Whatever it is, it's at the front door," he said, tossing down the hammer he'd been holding and heading down the crooked, narrow corridor to the front of the house.

Pamela hurried after him, ready for an excuse to take a break. They'd been working for more than an hour, and without air-conditioning, Birdie's house was beginning to feel like a sauna.

By the time she caught up with Joe, he had the front door open. Two people stood on the small porch. The man had on an elegant, unstructured suit of beige linen, the trousers pleated and the sleeves of the jacket rolled up one cuff. Despite the summer heat, his charcoal-gray shirt was buttoned up to his Adam's apple, although he wasn't wearing a tie. His dark hair was so impeccably groomed it might have been clipped with manicure scissors, one strand at a time.

The woman beside him was equally impressive. She wore a plain black shift that was so simple in its lines, Pamela knew it had to have cost a fortune. Her hair was shorter than the man's, and it had been moussed into a profoundly chic arrangement around her face. Both she and the man wore horn-rimmed sunglasses with small, round lenses. The woman also wore bright red lipstick.

They looked to Pamela like refugees from some terribly precious boutique. Having spent the past month in Key West, she'd been lulled into the prevalent belief that shorts and T-shirts were the ultimate in fashion. She hadn't seen anyone dressed with such slavish deference to haute couture since she'd left Seattle.

The stylish couple fell back a step at the sight of the

two grungy, dust-covered workers. "Joyce, Lawton," Joe mumbled through his bandanna, then tugged it off. "So, you finally decided to roll into town." He doffed his cap and hurled it down the hall behind him.

"We arrived last night," the woman said. Pamela wished she could see the woman's eyes, but the lenses of her sunglasses were too dark. "We're staying at the Reach Resort. We went to your house. A very peculiar old woman was there."

"She had peacock feathers fastened to her sleeves," said the man.

"There was a little girl with her. She had feathers braided into her hair. They were stomping barefoot in a mud puddle at the back of your house, carrying bunches of dandelions and chanting strange things. They said we'd find you here." The woman regarded Joe critically, her bright red lips pressed together in disapproval.

"Yeah, well..." Joe dusted his hands on the seat of his jeans and extended his right hand to the man, who shook it without much enthusiasm. "That little barefoot girl is Lizard. I guess you didn't recognize her."

The woman turned and glared at the man. "I told you that was her."

"She didn't look anything like the photo we got last Christmas." The man glowered at Joe. "Whose picture did you send us at Christmas?"

"That was Lizard, without the feathers."

"Elizabeth," the woman corrected him.

"She prefers to be called Lizard." Joe eased Pamela's bandanna down over her chin, then slid his arm around her waist. "Pam, these are the Prescotts, Lizard's aunt and uncle from California. Joyce, Lawton, I'd like you to meet my wife, Pam."

A long, stunned silence ensued. "Your wife?" the woman scoffed.

"Yeah. My wife. Lizard's aunt by marriage."

Joyce glared at Lawton again. "Why weren't we informed of this?"

Lawton, in turn, glowered at Joe. "Why weren't we informed of this?"

"I didn't know you cared. Anyway, I figured if I'd sent you an invitation to the wedding, you might have felt you had to buy us a gift. I thought I'd do you a favor and spare you the expense."

Pamela caught the glint of amusement in his eyes. He ought to have been baring his teeth and growling; these were the people who wanted to take Lizard away from him.

It was her job to see that they didn't. In spite of the ghastly first impression she must be making, she wasn't going to let the Prescotts daunt her. After all, she was a professional, an upwardly mobile woman with two university degrees. A supercilious couple costumed by Armani couldn't faze her.

"How do you do," she said cordially, extending her hand. "Jonas has told me so much about you."

"He hasn't told us anything about you," Joyce retorted.

Joe opened his mouth to respond, but Pam answered for herself. "There really isn't much to tell. We met, we fell in love and we got married."

"The impact this could have on Elizabeth—"

"Has been quite positive," Pamela said with breezy certainty. "She's been happier than ever."

"She has feathers in her hair," Lawton muttered.

"And I have plaster dust in mine," Pamela said sweetly, pulling off her cap and riffling her fingers through her sweat-damp hair. "That's why God gave us shampoo."

"As you can see," Joe broke in, "we're in the middle of some work here, doing repairs on the peculiar old lady's house, because she's a good friend of ours. So, Lawton, Joyce—" he nodded to each in turn "—it's great seeing you, and why don't you have your lawyer call my lawyer."

The four of them squared off for another awkward minute, and then the Prescotts beat a retreat. Only when they'd reached the Infiniti parked at the curb did Pamela feel Joe's hand furl into a fist at the small of her back.

"Charming folks," she said.

"They've got money," Joe grunted, as if that would be the deciding factor in who won custody of Lizard.

"They didn't even recognize Liz."

"All they've seen of her for the past three years is snapshots. And they're right—I cleaned her up some for the Christmas photo."

"Jonas, look at them! Can you imagine them letting Lizard plant herbs in their backyard?"

He sent her a quick, ironic look and then spun around and entered the house. "I'd better call Mary DiNardi and let her know the boom's about to fall," he said.

Pamela lingered in the doorway for a moment. She could guess what that look of his said: that when she'd first walked into the Shipwreck one month ago, she'd been no more prepared to raise a child than the Prescotts were today.

But she'd changed. She'd put away her silk blouses and tailored trousers. She'd forgotten about nail polish and nights at the ballet. She hadn't listened to Mozart in a month; she hadn't eaten steamed asparagus or sipped a properly aged Bordeaux. But she'd learned how to tramp through the mud and herd an unruly child through a store, how to tune out the whining and accept Lizard's candor without taking offense.

If she could learn, why couldn't the Prescotts?

They didn't have the same incentive she had, she answered herself. They would be doing it only for themselves. Pamela wasn't doing it for herself, or even just for Lizard.

She was doing it for Joe.

Not because she'd made a deal with him, she realized. Not because he'd offered her his name as a shield. Not because he trusted her—she wasn't entirely sure he did. Not even because of last night, which Pamela was still convinced had been a major mistake.

She was mothering Lizard, scolding her, finger painting, collecting sea gull feathers on the beach with her and staying up late at night to discuss her well-being with Joe because, somehow, Lizard and her uncle had come to matter more to Pamela than her expensive condominium and everything that went with her former lifestyle.

In the past eight years, she had designed buildings, received plaudits, earned bonuses in her work—but that had all come easily to her. She had spent her life training for it, studying, developing her innate talents as a draftsman and an artist. Maybe she had a gene for architecture somewhere inside her, but everything she'd ever accomplished had been well within her abilities, completely under her control.

Lizard was different. Dealing with her didn't come naturally to Pamela; she had no training, no talent, little control over what Lizard did and even less control over how Pamela herself felt about it. But she was doing it for no other reason than to make another person happy.

Two other people: Lizard and Joe. Her temporary family. She was doing it for them.

And no snooty, swanky interlopers were going to convince her to give in to their wishes without a fight.

CHAPTER FOURTEEN

THE PRESCOTTS' ARRIVAL on Key West resembled a solar eclipse, blocking out Pamela's other concerns and throwing the world into shadow. She had no time to worry about her relationship with Joe, her situation back home in Seattle, or even her plans for Birdie's house. Her thoughts zeroed in on one subject only: the battle for Lizard.

Joe spent the afternoon at Mary DiNardi's office on Eaton Street, plotting strategies and working out schedules. Pamela spent the afternoon with Lizard at the beach. She supposed there were things she ought to be doing—cleaning the house, tidying the yard, buying Lizard a wardrobe of respectable feather-free clothing—but somehow, none of those activities seemed as important as making sure Lizard had a happy afternoon.

Pamela wasn't used to exerting herself to make a child happy. She tried to remember what her life had been like not so very long ago when all her energies had been devoted to her career, her adult friends, her memberships in museums and subscriptions to the opera. In those days, she used to grimace when she saw children entering a theater with her or sitting near her on an airplane, because she knew they would be noisy and disruptive. She used to pride herself on the order in her life, the dependability of her surroundings. She used to go for days—for years—without ever considering the significance of pink food.

But now that placid existence had vanished. Pamela could no longer control the flow of events that coursed around her. She was geared to the needs of others—most particularly, the needs of a demanding, occasionally obnoxious and chronically messy little girl. And the strange part was, Pamela was too busy worrying about that little girl's needs to mind.

The phone was ringing when they got back from the beach late in the afternoon. During the walk home, Lizard had groused about having to keep her swimsuit on, but Pamela had stood firm in her view that Lizard had to behave modestly—at least when it came to her body.

Modesty in all other matters seemed beyond Lizard. "I'm the smartest kid I know," she boasted when Pamela expressed surprise at her ability to identify the different types of palms bordering the beach. "I'm smarter than Megan, even. She's my best friend, but I'm smarter than her. Ask anybody. Even Birdie, she'll tell you how smart I am. And she knows boo doo, so she oughtta know."

Pamela heard the shrill, rhythmic peal through an open window and hustled Lizard up the front walk. "Maybe you're smart, but right now you're as slow as molasses. That could be your Uncle Joe calling us. Let's pick up the pace."

Just to be contrary, Lizard chose that moment to drop the bag containing her beach toys and chase after a butterfly flitting among the rhododendrons. Ignoring her, Pamela raced up the front steps to the porch, unlocked the door, charged into the kitchen and dived for the phone, eager to answer before Joe hung up.

Unfortunately, it wasn't Joe. "This is Mona Whitley," the social worker's voice chirped through the line.

Dear Lord, Pamela thought a few minutes later, after Ms. Whitley had explained to her that in order for her to observe the Prescotts interacting with Lizard, Pamela would have to host a get-together with Lizard and her long-lost relatives tomorrow morning at nine o'clock.

Lying through her teeth, Pamela assured Ms. Whitley that this would be no trouble whatsoever. She glanced at her watch. After five. Lizard was still outside; through the kitchen window Pamela could see her, armed with her plastic bow-and-arrow set, blithely firing arrows at the butterfly. Pamela considered calling Lizard inside for a bath, but wrestling the kid into the bathtub was more than Pamela could handle right now. The realization that Lizard's life—or, more accurately, *Joe's* life—was about to cave in, zapped Pamela of energy.

She recalled the last time Mona Whitley had paid a call on the Brenners. Pamela had knocked herself out to make the house and Lizard presentable. Joe had knocked himself out to convince Ms. Whitley that he and Pamela were madly in love, even though, at that time, Joe could barely tolerate her.

Obviously that had changed. Especially if last night counted for anything. Would he kiss her again in front of Ms. Whitley? Did he *want* to kiss her again? Did she want him to? Would kissing him lead to something more once Ms. Whitley and the dreaded Prescotts had gone? Would it throw her emotions into even more disarray?

Had Pamela ever wasted so much mental effort trying to figure out a man before?

Since Joe hadn't called her, she telephoned him at the Shipwreck. After three rings, Brick answered. "Hi, it's Pam Brenner," she said. "Is Jonas there?"

Brick grunted something and set the phone on the bar with a loud thunk.

She heard the sounds of early tavern traffic, a low babble of voices and the muffled strain of music from the jukebox. She recognized the song at once: "Stand by Me." It sent a tremor of longing through her. Life had seemed so complicated the day she had married Joe—but in fact it had been much simpler. Now life *was* complicated, but one thing was crystal clear.

She had to help keep Joe and Lizard together. She had to stand by Joe.

Really, very simple.

She heard his voice through the line. "Pam?"

"I just got a call from Mona Whitley," she said, then reported on the following day's agenda.

Joe cursed. "I've been waiting for this to happen for so long," he confessed. "Now that it's finally in the works, I can't stand it."

"I know." She sensed the sadness and frustration in his tone and felt a powerful desire to reassure him. "Joe, those people—the Prescotts—they aren't cut out for dealing with Lizard. It doesn't take much perception to realize they aren't child-oriented."

"They're rich," he said laconically.

"So what? You're not exactly poor."

"I could shave every day and I'd still be a bum."

"No," she said, refusing to let him label himself the way she'd once labeled him. "You're a good father. Or uncle. No, *father.* That's what you are to Lizard."

"Yeah, sure," he muttered.

"What did your lawyer say?"

He cursed again. "In twenty words or less? She said the law was a funny thing, and she hoped I could hang on to my sense of humor."

"We'll get through this, Jonas," Pamela promised. "I'll do whatever I can to convince the courts that Lizard belongs with you."

He said nothing for a minute, then murmured, "Thank you." Just two small words, yet they conveyed so much. She heard the catch in his voice, the slight waver, and felt a closeness to him far more profound than the closeness she'd felt during those few intense minutes last night when her body and his were locked together in love.

This was it, the main event, the reason Joe had taken her in and given her his name. She would do whatever she could, and he would trust her.

"Come home early," she urged him. "You'll need a good night's sleep."

"I'll try," he said, and hung up.

Pamela lowered the phone into the cradle and let out a long breath. She felt oddly shaken. The last part of their conversation had been strangely personal, the sort of solicitous back-and-forth a husband and wife engaged in.

She reminded herself once more of the terms of her marriage to Joe. They weren't going to become involved. Their wedding was strictly for show. Behind closed doors they would remain separate.

When had she lost control of the ground rules? When had she lost control of her own feelings? Why did she care, to the depths of her soul, what happened to Joe and his niece? Why did she feel her heart wrenching in sympathy for him? Why did it seem as if his losing Lizard would hurt Pamela as much as it did him?

And however it ended up, once it was all behind her and Joe, how would she ever be able to find her way back to the life she had loved in Seattle?

A thump at the window startled her out of her ruminations. She glanced across the kitchen and saw the suction tip of one of Lizard's arrows sticking to the outside surface of the pane.

She should have been incensed at Lizard's wild play. The window could have been shattered, for heaven's sake. Lizard could have gotten cut by flying glass.

But all Pamela thought, as she strolled to the back door to call the girl inside for her bath, was that Lizard was a splendid shot.

THE NEXT COUPLE OF DAYS slid by in a blur. Joe could hardly remember going to the Shipwreck, chatting with the customers, tapping the kegs and tallying the receipts. All he remembered, as he reviewed the period since the Prescotts had shown their hoity-toity faces on his island, were the signs, as bright as the neon lights on Duval Street, that he was going to lose Lizard.

Joyce and Lawton were just so damned nice to Lizard. The morning they came to play with her under the watchful eye of Mona Whitley, Joyce adopted a cloying singsong voice and made such a fuss about each and every one of Lizard's ratty old stuffed animals, Joe couldn't believe the kid was taken in by it. Usually Lizard had a built-in hypocrisy detector. But she fell for Joyce's gushing: "Oh, so this is your stuffed manatee! Why, isn't he just adorable! What's his name? May I shake his hand—or is it a flipper?"

A few minutes of that, and Joe was ready to lose his breakfast. He wondered why Lizard played along, but the fact that she did made him even more certain the court was going to decide in favor of the Prescotts.

Sickened by the prospect—to say nothing of Joyce's saccharine behavior, Joe headed downstairs, where he discovered Lawton and Mona Whitley seated on the living room couch, drinking Joe's coffee and yakking like long-lost friends. When they weren't exploring their shared passion for golf, Lawton was describing the school system where he and Joyce lived. "The Hillsborough public schools are among the best in the country," Lawton bragged. "But with state budget cutbacks, we might choose to send Elizabeth to private school instead. There are several fine preparatory schools within a reasonable distance of our house. Elizabeth would receive the best education money can buy. Do you think she'd like to be called Betsy? She seems like such a Betsy to me."

"She likes to be called *Lizard*," Joe interjected, which won him a reproachful look from Mona Whitley.

That was the first day, a day Joe dealt with by heading for the Shipwreck as early as he could and submerging himself in his work. He insisted on staying until closing time, hopeful that Pamela would be asleep by the time he got home. He didn't want to have to talk to her, to reveal how miserable he was. He didn't want to confront the truth that it would be much easier for him to get through the night if he had her in his arms.

The following day, the Prescotts took Lizard out for a while, with Mona Whitley chaperoning. "They're going to win," Joe groaned to Pamela once he no longer had to smile and wave at his niece as his loathsome in-laws ushered her down the front walk to their rented Infiniti. "They're going to take the Liz Kid away from me."

Pamela patted his shoulder and said, "We're not going to let them." She was wearing a pair of pleated culottes and a neat button-front shirt, obviously an effort to compete sartorially with the Prescotts. Joe hadn't seen her dress so well since she'd moved in with him and learned what life with Lizard could be like. Turning from the door, she said, "I'm going to change into some real clothes and then take a run to the supermarket. We're out of strawberry yogurt. Is there anything you want me to pick up for you while I'm out?"

He didn't want food. He wanted...*her*. Not her pity, not—at that particular moment—her body, but her forgiveness. Before she could reach the stairs he snagged her wrist, halting her. "Listen, Pam—I've been a real jerk since the Prescotts showed up."

"No more of a jerk than usual," she teased, although there wasn't much humor in her voice.

"I mean it. I don't know how you can stand being around me. I sure can't stand being around myself."

She smiled, a sad, beautiful smile. "The only thing I can't stand is your negativity. I haven't known you very long, but I think it's safe to say pessimism isn't your style. I wish you'd stop assuming the worst."

He gazed at her in the late-morning light. She appeared completely transformed from the frightened, waif-like creature who'd entered his bar little more than a month ago, searching for a husband to hide behind. Her eyes were bright with courage, her cheeks elegantly hollow, her hair brushed back and held behind her ears with tortoise-shell clips. The top button of her shirt was undone, and he could see the delicate flare of her collarbones at the base of her throat.

For one strange, fleeting moment, he found himself thinking that the worst thing in the world would be to lose *her*.

The notion was gone as soon as it registered, but it left in its wake a quiet warmth that comforted him more than all of Pamela's words, speeches and smiles. Joe and his wife were friends. Pamela had become his partner in a very real sense.

He pulled her gently into his arms and dropped a light kiss onto her brow. She tilted her face to look at him, and he realized that, while a few minutes with Pamela on the nearest horizontal surface would do a hell of a lot to improve his mood, holding her was nearly as effective.

"I bet you didn't realize what you were taking on when you married me," he murmured.

She met his steady gaze without flinching. "I was taking on a guy with an earring and a niece."

"And a double shot of negativity." He shook his head and grinned. "Not to mention a couple of scary in-laws."

"At least some of your in-laws are pleasant."

Thinking of Joyce and all the other pompous, snobbish relatives of his late sister's husband, Joe couldn't come up with a single pleasant in-law in the bunch. He frowned at Pamela's remark.

"Your mother- and father-in-law," she explained. "They're quite nice."

"Oh. Yeah." He cracked a smile. "They're three thousand miles away, and I have nothing to do with them. Of course I love them."

Pamela eased out of his loose embrace and sighed. "I think you'd like them, Joe. I miss them."

"Why don't you give them a call?" he suggested. Here he was, the only family she had for miles—unless you counted Lizard—and he'd done nothing to make her feel as if she belonged. "I'll even say hi to them," he added with a smile. It was the least he could do for Pamela.

She shook her head. "I haven't spoken to them since

I left Seattle. I was afraid it might put them in danger. Mick Morrow could pressure them to tell him where I am, and…'' She shuddered. ''It's just safer if they don't know anything, so I haven't spoken to them at all.''

''Why don't you call them now?'' Even if Pamela didn't think she was out of danger, Joe knew she was. That police detective in Seattle had convinced him.

Again she shook her head. ''No. But maybe I'll call my lawyer. I haven't talked to him in a while, what with the Prescotts showing up and all.'' She glanced at her watch. ''I could probably catch him at his desk. He tends to get into his office early.''

She departed for the kitchen, leaving him to shake off his lust. He stared through the front screen door at the empty yard, trying to guess what the Prescotts were doing with Lizard right now, what Mona Whitley was scribbling in her blasted notebook, what she would report to the judge.

''*What?*'' Pamela shrieked from the kitchen. ''My God! When?''

Joe sprinted down the hall to the kitchen, wondering what had set her off. When she pivoted to face him, the telephone receiver still pressed to her ear, her smile was brighter than the Florida sun. She looked utterly thrilled—and more gorgeous than a woman who was off limits to him ought to look.

''What's up?'' he mouthed.

She held up her hand, signaling that she would tell him in a minute. ''You're absolutely sure? And he's going to stay there?'' She listened for a few seconds, then erupted into a joyous little jig. ''Okay, okay,'' she said into the phone. ''Of course I'll sit tight.'' She recited Joe's phone number, then said, ''Keep me posted. And give my love to my parents. Make sure they know about this." She hung up, stared at the phone in disbelief for a minute, then launched herself into Joe's arms. "Mick Morrow's in jail!"

"Huh?" The impact of her mad dash into his arms knocked the breath out of him—or maybe it was just that her nearness, when she was so radiant and jubilant, took his breath away.

"Mick Morrow. The hit man. He's in jail!"

"Really?"

"He was stopped on a traffic violation, and when he refused to let them search his car they impounded it. They found a gun, so they rescinded his bail and locked him up!" She started another jig, but with her arms around Joe, it mutated into a kind of jitterbug.

"They found a gun on him?" Joe didn't think that particular detail was cause for mirth.

"But now he's locked up until his new trial. I'm safe, Joe. I'm safe!"

Joe was glad for her...but not without certain misgivings. Like, for instance, what were the implications of this hit man driving around with a gun? Had he been trying to track her down when he'd committed the traffic violation? How the hell had he gotten hold of a gun if he was under police surveillance? Had he intended to use it on Pamela?

If he had, he wasn't going to have the chance, thank God. She was thousands of miles away, while he was behind bars.

And Joe was still going to lose Lizard. Everything would work out perfectly for Pamela. She would return to Seattle, and Joe was going to wind up alone.

Being alone had suited him well enough for the first thirty years of his life—until he'd discovered that playing daddy for a little girl was more fun than being alone.

Then he'd discovered that marriage could turn a guy inside out and upside down, make him more willing to go the distance, to have faith in a woman, to take a chance on her....

Losing Pamela and Lizard at the same time was going to devastate him.

"So..." He extricated himself from Pamela's embrace, hating to remove her hands from him but knowing he had to. "The creep's in jail. What happens next?"

"My attorney will let me know," she said, still twinkling, reminding Joe of a sparkler on the Fourth of July. "In all likelihood, they'll push up the date of Morrow's new trial. I'll have to go back to Seattle to testify, but this time there won't be any slipups. They'll do the job right."

"So, you're going back to Seattle."

"For the trial," she said, abruptly growing sober as the implications sank in. "Lizard's fate will be decided before the DA in Seattle can start a new trial there. I'll be with you for the custody hearing. And if you win, and the Prescotts appeal, I'll be back in time for that. I'll only have to be in Seattle a couple of days." She peered up at Joe. Judging by her frown, he knew she was worried by what she saw in his face. "I'll get you through the custody battle, Jonas. I promised I would, and I will."

If he won. But what if he didn't? Unlike the Prescotts, he couldn't afford to drag the process through endless appeals. He would lose Lizard, and Pamela would have no reason to stay in Key West and pretend to be his wife. She would go back to Seattle to testify—and she wouldn't come back.

Negativity. Pessimism. That about summed up Joe's mood.

Without a word, he stalked out of the kitchen, no longer able to be in the same room with a woman whose elation was directly related to her chance to clear out of his life. He was angry, resentful, envious—and by storming out of the room he was acting like an ass.

But he wasn't going to stick around and let her see his heart break.

LIZARD CAME HOME that afternoon with a Barbie doll. "How nice," Pamela said through gritted teeth as Lizard displayed her prize. "Did the Prescotts buy that doll for you?"

Lizard—weed gardener, skinny dipper and feather fanatic—grinned proudly. "Uh-huh! Look at this, Pam. You can put these earrings on her by just sticking 'em through her ear. Isn't that awesome?" She proceeded to poke a doll-size earring through Barbie's ear, as if she were skewering one of Birdie's voodoo dolls. "I'm gonna name her Snoot, and tomorrow I'm gonna tape feathers all over her. She can be a biker."

"Wonderful." Pamela regarded the doll, still new and virginal in her dream-date dress, and sighed. She herself had owned a Barbie when she'd been not much older than Lizard. She had adored dressing her doll in a variety of outfits, fitting tiny doll shoes onto Barbie's permanently high-heeled feet and parading her around the house. But Pamela had been a very different child from Lizard.

What if Lizard discovered she actually loved playing with a fashion doll more than traipsing around Birdie's house with an army of cats, or gobbling pink victuals, or romping in the mud? What if Lizard turned into a child like Pamela—the kind who would thrive in the affluent suburban surroundings of her aunt and uncle's home in California?

"Did you have fun with the Prescotts?" Pamela asked carefully.

"Yeah. They bought me lick-rish, too."

Pamela watched Lizard romp back outside. She was glad Joe had left for the Shipwreck early, if only so he would be spared the sight of his niece waxing rhapsodic about the Prescotts' generosity.

Pamela's euphoria over Mick Morrow's incarceration had been short-lived. After Joe had left for work, she'd telephoned the DA's office in Seattle. He'd confirmed her lawyer's news and told her he was hoping to put together a new trial within a month or so. "Now that you're safe from Mr. Morrow," he said, "perhaps you'd be willing to tell me your whereabouts, so I can contact you when it's time to bring you back to Seattle to testify."

Pamela supplied him with Joe's address and telephone number. "I'm using the name Pamela Brenner now," she added.

"Oh?"

"Didn't my lawyer tell you? I got married."

"Yes, he mentioned something about that. A phony marriage, to help hide your identity. Well, you won't have to worry about hiding anymore."

Pamela nodded. In a sense, she felt she'd stopped hiding the minute she'd told the DA she was married. Now it was truly public information, not just in Key West but in Seattle. Now her marriage wasn't just legal; it was *real*.

Or maybe it had become real the night Joe had made love to her.

No. That had been an aberration, a bit of foolishness.

And if it had been an incredibly pleasurable aberration and foolishness, so what? A real marriage had to be grounded in love, and Joe had never said anything about love.

Refusing to dwell on her own tortured feelings about Joe, Pamela went off in search of Lizard. Exiting through the screened porch, she spotted the kid in the weed garden, taping two bright yellow dandelion blossoms to her doll's bosom. A third blossom was taped between the doll's legs, giving Barbie the appearance of a stripper about halfway through her act.

Pamela stifled a chuckle. Apparently acquiring a fashion doll had failed to civilize Lizard. "Nice outfit," she joked. "What do you think your Aunt Joyce would say if she saw it?"

"She'd hate it," Lizard predicted sagely.

Pamela allowed herself a small grin at Lizard's perceptiveness. "You're right. I think you'd better make sure Barbie—I mean Snoot—is always fully clothed when your Aunt Joyce is around."

"Why? I don't care if she hates it. She hates lots of neat stuff."

"Oh?"

"Like, she hates seaweed when it piles up on the sand and gets all smelly. She told me she hates that. And she hates the Three Stooges. She says they're dumb. Uncle Joe and I watch the Three Stooges all the time. And she hates the name Lizard. She always calls me Betsy, which is gross. And she hates strawberry yogurt. She's icky."

"She loves you very much," Pamela said, not thrilled at having to defend the woman to Lizard.

"Well…" Lizard taped a fourth yellow fluff of dandelion onto Barbie's pert ponytail. "If she loves me, she oughtta love my doll."

"I agree. But you should respect her feelings about certain things, Lizard. It's important that she sees what a good job Uncle Joe has done raising you."

"He didn't raise me. He's just my uncle."

"And he loves you, too, maybe even more than your Aunt Joyce. So it's important to make sure your Aunt Joyce and Uncle Lawton and Ms. Whitley all realize that Uncle Joe has taught you how to respect others and be polite."

Lizard eyed her askance. "That's icky."

"Courtesy isn't icky."

"No—I mean, all those people who have to realize things. It's icky. You know what? I'm gonna tattoo Snoot. You know what a tattoo is?"

Pamela suppressed a shudder. "Yes. How do you happen to know about them?"

"Kitty has one on her boob. Right about…*here*," she said, pointing to the left side of the doll's breast, just above the edge of the dandelion brassiere. "She let me see it once. It was neat. I think I'm gonna tattoo Snoot."

"I think you're going to take a bath," Pamela refuted her. "And then you and I are going to have some supper. How about tuna salad?" She didn't feel like making a big meal. The afternoon was hot and muggy, smothering her appetite. She felt overloaded, inundated by events: Mick Morrow's capture, her impending testimony, Joe's impending custody case, Lizard's gruesome treatment of her doll. Mixed together and garnished with a discussion of tattoos, the concoction made Pamela queasy.

"Okay," Lizard said, swinging her doll by its ponytail and jogging toward the porch. "But make sure you put the right amount of mayonnaise in. If you put in too much, it doesn't look pink. And I want a bagel, too." With that, she disappeared into the house.

Pamela gazed after her, feeling a tug that was part pride, part protectiveness and part something she might have called mother-love if she believed herself capable of maternal sentiments. Lizard was exasperating—but in a perverse way, that was one of her most appealing traits. She was uncouth and sassy and, in a word, *icky*—and Pamela honestly loved her for it.

The Prescotts would never view Lizard's bad behavior as lovable. Neither, Pamela feared, would the court. Ms. Whitley was going to declare Lizard a maniac and tear her from Joe.

Pamela couldn't let that happen. She would have to work on Lizard some more—make sure she scrubbed behind her ears in the bath, make sure she dressed neatly, make sure she didn't call her Barbie doll "Snoot" or Joyce Prescott "icky" in front of hostile witnesses. Pamela had married Joe for better or worse—something along that line, anyway—and she was now entering the "for worse" stretch with him.

She was simply going to have to make things work out.

"I'M COMING TO the Shipwreck with you," Pamela said.

"You? At the Shipwreck?"

Four days had passed since the Prescotts had come to town. Four days of sunny skies and apprehension, of meetings with Mary DiNardi and high tension in the house, of Joe spending as much time at the Shipwreck as he had when he'd been avoiding Pamela.

He wasn't avoiding her now. Over breakfast he reviewed with Pamela everything his lawyer had told him. He seemed to value Pamela's opinions. He definitely valued her ability to get Lizard to dress in pretty matching shorts and tops and to braid either all or none of her hair instead of just plaiting the locks at her ears.

Yet he sought refuge at the Shipwreck every night. Pamela doubted he was drinking there. In fact, the last time she'd seen him partake of liquor—a single bottle of beer—was the night he'd wound up making love to her.

She willfully closed her mind to the image. She didn't want to think about it, or dream about it, or find herself wishing for a recurrence. She didn't want to love him.

The Prescotts had taken Lizard to their resort for dinner tonight. Joe had protested, claiming that they were getting too much access to Lizard, but his lawyer had insisted that it was important for Lizard to establish some ties with the Prescotts, just in case she wound up in their custody. Hearing his own advocate mention such a possibility had sent Joe into a funk.

Pamela had no illusions that she could cheer him up by accompanying him to the bar. But she didn't want to sit home alone, worrying about him. She would accompany him to the Shipwreck, spend a couple of hours catching up with Kitty and nursing a glass of wine and then go home in time to greet Lizard when the Prescotts dropped her off.

"It's a public facility," she pointed out reasonably. "You can't tell me not to come."

Joe mulled over her assertion. "I wasn't going to tell you not to come. I just don't know what you'll do there."

"Listen to the jukebox," Pamela suggested. "Keep you company."

"I'll be working."

"Fine."

Evidently he could find nothing more to object to.

"Okay. But you've got to be home before the Prescotts get back with Lizard. If they come home to an empty house—"

"They said they'd be bringing her back at nine. I'll be home before then."

"Okay." He shrugged, then lifted the keys to his car and handed her the keys to hers.

The bar was already bustling with happy drinkers by the time she and Joe arrived, a little after five. Within minutes she lost track of the number of people who said hello to her—people she scarcely recognized. They all claimed to be friends of Joe's, or regulars, or former boyfriends of Kitty who'd been at the wedding.

The noise level rose as one hour shifted into the next. The jukebox blasted an eclectic mix of songs: U2, the Pointer Sisters, Tony Bennett, Sting—and, of course, Ben E. King warbling "Stand by Me."

Seated at a table at the rear of the room, Pamela sought Joe with her gaze as that song, their song, filtered through the thick, smoky air. Joe was apparently searching for her, too, because when their eyes met she felt as much of a jolt as if he'd crossed the room and kissed her. She wanted to promise she would stand by him forever. But that was a promise he had no use for. All he'd ever asked of her was that she stand by him during the custody fight.

Yet his gaze remained on her for the duration of the song. Brick seemed to sense his boss's distraction, because he picked up the slack and filled all the orders until the last plaintive notes faded away. Only then did Joe sever the unspoken communication between them.

She approached the bar, but Joe was suddenly very busy organizing his whiskey bottles. "Whenever that song gets played, he thinks of you," Brick confided, stringing together more words than Pamela had ever heard from him.

"Maybe he's just remembering what a good time we had at the wedding."

Brick grunted and shook his head.

Joe finished inventorying his whiskey. He shot a quick glance at the tacky steering-wheel clock hanging on the wall, then sent Pamela a fleeting smile. "You'd better head off. It's a quarter to nine."

"I'm on my way."

"Kiss Lizzie good-night for me."

"I will, Joe." Pamela was tempted to kiss him good-night, too. She saw the pensive glimmer in his eyes, and for a selfish instant wished his emotions were for her. But they were for Lizard, she knew. Lizard was the one who mattered to him.

Forcing a smile, she slid the strap of her purse over her shoulder and sauntered out of the bar. The streets were clogged with traffic, but Pamela made it to Joe's block by five minutes to nine—enough time to get inside, turn on some lights and wait for Lizard.

Not quite, she amended as she spotted the Infiniti parked in front of Joe's house. She accelerated down the street and drove into the driveway. By the time she'd turned off the engine and climbed out of the car, Joyce and Lawton Prescott had emerged from their rental car. Lawton's hand was clamped firmly around Lizard's wrist; he was practically dragging her toward Pamela. Something pink was spilled across the front of the Liz Kid's sundress.

"Hi," Pamela said in a falsely bright tone. "I'm sorry you had to wait. You got here a little early."

"We got here at eight-fifteen," Joyce snarled. "We've been waiting all this time. Another minute and we would have left her at the social worker's house. We've had just about all we can take!'' Lawton released Lizard with a slight shove, and Lizard flew into Pamela's arms.

Ignoring the adults, Pamela inspected Lizard for signs of damage. Besides the pink splotch on the bodice of her dress, her hair was matted and her neck was discolored with rings of dirt. She looked remarkably dry-eyed, though, and feisty and defiant.

''What happened?'' Pamela asked her.

''Nothin'.''

''That child is a beast,'' Lawton declared tersely. ''She ought to be sent to reform school.''

''Lizard,'' Pamela scolded. ''What did you do?'' *And whatever it was, will it persuade the court that Joe's an unfit parent?*

''It was her fault,'' Lizard said, pointing a grimy finger at Joyce. ''She asked me what I thought of her dress.''

''This is a Gianni Versace,'' Joyce erupted. ''It was bad enough that she told me it was gross, but then she deliberately spilled water all over it. This is silk. Water stains won't come out.''

''Perhaps a dry cleaner—''

''She ruined this dress for no good reason. Then she ran around the restaurant, throwing a tantrum. She humiliated us in front of the other patrons.''

''It was an icky restaurant,'' Lizard argued. ''They didn't even have *pisketti*.''

''Spaghetti,'' Pamela corrected her before addressing the Prescotts. ''She's rather young to be going to fancy restaurants.''

''We don't eat at fast-food joints,'' Joyce sniffed. ''Perhaps your idea of dining out is shouting your order into a microphone and driving up to the pick-up window, but we consider dining an important social experience— and we expect a well-bred child to behave properly in a restaurant. Elizabeth was horrible. She deliberately tripped a waiter.''

"I'm sure it wasn't deliberate," Pamela argued. "Was it, Lizard?"

"Uh-huh." The little girl nodded. "I did it on purpose."

"The waiter was carrying a chocolate soufflé," Lawton said.

"Needless to say, it collapsed because of her," Joyce added. "She's a spiteful, hateful child. She has no sense of decorum. She reduced me to tears."

"Lizard." Pamela tried hard to look indignant, but a rebellious smile stole across her lips.

"She is a heathenish beast," Joyce continued. "I don't see how we can possibly fit her into our lives if this is the way she chooses to behave."

"She's vulgar," Lawton added.

"Ordering a strawberry milk shake at a three-star restaurant. And when the maître d' came out to see what the ruckus was about, she called him a butt-face. I thought I was going to die!" Joyce whined.

"She isn't fit for society," Lawton concluded. "She's beyond redemption. There's nothing we can do for her."

"Excuse me..." Pamela was afraid of jumping to the wrong conclusion and then having her hopes dashed. "Are you saying you aren't going to ask for custody of Lizard?"

"Joseph can have her. She's obviously a Brenner."

"Tainted genes," Lawton concurred.

"A hideous child."

"She's a wonderful child!" Pamela argued, hugging

Lizard and not caring that some of the pink stuff—strawberry milk shake, no doubt—was rubbing onto her T-shirt. "And his name is Jonas, not Joseph."

"And my name is Lizard, not Betsy," Lizard shouted.

"Lizard suits you well, little girl," Lawton retorted. "You and your aunt and uncle deserve one another. We'll be leaving for Hillsborough in the morning."

Before Pamela could say another word, the Prescotts, dressed in their overpriced, water-stained apparel, strode regally back to their expensive rental car, climbed in and drove off into the hot, starlit night.

Too stunned to move, Pamela laughed. So did Lizard. Pamela closed her arms snugly around Lizard, and Lizard hugged her just as tightly.

"We ought to telephone your Uncle Joe," Pamela whispered, aware that her cheeks were damp with tears.

"Yeah. And then can I draw a tattoo on Snoot's boob?"

"You can draw all the tattoos you want on Snoot," Pamela promised, swinging Lizard high into her arms and carrying her inside the house.

CHAPTER FIFTEEN

LIZARD RULED the Shipwreck from her perch on the bar. In one hand she held a nonalcoholic Pink Lady; in the other she held her Barbie doll, its body wrapped in rubber bands and its hair woven into a lopsided braid with a feather glued to the tip. "It was great," she regaled anyone who wandered close enough to listen to her. "I tripped a waiter and he was carrying this chocolate stuff and it went flying everywhere and it looked like poop."

Pamela had heard her tell the story three times already that evening, so she wandered away from the bar to greet Mona Whitley, who was seated primly by herself at a table near the door. "I'm so glad you decided to stop by," Pamela said, settling into a chair across from Ms. Whitley.

Dressed in a decorous suit of gray linen, Ms. Whitley nursed her bourbon and eyed Lizard with less than complete approval. "It's past Elizabeth's bedtime," she observed.

Lizard frequently stayed up later than nine o'clock, but even though the custody battle was over, Pamela decided the social worker didn't have to know that. "This party is in her honor, so it would be a shame if she couldn't be here. Besides, she can always sleep late tomorrow."

Ms. Whitley appeared skeptical. "I'm still not convinced that the Prescotts wouldn't have provided her with a more stable environment.''

"Stability isn't everything," Pamela argued gently, surprising herself. Her life had been perfectly stable until a couple of months ago when her car had journeyed the last few miles of Route 1, depositing her on Key West. She used to treasure the stability of her existence. It indicated that she was in control of things.

Maybe someday she would want stability and control back in her life. But not tonight. Tonight belonged to Joe and Lizard.

"I really do think nine o'clock is too late for a five-year-old," Ms. Whitley persisted, although the words seemed to emerge from a great distance, through a dense fog. Pamela wondered how many bourbons the social worker had consumed.

"We'll be getting her home soon," Pamela promised, then rose and sauntered across the room, grinning and nodding as Joe's numerous friends shouted greetings and good wishes at her. A month ago they'd been toasting her wedding to him. Today they were toasting something much more significant.

Standing behind the bar, his earring glittering and his chin scruffy because he'd skipped shaving that day, Joe wore a quiet smile. He looked as if he couldn't quite believe his good fortune. Every now and then he glanced at his niece, who swung her legs, kicking the vertical panels of the bar, and who danced her Barbie doll among the glasses and bowls of pretzels until the doll's molded, high-heeled feet landed smack in the middle of a plate of sliced lemons, squirting citrus wedges and juice in all directions.

Joe didn't scold. He was obviously too happy to be

upset about a mess that was meager by Lizard's usual standards.

Noticing Pamela's approach, he signaled Brick to cover for him and strolled to the end of the bar. With a flick of his head, he signaled for Pamela to join him at the back door.

She edged past the crowd of revelers lining the bar until she reached Joe's side. He looked formidably handsome, and his blue eyes glowed, but not with lust, not for Pamela.

She could accept that. The fact was, Joe and Lizard were a team, a family, the rationale behind just about every step he had taken over the past few months—the past few *years*. Pamela had never been more than a means to an end, a peripheral part of the story.

Touching her elbow lightly, he ushered Pamela down the hallway to the back door and out into the small lot at the rear of the building. Pamela recalled the first time he'd brought her there—to propose marriage. The spotlight above the door still flooded the lot with a silver-white glare, highlighting the coppery streaks the sun had painted into Joe's tawny hair and casting his deep-set eyes in shadow.

They stood in the hot, sea-scented evening, enjoying the fresh breezes. A horde of souped-up motorcycles rumbled down the street, and Joe waited for the noisy caravan to pass before addressing Pamela. His smile became sheepish, yet there was an edge to it, something she couldn't identify. "It's a good party, isn't it?" he said.

"It's a wonderful party. How did you organize it so quickly?" She knew Joe had spent most of the day at Mary DiNardi's office, finalizing the paperwork that would enable him to adopt Lizard formally. Pamela her-

self hadn't even known there would be a party until Joe
had called her at five that afternoon and told her to bring
Lizard down to the Shipwreck for the festivities.

"Kitty threw it together. She was almost as excited
by the news as I was." He shook his head, disbelief
rising to the surface again. "Pretty amazing, isn't it?"

"What's amazing? Kitty being excited?"

"Life in general." He seemed to wrestle with his
thoughts. He gazed past Pamela, as if unable to look
directly at her. "I got Lizard without a fight, and your
thug is in the slammer. It turns out you and I didn't have
to get hitched after all."

The thought hadn't occurred to Pamela, yet she
couldn't deny it. The very issues that had compelled her
and Joe to latch on to each other had resolved themselves. She and Joe wouldn't have to pretend to be married any longer to satisfy judges and social workers. Pamela wouldn't have to stay in Florida to elude Mick
Morrow. With the reasons for this marriage dissolved,
the marriage itself could be dissolved as soon as she and
Joe agreed to it.

His thoughts apparently paralleled hers. "So, what
happens now?"

She peered up at him. He'd shifted his gaze back to
her, and she understood what was lurking beneath his
hesitant smile. Lizard's custody was settled; now he
wanted everything else settled, too.

Pamela wasn't ready to settle things with Joe, not until
she knew which way to settle them. She had made love
with this man, weathered his moods, bonded with his
niece. She'd temporarily abandoned her career—and
ever since she'd crossed paths with Jonas Brenner she
hadn't given a thought to the strip-mall project she'd had
to give up when she left Seattle. That realization startled

her. Her career had once meant everything to her. But now things weren't quite as simple.

She wished she could read Joe's mind. He wasn't asking her to stay; he wasn't telling her to leave. If he did either, she wasn't sure how she would respond. He wanted to know her plans, but for once in her life, she didn't have any.

"I'd like to complete work on Birdie's house," she said. "I can't very well leave it half done."

He continued to stare at her, his face inscrutable. She wished he would ask her to stay—and then she recoiled from the thought. How many times did she have to convince herself that theirs wasn't a real marriage, that her home and her life were at the other end of the country?

"I'll help you finish it," he offered. "The two of us working together, we ought to be able to do the job in a week."

"Well, then there are the uneven floors. And I wanted to widen that front hall...." As long as she kept tinkering with Birdie's house, she wouldn't have to go home.

"Whatever you want," Joe said, as if once again keying in on her thoughts. "You want to stick around, it's no problem. You're welcome to stay for as long as you want."

That wasn't what she longed to hear. She didn't want to be *welcomed*—she wanted to be *needed*. She wanted Joe to beg her to stay because she was good for Lizard, because he liked having her around. Because he loved her.

Oh, God. She must be insane, yearning for something so inappropriate, so illogical.

"Well," she said briskly, "let's finish Birdie's kitchen and then see." Perhaps if she stuck around long enough to complete the construction job, Joe would decide he wanted her to stay after all. Perhaps she could seduce him, and...

The hell with that. She wasn't going to knock herself out trying to convince him that he needed her. She would finish Birdie's kitchen because a professional didn't walk away from a project until it was done. But given Joe's lackadaisical attitude, she concluded that he didn't deserve a part of her future. She'd do her job at Birdie's and leave. She wouldn't let herself mourn over it, either. She would remain in control, her old, pre-Jonas self.

Joe seemed on the verge of speaking—although Pamela wasn't sure she wanted to hear anything else he might have to say. Before he could utter a word, Kitty swung open the back door and announced, "The Liz Kid fell asleep."

Joe laughed. "Impossible. How could she fall asleep when she's got a captive audience?"

"Maybe she was tired. I think you better take her home, Joe—she's sprawled out on the bar and we can't work."

"All right." He checked his watch and gestured for Pamela to accompany him back inside. "Let's get the monster home."

Lizard was, indeed, sprawled across the bar, one of her braids lying in a bowl of cocktail peanuts. The raucous voices and thumping music had no effect on her. Her slow, rhythmic exhalations caused the feather in her doll's hair to quiver.

"Keep partying," Joe urged his friends. "I've got to dispose of the body and then I'll be back." He heaved the slumbering child into his arms and balanced her over his shoulder. Her arms dangled down his back; Pamela caught the doll as it dropped from Lizard's limp fingers. He glanced at her over Lizard's rump. "You want to stay? I could get Birdie to stay with Lizard till we leave the party."

"No, I'll go home with Lizard," Pamela said, suddenly anxious to distance herself from Joe and all his friends. "I'll stay with her, and you can party all night long if you want." She pressed her lips together, repressing her anger. No matter how hurt she was by Joe's failure to express any emotion for her, she didn't want to interfere with his celebration.

Acknowledging the crowd with more smiles and nods, they made their clumsy way out of the bar and down the street to Joe's car. Joe arranged Lizard across the back seat, somehow managing to get a seat belt around her, while Pamela took her place in front and struggled to suppress her bitterness. Really, she shouldn't resent Joe. He was offering her the escape he assumed she wanted; he probably thought he was doing her a favor. If she would rather stay in Key West, it was up to her to let him know. And even if things had been perfect between her and Joe, she wasn't sure she'd rather stay.

Joe cruised through the lively downtown boulevards to his quieter neighborhood. It was nearly ten o'clock. Anyone still awake at that hour was no doubt carousing in Old Town. The houses lining the residential streets were mostly dark and peaceful.

Reaching his house, he pulled into the driveway and turned off the engine. "Why don't I run ahead and open the front door?" Pamela suggested.

"Thanks." Joe climbed out and opened the back door to attend to Lizard.

Pamela removed her key from her pocket and strode up the front walk. She had forgotten to leave on the porch light—not surprising, since the sun had still been high above the horizon when she and Lizard had left for the Shipwreck. She scaled the porch steps carefully in the dark and tugged on the screen door latch.

A gloved hand reached out from the shadows and clapped over her mouth before she could scream. The cold barrel of a revolver jammed into the vulnerable skin beneath her chin. A rumbling voice rasped, "Greetings from Mick."

ONE OF THE GREAT mysteries of the world, as far as Joe was concerned, was why a kid weighed more asleep than awake. He hoisted Lizard over his shoulder, where she joggled and shifted like a forty-pound sack of potatoes. Her feet pounded against his ribs; her hair snagged in the stubble of his beard. He couldn't wait to dump her onto her bed—and then maybe talk to Pamela some more, away from the noisy activity of the bar.

One of the other great mysteries of the world was the way a woman's mind worked—or didn't work. As he lugged Lizard up the front walk, he reviewed the few minutes he'd spent with Pamela in the lot behind the bar. What did she want? Why couldn't she tell him? Her eyes said she wanted to stay on in Key West, but her words implied the only reason she wanted to stay was to work on Birdie's house.

And that wasn't much of a reason.

As soon as he got rid of Lizard, they'd talk it out. Or make love. If the past was any indication, they'd understand each other just fine once they had their clothes off.

Why hadn't she turned on any lights? he wondered as he neared the house. The porch was black with shadows, and he worried about tripping on the steps and jostling Lizard. "Pam?" he called softly.

Pamela said nothing.

When he was just a few yards from the bottom step,

his eyes adjusted to the gloom and he saw her—standing beside a goon wearing a ski mask and leather gloves and holding a gun to her throat.

Joe froze. Above the gloved hand clamped over her mouth, Pamela's eyes glistened with terror. She stood very still, locked inside the curve of the goon's arm.

"Don't move," the goon ordered him.

"I'm not moving." Joe's voice came out a breathless croak.

"No need to get you and the little girl involved," the goon said. "Why don't you go back to your car and clear out, and Miss Hayes and I will take care of business."

Joe shifted his gaze to Pamela again. Besides terror, he saw resignation in her eyes, and resolution. "Pam—"

She moved her jaw and mumbled something. The goon lowered his hand to permit her to speak. "Just go," she whispered. "If you stay he'll hurt Lizard."

"Pam—"

"This is between the lady and me," the goon said reasonably. "Actually, it's between the lady and a friend of mine, Mick Morrow. You and the little girl have nothing to do with it. Why don't you get going so I don't have to hurt you."

"Take Lizard and go," Pamela pleaded. "Just do as he says, Jonas. I don't want anything to happen to Lizard."

Deep in Joe's gut, emotions began to churn. Pain, rage, dread and a hefty dose of self-loathing at the possibility that his phone call to the Seattle police—his distrust of Pamela—had brought this villain to his doorstep. But he kept his tone calm and even as he said, "Okay, we're outta here."

It tore him apart to leave Pamela, to turn away from

her fearful gaze. What would she think of him for walking away?

But he had to consider Lizard. He couldn't do anything as long as he had his niece slumped over his shoulder. Lizard's safety was the most important thing. Joe was sure Pamela would agree.

He strode back to the car in quick but measured steps. His brain raced ahead at breakneck speed, considering strategies, discarding them, wondering how in God's name he could save Pamela without jeopardizing Lizard. Behind him he heard nothing more than the shriek of crickets.

He lowered Lizard gently onto the back seat of his car and closed the door. Glancing toward the porch, he saw the gunman ushering Pamela down the steps. The two of them moved awkwardly, the gunman keeping her pinned to his side with one huge gloved hand and the gun against her neck with the other.

Joe slipped in behind the wheel and started the engine. Pamela sent him a searing look, and he knew in that instant that she despised him for abandoning her. He wanted to roll down the window and remind her that he couldn't have dropped Lizard on the lawn and taken on an armed killer with his bare fists. He wanted to beg her not to give up. He wanted to tell her that if anything happened to her he would die.

Instead, he jammed his foot down on the gas pedal, jerked the steering wheel to the left and careered across the front lawn, aiming straight at the gunman and praying that Pam would be able to get out of his way in time.

The sudden swerving of the car tossed Lizard off the back seat, waking her. "You're driving on the grass!" she yelled.

"Hush," he said. "Get down." Joe forced himself to

concentrate on the thug who held Pamela hostage. Instead of releasing her, he was trying to drag her across the yard toward the rhododendrons abutting the porch. Joe yanked the steering wheel the other way, chasing the masked man. The car's headlights offered perplexing glimpses of trees and flowers; the tires bumped and skidded on the grass.

The thug still had the gun, although he no longer held it to Pamela's neck. His fingers circled her upper arm as he dragged her away from the porch, toward the street. Joe noticed the unfamiliar car parked at the curb.

He also noticed a few other cars on the street. Some of his neighbors must be home. Joe slammed his fist against his car horn, figuring it couldn't hurt to rouse some attention.

The sudden bleat of the horn startled the gunman. He flinched, and Pamela at last wriggled free of his grasp. Joe assumed she would flee, but he didn't stop to follow her progress. His attention was on the thug.

Lizard clutched the back of the front seat. "Blast the horn again, Uncle Joe! Hit the guy! This is fun! Kill the sucker!"

"You're a bloodthirsty little brat," Joe muttered, although he shared her vindictiveness a hundred percent. As the thug lunged toward his own car, Joe gunned the engine and headed after him. Frantic, the man tried to climb up the side of his car, but Joe plunged forward, closing his eyes an instant before impact. Sure, he wanted to kill the sucker. He just wasn't sure he wanted to watch himself do it.

His car hit the thug's with a loud crunch of metal that flung Joe against the steering wheel, causing the horn to blare into the night. "Lizard?" he wheezed, wrestling with his breath. "Lizard, are you all right?"

Her answer was a giggle of delight. "That was *awesome!* Let's do it again!"

Joe coughed a few times. "Not a chance, toots. You stay here. I'm gonna get out and check the damage and see if I'm going to be charged with vehicular homicide."

"What's *vick-you-ler home-side?*" Lizard asked.

"You don't want to know." Joe moved slowly, mentally inspecting each limb and joint to make sure he hadn't done any serious harm to himself in the collision. He was only slightly relieved to discover, as he emerged from his battered car, that the thug was alive, trapped between the mangled chassis of his car and Joe's. He was moaning, though, and cursing a blue streak. His ski mask was askew, revealing the lower half of his face. A trickle of blood leaked from the corner of his mouth.

"What the hell is going on?" An irate male voice reached Joe from the street. Straightening up, he noticed several neighbors swarming down the block to witness the excitement.

"Would somebody call the police?" Joe asked, still sounding a bit breathless.

"I already did," Birdie squawked. "This is how you celebrate?"

Lizard took Birdie's question at face value. "This was better than the party," she squealed in delight as she leapt from the car. "Isn't it awesome?"

Joe heard the whine of a siren in the distance. Assured that the thug wasn't going to get away, he staggered across the lawn in search of Pamela. He found her seated on the porch steps, her head propped in her hands and her cheeks stained with tears.

He dropped onto the step next to her, arched his arm around her and drew her against him. A tremor of panic seized him, then vanished. She was alive. He hadn't lost her.

"You okay?" he whispered into her silky blond hair.

She sighed. "I threw up."

"I don't blame you."

"I thought..." A low sob escaped her, and she covered her eyes with her hands, as if she didn't want him to see her weep. "I thought you were really going to go away and leave me."

Joe tightened his hold on her. "Just because that was what you told me to do? Since when do you think I'd actually listen to you?"

She issued a soggy laugh. "I told you to leave because I was afraid for Lizard."

"Well, if anyone came close to killing her, it was me, not him. Looks like I did some major damage to the lawn, too."

"The lawn looks beautiful." Pamela nestled closer to him. "And Lizard's pretty tough. Tougher than me, for sure."

"You're the toughest woman I've ever known," Joe told her, closing both arms around her and feeling her shiver in his embrace.

Bright red lights pulsed across the front yard as a police cruiser pulled to a screeching halt behind the two mangled cars. A police officer stalked up the front walk, and Joe knew he was going to spend the next several hours answering questions. The authorities would need to know what happened, who the gunman was, who had sent him and why.

But the questions could wait for a few minutes. Right now, Joe couldn't imagine anything more essential than holding his wife.

CHAPTER SIXTEEN

PAMELA SAT on the leather couch in her living room, weary after having given a full day of testimony in court. Her feet hurt from the high heels she'd worn. Back in Key West, she'd lived in sandals.

Forget about Key West, she ordered herself. She was in Seattle now. Home. Because the district attorney's office had ghastly proof that Pamela's life was in danger, he'd insisted that the court schedule Mick Morrow's new trial immediately, and Pamela had returned to testify. She supposed she would have to fly back to Florida to testify against the hit man Mick had hired to get her, but she couldn't think that far ahead.

Not tonight, anyway. Tonight, after having seen her foe in court, having spoken out against him, having spent too much time wondering whether her life would have been better if she'd never opened her mouth in the first place, she wasn't going to do anything but rest.

Mozart's *Jupiter* Symphony swelled into the room from the speakers of her sound system. The glass of milk she sipped made her stomach churn. The glass-topped tables gleamed from their recent cleaning; her knick-knacks bespoke taste and class; and as soon as her parents had heard she was returning to Seattle, they'd gone to the condominium and replaced all her dead plants with live ones.

A tear seeped through her lashes when she realized

how much she missed the chaos of life with Lizard, of spilled cereal, smeared finger paint and girlish giggles. And the chaos of life with Joe, whose soul she could never read and whose heart she could never trust. The man who had saved her life.

She'd left the island the day after the attack. The police in Key West had alerted the DA in Seattle, and he had told Pamela to come west as soon as she could. He felt the Seattle police could protect her. Sure, she'd thought—now that they no longer considered her paranoid and hysterical.

She'd spent her last Key West night in bed with Joe, not making love but simply being held. He'd been so steady, so comforting as she trembled beside him, fighting anguish and nausea and waves of dread. When she thought about how close she'd come to dying, she'd burst into tears. When she thought about how Joe had saved her life, she'd burst into tears. It had been a very wet night, not the least bit romantic, yet by the time she'd finally drifted off to sleep she'd been absolutely convinced she loved him.

Which made it imperative that she leave as soon as possible. She had hoped that once she was back in Seattle, the physical distance between her and Joe would help her to regain her perspective. It helped to remember that before the hit man had shown up on Joe's front porch, Joe hadn't asked her to stay and make a real marriage with him. What he'd done hadn't been done out of love. He'd saved her life only because he was a decent fellow with a few heroic impulses, the same heroic impulses that had compelled him to take in his niece and fight for her.

Heroism wasn't the same thing as love.

But meanwhile she felt like hell.

Don't think about it, she ordered herself. *Get through the trial and then you can plan the rest of your life.*

Through the lilting strings of the Allegro first movement, she heard the doorbell ring. In the week she'd been back, a few neighbors had dropped by to see how she was doing. Her colleagues at Murtaugh Associates had sent her flowers, and Richard Duffy had phoned to tell her the strip-mall project was coming along nicely. She'd spent several evenings at her parents' house and a day reviewing her testimony with her attorney and the DA. By now, she figured, anyone who had wanted to welcome her home would have done so.

She stood, smoothed the sash of her silk robe around her waist and crossed barefoot to the door. Peeking through the peephole, she saw more flowers. She wondered why the doorman hadn't accepted the delivery for her or signaled through the intercom that she had a visitor.

Pamela carefully slid the chain lock into place before she cracked the door open and peered out.

The flowers were roses. The delivery man was Jonas Brenner.

"Hi, Pam," he said.

He looked remarkably tan compared to the sun-deprived citizens of Seattle. His hair was the wondrous tawny shade she remembered, thick and much too long. His eyes were the marvelous blue she'd fallen in love with. His earring was the same dangling ornament he'd worn at their wedding: a tiny gold heart.

And then there were the roses, three of them. Red.

Pamela released the chain and opened the door wider. "Come in," she said, feeling unexpectedly awkward. She had to remind herself that Jonas Brenner was her husband. But her life in Key West seemed so far away, so alien to her life in Seattle. Joe didn't belong here.

He stepped inside. He had obviously groomed himself carefully for this visit. His cheeks were freshly shaven, and he wore his khaki trousers and a crisp white shirt. As he handed her the flowers, he scrutinized her intensely. "You look awful," he said.

She ought to have been insulted, but she only smiled weakly. Leave it to Joe to opt for honesty. She *did* look awful, and she knew it. "I've had a long day," she explained, crossing to the credenza to find a bud vase.

"Today was your first day of testimony, wasn't it?"

She had phoned him a few days ago to let him know, in the vaguest terms, what was going on. She'd talked for a few minutes about the trial and asked how Lizard was doing. Joe hadn't told her he missed her, and she'd tried to convince herself afterward that it was just as well.

Answering his question with a nod, she went to the wet bar to add water to the vase. Then she set the flowers on the coffee table. Three was an unusual number—roses usually came singly or in dozens. Staring at the graceful trio of buds made her think of the Brenner family: Jonas, Lizard and Pamela.

Except that the Brenner family was no longer a trio.

"Would you like a drink?" she asked, the perfect hostess.

Joe continued to stare at her, his smile contradicted by the frown pinching his brow. "You really look terrible, Pam."

"Thanks," she said, forcing a laugh. "I'm so glad you traveled all this way to tell me. Where are you staying, by the way?" She'd be damned if she would put him up for the night, not when he was standing in her living room insulting her.

"Are you sick?" he persisted.

"Seriously, Jonas—why are you here?"

"To see you," he answered simply. "This is some swanky place you've got."

"Thank you." That was exactly what it was: a swanky place. Elegant, sterile, swanky.

"It wouldn't survive ten seconds with Lizard in it," he remarked, appraising the glass-topped tables and the modern sculptures.

"Did you bring her with you?"

"No. She's staying with Birdie." He eyed a chair, and Pamela indicated with a wave that he ought to sit. She lowered herself back onto the couch and brushed her hair out of her face. "I'm worried about you," he said.

"I'm safe," she assured him. "No more hit men are after me. I know I look like hell, but as you said yourself, I've been testifying all day, sharing a courtroom with Mick Morrow. I—"

"No," Joe cut her off. "I'm worried about *you*. The one time you called, you talked about everything but us. When I got off the phone, I just had this—I don't know, this premonition that you weren't coming back."

Pamela studied him in the clear light from her halogen floor lamp. He appeared apprehensive. "A premonition?"

"Damn it, Pam—I don't want to force you into anything, but we've got to talk. You've been gone a week, and Lizard's been moping, and I..." A helpless laugh escaped him. "I've been moping, too. I don't know—I didn't think this was the sort of thing we ought to talk about on the phone. So I came to Seattle to ask you, are you coming back?''

Beg me to and I will, she almost said. "I don't know."

"Maybe the Seattle climate isn't good for you. You look so pale."

"I'm not pale."

"Have you been having nightmares about that ass who attacked you at my house?"

"No." She'd been having nightmares about how she was going to straighten out her life.

"Then what is it? What's going on?"

"I told you. The trial, the testimony—"

"Trials and testimony don't make you pale."

"I'm pregnant," she said.

The first movement of the symphony chose that moment to end, leaving the living room in silence. Joe's eyes grew bright with astonishment. "You're kidding."

"No. I'm not."

"You mean from that time on the screened porch?"

"That was the only time there was," she pointed out.

"Why didn't you tell me?"

"I was going to," she hedged. "I just found out. After the trial was behind me, and..." Damn it, Joe deserved equal honesty from her. "Maybe I *wasn't* going to tell you. Our marriage wasn't a love match, Jonas. We both got what we wanted from it. We had agreed from the start that we would get a divorce as soon as you had Lizard free and clear and I was no longer running for my life. Well, you've got Lizard, and Mick's going to be convicted this time, and I'm not going to force you to remain in a marriage that was never meant to be."

He practically flew out of his chair and dived onto the couch next to her. That she'd kept the news from him didn't seem to matter to him. That she'd chosen not to pressure him to accept a responsibility he might not want seemed to have no significance. He hauled her into his arms, onto his lap and kissed her with such vehemence she couldn't breathe.

He was grinning when he pulled back. "We're having a baby? I can't believe it! Man, how many parties can we hold at the Shipwreck? My pals are gonna start getting sick of them."

"What party?" His kiss had shaken her deeply. It was full of passion, full of exuberance—full, perhaps, of male pride. But where was the love? "Jonas, this baby—"

"Our baby," he whispered reverently.

Evidently he wasn't thinking of all the implications, all the obligations. "We didn't plan it, Jonas. It was an accident. I'm not going to hold you—"

"You damned well are going to hold me," he retorted—and in fact she *was* holding him. If she let go, she might tumble off his lap and onto the glass-topped table. "When are you due?"

"March."

"Wow." He kissed her again, more tenderly. His lips caressed her mouth, her cheeks, her brow. He skimmed one hand down her body, tracing the curve of her breast before he came to rest against her still-flat abdomen. "Oh, Pam...are you still allowed to have sex?"

"Allowed? You mean, because I'm pregnant?" She hadn't even thought to question the doctor about that. Sex hadn't seemed a very real possibility until Joe had walked through her door.

"Later," he murmured, kissing her lips again, so sweetly, so softly, she felt herself go sweet and soft inside. Why later? she wanted to ask. Why not right now, this instant?

No. Just because he could turn her on with a few kisses didn't mean everything was right between them. They wouldn't have sex this instant, and they wouldn't have it later. Not unless they'd worked a few things out.

Joe was apparently already trying to do that on his own. "You're gonna have to give up that bedroom at the end of the hall, you know. We'll need it for a nursery."

"Slow down, Jonas." She eased out of his arms and shoved herself to her feet. Joe still hadn't even hinted that he loved her. How dare he rearrange her living space? "What makes you so sure I want to go back to Key West after I'm done here? This is my home. This 'swanky place,' as you call it, is my home."

He surveyed the spacious, impeccably decorated room and snorted. "You really want to live here? Lizard would hate it."

Pamela couldn't argue with that. "Maybe."

"It's so...so *cold*," he concluded. Then, reading her dissatisfaction, he switched gears. "But we can work it out. I'm sure there are bars here. I could get good money if I sold the Shipwreck, and maybe I could find an establishment to invest in here. Or I'd tend bar for someone else. I mean, it's awfully rainy here, and I bet the beaches can't compare to what we've got—to say nothing of the fact that you can probably go swimming only about two months out of the year. But at least you wouldn't have to worry about Lizard running around bare-ass. She'd be too cold."

It wasn't just Seattle's climate Joe was talking about, Pamela realized. It was her condominium, chilly in the absence of a child, in the absence of noise and havoc and love.

"You'd rather live in Key West than Seattle, wouldn't you?" she said.

Joe grew solemn. "I'd rather live with you," he said. "Where doesn't matter."

"Do you mean that?"

He gathered her hand in both of his and pulled her back onto the sofa next to him. This time he didn't kiss her, but simply held her hand sandwiched between his. His thumb traced the thick gold band he'd placed on her finger less than three months ago. "Until you left, I wasn't sure," he admitted. "But once you were gone, Lizard and I could hardly function. The house felt different. It felt empty." He sighed. "I didn't want to do a number on you, so I tried to pretend I didn't mind your being gone. I figured you were glad to be rid of me. I'm no bargain."

"Who would want a bargain for a husband?" she teased gently.

"But..." He let out a long, pensive sigh. "Truth is, I'm a selfish guy. And Lizard is a very selfish kid. And we need you. Both of us." He sent her a meek grin. "Me more than her."

"It's nice to be needed," she conceded. When he didn't speak, she averted her eyes, willing him not to see her disappointment. "But being needed isn't enough, Jonas."

He slid his hand under her chin and guided her gaze back to his. He was smiling, but it was the most earnest, soulful smile she'd ever seen. "You want to hear me say I love you? Of course I love you. I thought that was obvious that night on the porch."

"What happened on the porch wasn't love," she argued. "It was sex."

"It was a hell of a lot more than sex," he shot back,

his eyes straying to her abdomen. "As it turns out, it was more than even I realized. But Pam..." He lifted his gaze to her face once more. The amusement in his eyes was gone, replaced by ardent sincerity. "I fell in love with you when you lit into me about Lizard. You cared as much about her as I did, and I realized that nothing else mattered. You were the woman for me. Making love was only my body telling you what was in my heart."

This time it was Pamela's idea to snuggle into his lap, to cover his mouth with hers and kiss him, deeply, passionately, her lips telling him what was in *her* heart. He responded with pleasure, with arousal, with love.

"You want our baby?" he murmured once they'd come up for air. He cradled her cheeks in his hands and peered intently into her eyes.

"Yes," she swore. "Do you?"

"More than just about anything." He kissed her again, a light, sweet kiss. "How much longer do you have to stay in Seattle? I want you home."

"I want to come home." She sighed. "Just a few more days of testimony and then they'll let me leave."

"I could stay a few days," he told her. "I could even meet those wonderful in-laws you tell me I've got."

"We could exchange vows in my parents' church."

"If you want to."

"I want to," Pamela said, resting her head on Joe's strong, firm shoulder. It wouldn't have to be the formal white wedding she'd always dreamed of. She'd already had a wedding—a strange, funky, wonderful wedding. And when all was said and done, a wedding wasn't as important as the marriage it created.

She closed her eyes, feeling content for the first time since the doctor had told her she was pregnant, since the

DA had told her Mick Morrow's trial was going forward, since she'd fled Seattle for Key West so many weeks ago—since she'd been old enough to imagine falling in love. She couldn't really say her life was under control, but having her life under control no longer seemed terribly important.

"You think the church organist can play 'Stand by Me'?" Joe asked.

"If she can't, we'll sing it ourselves."

"Yeah," he agreed, then kissed her lips and tightened his arms around her. "We'll sing it, and then we'll go home together."

Pamela felt as if her marriage was truly starting right now, in Joe's embrace, with his baby in her belly and his love in her soul. "Yes," she vowed. "We'll go home together."

American HEROES
AGAINST ALL ODDS

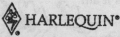

HARLEQUIN®   Silhouette®

Please address questions and book requests to: Harlequin Reader Service U.S.: 3010 Walden Ave., P.O. Box 1325, Buffalo, NY 14269 CAN.: P.O. Box 609, Fort Erie, Ont. L2A 5X3

PAHGEN

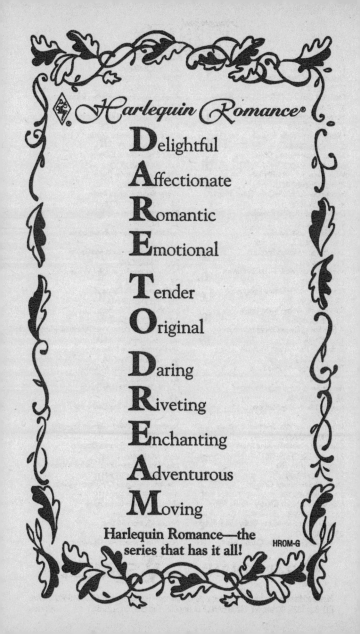

Harlequin Romance®

Delightful

Affectionate

Romantic

Emotional

Tender

Original

Daring

Riveting

Enchanting

Adventurous

Moving

Harlequin Romance—the
series that has it all!

HROM-G

HARLEQUIN PRESENTS®

**The world's bestselling romance series...
The series that brings you your favorite authors,
month after month:**

Helen Bianchin...Emma Darcy
Lynne Graham...Penny Jordan
Miranda Lee...Sandra Morton
Anne Mather...Carole Mortimer
Susan Napier...Michelle Reid

and many more uniquely talented authors!

Wealthy, powerful, gorgeous men...
Women who have feelings just like your own...
The stories you love, set in exotic, glamorous locations...

HARLEQUIN PRESENTS,
Seduction and passion guaranteed!

Visit us at www.romance.net

Harlequin® Historical

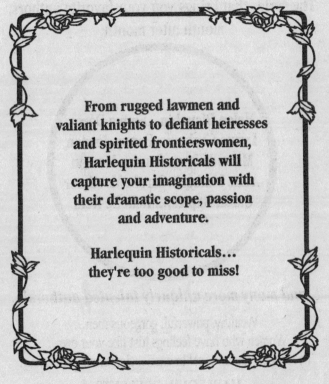

From rugged lawmen and
valiant knights to defiant heiresses
and spirited frontierswomen,
Harlequin Historicals will
capture your imagination with
their dramatic scope, passion
and adventure.

Harlequin Historicals…
they're too good to miss!

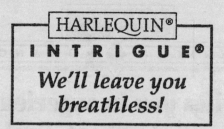